CURSED HEART

DAUGHTER OF AIR #4

JADE KERRION

Cursed Heart / Jade Kerrion—1st ed.

Cover Design by Rebecca Frank

CHAPTER 1

A clenched fist pounded on the door. "What the hell is going on in there?"

Varun Zale did not lie easily or well, but he had more or less given up on telling the truth. He ripped the scorched gloves off his hands as he frantically stamped out the last of the sparks smoldering on the rubber mats lining the steel floors. "Nothing!" he shouted. He swallowed hard against the outright fib. Lying was easier if he didn't have to look anyone in the eye. "Everything's all right here."

He didn't release the breath he was holding until he heard Jackson's disbelieving snort and the quiet thud of his boots as the first mate returned to the bridge of the marine research vessel *Veritas*.

Varun stared down at his hands—his seemingly normal hands—that had spontaneously burst into flame. Heat still simmered on the palms of his hands. Sparks frittered if he brought his fingertips too closely together.

His head throbbed from the certainty that he was in a crap load of trouble. He hadn't been anywhere close to understanding the basics of being an earth elemental. The last thing he'd needed was Nergal's stolen fire magic further complicating his life.

He should have known better than to stand on the receiving end when the goddess of the underworld cut Nergal's fire magic out of him.

Too late now; he grimaced. He was stuck with part of Nergal's power.

And if it made Nergal, the Sumerian god of pestilence and the former god of fire, easier to take down, then Varun considered the complication well worth it.

As long as he didn't accidentally burn anything down.

He slept poorly that night, waking in the early hours of dawn when the *Veritas* finally pulled into Fox Point Marina. Varun abandoned the concept of sleep and paced the deck, staring at the unblinking lights of Providence, Rhode Island, until daybreak. If only Ginny Waters, his close friend and a professor of ancient history at Brown University, picked up her phone or answered his e-mails, he could have saved himself a trip out here.

But now that he was in Providence, which was almost as much home as the Greek island of Kalymnos, he was grateful for the familiarity, the almost-serenity; thankful for the momentary relief from pounding disquiet, so acute, so vivid, it skimmed close to a 24-7 panic attack.

God knew, peace of mind had been in desperately short supply ever since he escaped from the underworld.

Without Ashe.

He wasn't even certain which predicament he ought to have been more worried about—that he, a nascent elemental, was expected to deal with the bitter and thwarted god of pestilence, or that Ashe was in the underworld with several of the immortal Illojim, without anyone to temper her compulsion to make bad decisions and eternal enemies.

Varun inhaled deeply and braced against the tension tightening his shoulders. He shook his head. The low growl of his stomach reminded him that he had not eaten dinner, or lunch yesterday. He needed a snack and a huge dose of caffeine if he were to talk to Ginny without behaving like a zoned-out zombie. It was too early for the ship's chef to be awake, but Varun figured he could cook up bacon and eggs without screwing up. He thought he miscalculated when he ignited the gas stove by snapping his fingers, but thankfully, the fire stayed contained to the burner. *Score one for not burning down the kitchen. Or the ship.*

He managed a few mouthfuls of his breakfast, gulped down his coffee, then disembarked from the *Veritas*. Ginny was something of an early bird too, and he wanted to catch her before class. Within minutes, he was in the heart of the city, heading toward Brown University. Varun strode across the campus toward Rhode Island Hall, careful to hold his hands away from his body. He could not afford to spontaneously ignite his clothes, or anything else for that matter.

Ashe—once a mermaid, now a Daughter of Air and the Lady of the Ocean—had told him that elemental magic was built on a relationship with the elements, not on laws and rules. But now that he was an elemental, he suspected she had left out vast chunks of information.

She tended to do that—her thoughts instinctively filtering out anything that she did not consider important or relevant. She also had a penchant for asking the wrong questions, and getting terrible, misleading answers as a result. She was frequently grumpy, always irritable, and occasionally snappy.

He was also in love with her, and he was not entirely sure why.

Varun was honest enough to admit his fascination had begun as scientific curiosity. He was a scientist, and Ashe—the mute captain of the *Veritas*—defied explanation. She breathed underwater, her kiss ushered air into struggling human lungs, and the soles of her feet were covered in blisters.

Exactly like the Little Mermaid from Hans Christian Andersen's stories.

Yet, the wind danced around her, obedient to her whim. The waves rose and fell according to her wishes. And she was perfectly capable of churning air and water into a furious, gigantic, unstoppable waterspout.

But that was not why he had fallen in love with her. He was still trying to figure that part out.

He was also working through the details of what he was—exactly.

Ashe had told him that elemental magic belonged only to specific species—air magic to the sylphs, water magic to the nymphs, earth magic to the gnomes, fire magic to the imps.

But Varun now controlled—and he used that term loosely indeed—both earth and fire magic.

He had gained the former when Duggae, a gnome sacrificed his life to save Varun's. Duggae's powers had transferred to Varun when the cursed dagger, the *Isriq Genii*, pierced both their hearts. He had won the latter from Nergal, the psychotically jealous alien god-wannabe.

Varun did not know what to do with the power he now possessed. Humans were never intended to be elementals. And without Ashe, he had no idea how to find the other elementals. Was there a school of elemental magic, or did all those species instinctively know how to manipulate their power and their elements? Was he doomed to walk awkwardly for the rest of his life, trying not to touch anything with his hands?

Until he got answers, his best bet was to avoid accidents.

And to obtain answers, he needed Ashe. He had to free her from Irkalla—the Sumerian underworld where she was trapped.

After their last battle with Nergal, the Sumerian god had fled Irkalla, destroying the gates as he passed. As the gates collapsed, Ashe used the wind to hurl Varun, Ondine, and Zamir through the gate and back onto Earth.

Of the three, only Varun arrived, questionably intact. Ondine lapsed into a coma as the spirit that had possessed her, Neti, fled back into the underworld to be with his mistress, Ereshkigal. And Zamir, Ashe's son for whom she had risked everything, had simply vanished. Zamir had been a soul. Returned to Earth, but without a body, there was nothing of him to see or to touch. Varun assumed that Zamir was still around—somehow—but he had no way of finding him.

The world's going to hell, and the only person who knows what's going on is a human who doesn't know what to do.

Varun flexed against the tight muscles in his shoulders as he walked across the empty quadrangle. The promise of a beautiful day should have lured the undergraduates and even some of the graduate students out onto the lawn. Fear of the spreading infection, however, kept most people indoors, cloistered away in their homes, frantically scrubbing all surfaces with disinfectant. Clinics and emergency rooms were filling up with people coughing up blood-streaked, black-speckled phlegm.

Nergal.

The god of pestilence was making his presence felt. Varun had no proof, but he was certain of it. The ocean had succumbed first, and now the Earth was under attack. Unless he found a way to stop Nergal, the Earth would fade into the lifeless gray of Irkalla.

Free Ashe. Get my act together. Stop Nergal.

It was a beautiful, simple three-step plan. How hard could it possibly be?

Ginny Waters was the key to the first step. If any dusty old manuscripts contained hints on how to escape from the underworld, Ginny would know it. Rhode Island Hall, which housed the archeology and ancient civilizations departments, however, was quieter than a graveyard. Varun occasionally glimpsed movement behind the glass panels of closed office doors, but no students lingered in the corridor. At the other end of the hallway, a janitor, his nose and mouth covered by a mask, slopped water over the floors with his mop. The lemon scent of Lysol filled the air.

It was not enough to overcome the stench of fear or the stink of emptiness.

Varun walked up the stairs, his footsteps echoing hollowly against the curved stairwell. Yellow—the only glimpse of bright color in the muted hues of the hallway—

immediately snapped his attention to the police tape barring entry to Ginny's office door.

His mind stumbled over a tangle of curse words. What happened?

He raced down the stairs. The janitor was still mopping the floors, but he paused his work and waved Varun away, as if swatting at a fly. "You been coughing or anything?" the man demanded in a surly tone.

"No, not me," Varun said. "I went to see Dr. Waters. There's police tape across her office door. What happened?"

"You didn't hear? Not from around here, are you?"

"I graduated from the marine science department—Dr. Henderson was my thesis advisor—but I've been traveling. I just got back."

"Oh." The janitor's furrowed brow relaxed when he realized Varun was a Brown University graduate too. "It was just last week. She vanished. They found her bag near her car, which was parked in the faculty lot. Her wallet was still in her bag—credit cards, cash, everything—but her laptop and tablet had been taken." The man shrugged. "Police started looking for her, but then people started falling sick, and everyone's more or less forgotten. The cops are busy directing traffic around the hospitals. Bigger shit happening, you know."

"Right…" Varun nodded slowly. "When exactly did she disappear, do you know?"

The man frowned. "Might have been last Wednesday. No, that was the day I was off. Thursday night, that's when. I was here on Friday morning when the students first complained that she hadn't shown up for class. They went looking—at least those who didn't just skip out on class right away—and that's when they found her bag near her car."

Varun grimaced. *Thursday*.

That was the day he and Ashe had spoken to Ginny.

It was entirely possible that he was the last person who had spoken to Ginny before she disappeared.

CHAPTER 2

The *Veritas,* with its gleaming, no-nonsense white hull and array of monitoring equipment on its wooden deck, stood out among the pleasure yachts in Providence Harbor. The quay, a tourist destination, was mostly stripped of life. A few couples walked along the boardwalk, keeping a safe distance from others. A handful of stores remained open, but the employees watched warily from behind glass windows, obviously hoping that no one would stop by.

Varun clenched his fist. The palms of his hands, always warm now, suddenly felt hot. *No, no.* He unfolded his fingers. *No fire. Don't burn down anything.*

Especially not when the fire department was distracted dealing with the crises of widespread sickness in the city.

He strode down the pier toward the *Veritas,* then jerked to a stop in front of the ship. "What the hell?" he grumbled as he yanked out his smartphone and tapped in a number from memory.

Henry Jackson, the first mate of the *Veritas,* picked up immediately. "Ho, Varun. You're back?"

"Not quite. Where's the gangplank? I don't have time for a swim in the harbor today."

From behind the darkened glass windows of the *Veritas,* Varun saw a waving arm motion. "Be out in a second," Jackson promised.

A middle-aged African American man emerged from the bridge, his cap tipped low over his eyes. He wore a tight smile over his neatly trimmed goatee—actually the smile was closer to a grimace. He extended the gangplank for Varun and pulled it back as soon as Varun stepped onto the *Veritas.* "Just being careful," he said, not even going through the pretense of an apology.

"Did you think you were going to get swarmed?"

Jackson shrugged. "You could see it in the eyes of people passing by. They're thinking it might not be a bad idea to be out at sea if all hell breaks loose on land."

"Well, the sea's not doing great either."

"But they don't know that, do they?" Jackson asked. "Did you get in touch with the person you were looking for?"

"Not quite. She's missing," Varun said. "She went missing that night after Ashe and I spoke to her."

Jackson shook his head. "You're like the herald of bad luck, aren't you? You get on board, and we get storms like nothing we've ever seen, two volcanic eruptions, and not to mention all that weird shit, like warriors on oversized panthers flung into the sea."

Varun started to say, "It's not me—"

"It's the captain, isn't it?" Jackson finished. He crossed to the other side of the *Veritas,* rested his elbows against the rail and stared out at the sea. "Damn, but that crazy Ondine girlfriend of yours was right, after all."

Varun bit back the instinctive protest. Ondine was not his girlfriend, at least not anymore. And she hadn't been crazy.

She had been possessed.

Big difference—although perhaps not to Jackson.

Who cared about the cause when the symptoms were identical, and the result the same?

Varun hunkered, shoulders slumped, next to Jackson. Several moments passed before he broke the silence, choosing his words with care. "Jackson, what do you think the captain is?"

"Figured you knew," was Jackson's easy reply.

"I do."

Varun said nothing else, which oddly, drew Jackson into speaking again. The older man shrugged. "Got my money on a mermaid of some sort. She's as pretty as the old stories say they are, especially with her blue and green hair, but I always thought they'd be...*friendlier.*"

Varun chuckled.

Jackson continued. "Also figured mermaids would be vain and self-absorbed, but not our captain."

Varun frowned; was he hearing pride in Jackson's voice?

"Never seen her look into a mirror or glance up at the glass to check her reflection, and she's gotten the *Veritas* clean through every storm we've faced." The first mate glanced sideways at Varun. "Mermaid or not, she's a hell of a captain. That's worth something, and if you're on a ship, it's worth everything having a captain you can trust." Jackson paused for a breath. "Where is she?"

"Stuck…somewhere."

"You know where?"

Varun nodded.

"You know how to get her out?"

"I'm working on it."

Jackson's brows drew together. "That's where you went, isn't it? To get information."

Varun nodded as he ran through the mental debate of what to tell, and what not to.

Jackson's quiet affirmation, "We'll get her out," cinched the deal.

"Okay," Varun said. "Just listen for a bit. It's going to sound crazy, but it's all true."

To Jackson's credit, he listened in silence, although his eyes widened and his expression blended both skepticism and disbelief. When Varun finished speaking, Jackson concluded with, "So, the captain's stuck in the underworld, and we need to find this professor to have any chance at all of opening a door back down there."

"That's the gist of it."

"And is there anything else you need to tell me—like how you lit the stove in the kitchen this morning?"

Varun winced. "You saw that?"

"Video cameras," Jackson said. "Got them all over this ship, mostly for safety reasons. Can't have a kitchen going up in flames when the ship's over open water." He turned to face Varun, his tone so casual he could have been discussing restaurant menus. "I get that the captain is some sort of… being that controls air and water—makes a whole lot of sense now, in fact. But what about you? Are you a different sort of thing?"

Time for the truth. "When I got on this ship two weeks ago —" Damn, had it only been two weeks? "—I was completely human, completely ordinary."

"And now?"

"I'm supposed to be able to control earth and fire."

"The other two elements." Jackson sucked in a deep breath. "And what do you mean by 'supposed to.'"

"Meaning, I don't really know what the hell I'm doing. Humans aren't supposed to have elemental magic. I stumbled into it entirely by accident. Ashe was helping me not screw up, but—"

"All the more reason to find her quickly before you set the ship on fire. The accident in your lab last night—it wasn't a Bunsen burner, was it?"

"No."

"You need someone to watch your back, Varun."

"Are you signing up for the job, Jackson?"

"Maybe." The first mate turned his back on the ocean. He looked relaxed, but the taut line of his shoulders made a lie of his stance. "Seems to me the professor disappeared because someone thought she knew too much."

"I hardly told her anything."

"Doesn't matter." Jackson shook his head. "Only thing that matters is what that *someone* believed." His lips pressed into a thin line. "And it seems to me that if you're one of the few folks who really does know what's going on, then you're really in deep shit."

"Thanks."

"I got you, man. The crew—you can count on them, too.

They won't ask too many questions, unless you actually set things on fire, but they'll keep you from being outnumbered. Where do we start?"

"We find Ginny. And I think I know who's got her." He scowled. "I don't know where to find them. But I know someone who might."

~

"You're asking me to do *what*?" Cynthia demanded.

Varun held the smartphone away from his ear and winced at the shrill note in his former classmate's voice. "I know it's not much to go on, but you helped me track down the source of the dead spots in the ocean two weeks ago, and I thought—"

"It's *nothing* to go on," the FBI analyst snapped back at him. "We're neck deep in a crisis here, Varun. America—and the world—is going to hell and no one knows what's going on or how to stop it. I don't have time to research weird iconography."

"I know what's going on, Cynthia, but I haven't a damn chance of stopping it unless I find the people who *matter.* This weird iconography is the only clue I've got."

Cynthia snarled. Varun could easily imagine her narrowed eyes and bared teeth. Cynthia and Ashe, he suspected, would probably get along fairly well together. "Fine." She grated out the word. "What am I looking for?"

"An eight-pointed star."

"Are you kidding me? That's everywhere!"

"In conjunction with a Mesopotamian cult—"

"Ishtar."

Varun stiffened at Cynthia's whispered word. *Ishtar* was one of Inanna's later derivations. "What did you say?"

"The Temple of Ishtar is a cult that worships the Akkadian goddess, Ishtar."

"I didn't know the FBI tracked cults."

"We track everything, and cults, with their disproportionate population of deluded people, can be problematic. The Temple of Ishtar has two symbols—the eight-pointed star and the lion."

"Has the cult been problematic?" Varun asked tightly.

"Not usually, but several cult members were arrested a little over a week ago in Baghdad following the destruction of an abandoned department store. They were also blamed for trampling over excavation sites in Mari; it's an ancient city near the Euphrates."

"I know Mari. I was there."

Cynthia inhaled sharply. "Were you in Baghdad too?"

"Yes."

"And they attacked you? Both times? Well, it looks like you might have identified your attackers, then. Why is the Temple of Ishtar after you?"

"What can you tell me about them?"

Cynthia humphed. "I don't like it when you answer my questions with questions."

"I don't know why they're after me. I'm looking for answers, and maybe they're trying to stop me from finding them. They've been following me, and if they realized that I came here, to talk to Ginny, then it's more than likely they're the ones who've taken her. Do you know where I can find the cult?"

"Their only known base of operations is near Crystal,

Colorado. Crystal was a mining community way back when, but the 1893 silver crash emptied the town. It's possibly one of the most picturesque ghost towns in Colorado—rivers, rapids, all that stuff—but it's also very nearly inaccessible. The roads are rough. You're almost better off making the six-mile hike than driving in with a four-wheel-drive."

"You *are* a font of random information, Cynthia."

"I'm with the FBI. It's what I do. Obviously, their headquarters is not on any map, but I'll send you the coordinates." Cynthia paused. "Don't think you can do this alone, Varun. Fanatics are the worst sort of people to take on."

"Fanatics? So they're not just deluded."

"No, deluded is believing they're descendants of Atlanteans."

His jaw dropped. "They—what?"

"They believe they are descended from the people who escaped the destruction of Atlantis."

Varun ran his tongue between his teeth. "Really? *Atlantis*?"

"Like I said—deluded. I'm not interested in delusions, Varun. If you want to believe in rainbow-colored fairy unicorns, go for it. As long as no one's getting hurt, you can believe in anything you want. But when people get hurt and die, delusions cross the line into fanaticism, and that makes the FBI sit up and pay attention. We would have sent an agent to check it out, except that we have the makings of a pandemic on our hands. No one's got the time, and now you're telling me that *this* is the source of the problem?"

"They're not the source of the problem, but they may have a key to the solution."

"I don't think I can spare anyone to help."

"You don't have to." Varun glanced over his shoulder. Jackson, who had been listening in to the call, nodded. "My back's covered."

"All right, then. Just be careful. Don't kick up too much shit, or the FBI will start paying attention to you, and that's never a good thing."

"You should know."

"I do. Be safe." Cynthia hung up without saying goodbye.

Varun set down his phone and met Jackson's eyes. "If I could, I'll bet all of Ondine's trust fund that Ginny's out there."

Jackson nodded. "Let's go."

"It'll be dangerous," Varun warned.

"So what are we waiting for?"

CHAPTER 3

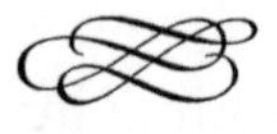

Crystal, Colorado, was as picturesque as Cynthia had promised. The cooling weather blanketed the mountainside with red, yellow, and orange foliage set against a brilliant blue sky. Far from the reach of civilization, it was easy to forget that the world was convulsing beneath the threat of a pandemic no one understood. The ghost town of Crystal, perched beside rock-filled rapids, was charming in a dilapidated way, the log walls of its crumbling buildings blending into the trees that surrounded them.

The headquarters of the Temple of Ishtar was a mile east of Crystal, away from the river, down a path that existed only if one squinted hard and used a great deal of imagination. "Are you sure it's this way?" Jackson asked for the third time in ten minutes, his knuckles white upon the steering wheel of the four-wheel drive Range Rover.

"No, I'm not sure it's this way," Varun retorted. "There

isn't any road to speak off, but we're getting closer to the coordinates Cynthia gave me."

Jackson took his eyes off the path for an instant to glance down at the map on Varun's smartphone. "We should be over it any time now." He glanced around, eyes narrowed. "Wouldn't you say this area looks rather conveniently cleared of foliage?"

Varun followed Jackson's gaze. Now that the older man had mentioned it, the area did look more like an open patch of grass, surrounded by trees.

The last time he had seen something like this, he had been in Atlantis, standing over the aether core and the Sphere of the Elements.

His heartbeat racing, Varun stepped out of the Range Rover and walked around the clearing before kneeling to examine faded parallel tracks in the grass. "Could be a helicopter landing pad."

"Sure beats driving up here. It'd be hell through the snow. Question is, the helicopter lands here, and then what? Where do the people go?"

Varun inhaled deeply, drawing the crisp air into his lungs. "Come on now," he murmured under his breath. "Do your thing." He touched the earth.

It wriggled beneath his fingertips like an affectionate puppy. The layers of the earth whispered, and the answer came to him as if he had always known it. "There's an old mining shaft down here. It goes several layers deep. They've reinforced it, changed it, molded the earth around it. That's where they are." The earth rippled, and he followed the movement to a patch of grass that did not look any different from any other. "The entrance is here."

Jackson parked the Range Rover on the edge of the clearing then joined Varun. Careful examination revealed a section of fake grass, no larger than a fist. Beneath it, a large steel D-ring attached to a well-oiled hinge allowed Jackson to pull up a grass-covered manhole-like cover. Jackson peered down the ladder extending into the darkness, then with a grim look on his face, called in the details to the two other Range Rovers, manned by the *Veritas* crew, located about a half-mile away. "If we're not out in an hour, assume it's gone to shit, then you come find us, all right? Bring all you've got."

"Gotcha," Corey, the ship's medic, replied over the satellite phone. He sounded tense, even nervous. "One hour. Starting now."

Varun clambered down the ladder. His heart skittered. Damn, but he hated heights, especially when he did not know how far the fall was. The sunlight flittering through the open manhole cover scarcely provided enough light to guide his steps.

The tunnel suddenly filled with florescent light. Varun winced against the soft glow. "What—?"

"Light switch. Right here, near the top," Jackson said.

It hadn't even occurred to Varun to look for such a thing.

"Want me to go first?" Jackson asked.

Varun inhaled deeply then shook his head. "No. You guys are already risking your necks for something that isn't your problem—"

"Last time I checked, we're all still living on this Earth, which makes it all our problems."

Varun managed a tight grin. "Of course, but I'm still going first." With his barely-there elemental magic, he could at least muster an instinctive defense, or a panicked offense.

He drew another deep breath, and this time, smelled the earth—fragrant, warm, and familiar, like a lover returning to his bed. It steadied him as he climbed down the ladder, and stripped away enough of his fear of heights for him to look around and marvel at the long steel bars reinforcing the mine's rickety structure.

"Feels like we're at least three hundred feet deep. How much farther?" Jackson's voice drifted above Varun's head.

"Not much more. The mine goes far deeper, but only the first two layers have been built out. We're almost there." He caught a glimpse of a platform, but climbed down through the opening in the hole to find himself in an enclosed room. Only then did he step off the ladder, which descended into deeper darkness.

"Not exactly handicap friendly," Jackson remarked as he joined Varun in the room. He rolled his shoulders, then tugged a handgun from a concealed holster. His grin bared white, straight teeth. "Just in case."

Varun cracked open the door and peeked out. Ornately decorated doors, each marked by chest-tall statues of a long-tailed animal, flanked a long passageway. No one seemed to be about. Varun swung the door wide and stepped out; Jackson behind him.

"Posh," was Jackson's only remark.

Varun would have chosen, "Gaudy." Turquoise and gold —in his opinion—did not lend itself to a soothing ambiance. He brushed his hand over one of the statues; the smooth, gleaming metal was as alluring as gold but stronger than steel. It had to be orichalcum. That rare metal, one of the cornerstones of the Atlantean maritime empire, was more proof of the cult's ties to that lost civilization. The rows of statues, combined with the lion and eight-pointed star motif repeated along the walls pushed the overall impression from "gaudy" to "over-the-top."

Jackson touched one of the lion motifs on the wall. "Metal of some sort. It's soft; could even be gold." His gaze swept along the length of the corridor. "At the very least, it's gold leaf. And the blue and gold isn't just a paint job. It's textured, like a woven material worked into the concrete." His eyes narrowed. "They've put a lot of work into making an abandoned mine look pretty." His grip tightened on his gun. "Do we check every door?"

Varun nodded. If Ashe were here, she would have sent in a little breeze to check out the occupants of each room. Unfortunately, if he had any surveillance capabilities as an earth and fire elemental, he had no idea what they were. "Ginny's a prisoner. They wouldn't leave her in an unlocked room. Just check the handle. If it turns, there's no need to open it. I'll check this side. You take the other."

Keeping pace with each other, they tested the doors. Varun's breath caught when he heard conversation within one of the rooms. Three…perhaps four distinct voices. He met Jackson's eye and held up four fingers. Jackson nodded grimly. He crossed the corridor and knelt in front of the door. From his pocket, he took a hardened gray putty, attached it to both ends of a wire, and then pressed the putty against the door and the doorframe.

Jackson gestured with two fingers. *Keep moving.*

None of the doors along the corridor were locked, but several rooms were occupied, judging from the sounds behind the closed doors. Jackson wired each room. Varun covered Jackson as the older man worked; his gaze flicked from one end of the corridor to the other, but no one seemed to be moving around.

Yet.

They continued down the passageway to a T-junction. Varun glanced down both ways—and saw a crowbar propped beneath one of the door handles, jamming it. *Ginny.* He hurried toward the door, but Jackson grabbed his upper arm. "Let me," he whispered.

Jackson visually examined the crowbar and the entire doorframe before nodding. "I don't think it's trapped. It's just to keep this door from opening out. Either your friend is in there, or some seriously bad-ass shit." He looked up and met Varun's eyes. "Ready?"

Varun nodded.

Jackson pried the crowbar off the door. The handle didn't turn.

Locked *and* jammed shut.

Either Ginny was a hell of an escape artist or there was, as Jackson said, seriously bad-ass shit behind that door.

"One sec." Jackson took two thin pieces of wire from his utility belt and slid them into the lock, jiggling gently.

Varun frowned. "What did you say you did before you were first mate of the *Veritas*?"

Jackson shrugged. "Don't recall ever saying anything along those lines." The lock clicked. Jackson put away his tools, and with his handgun tight in his grip, he pressed down on the handle and quietly pulled the door open.

In a small bedroom as gaudy and pretentious as the corridor, a slim figure slumped across the bed. "Ginny?" Varun hurried forward. He turned her over gently. Both her wrists and ankles were cuffed, and her face was pale and marred by a huge blue-black contusion on one side of her forehead. Even in sleep, her features were pinched, as if her pain went deeper than that quick physical examination warranted.

"No broken bones," Jackson concluded. "But her pulse is accelerated and erratic. No way to tell if she's had a concussion. Although considering the size of that goose egg, I'd say it's more than likely." He dug in his utility pouch for a small key, narrow and oddly shaped. "Opens most standard-issue cuffs," he said as he tried it on Ginny's handcuffs.

The steel cuffs clicked and snapped apart.

"Is there anything you can't do, Jackson?" Varun asked.

"Can't fold a fitted sheet. Damn tricky buggers, those things."

Ginny whimpered softly. Varun leaned over her. "Ginny, can you hear me?"

Her eyes flashed open. Her rapid inhalation of air was like that of a panicked animal. Jackson clamped his hand over her mouth to silence her scream, and she stiffened, fear blinking through her eyes.

"It's all right," Varun spoke in an urgent whispered. "It's me. This is Jackson—first mate of the *Veritas*—and my buddy. We're here to get you."

Her gaze shuttled between Varun's face and Jackson's. Her eyes remained dilated and unfocused although the terror slowly faded. Jackson loosened his grip over her mouth. Her tongue darted out to wet her cracked lips. "Varun?"

"Come on. Let's get out of here. Can you stand?"

Ginny was not stable on her feet, but she could stand with support and even walk. "I feel..." She reeled, and Varun tightened his grip around her waist. "I feel so odd."

"They hit you on the head. You've probably got a concussion."

She pressed her hand against her chest. Her shoulders hunched as if against intense pain. "So hot. And so cold."

"We've got a medic waiting. We've just got to get you out of here. Come on."

Jackson led the way, his handgun held ready. Varun followed, guiding Ginny from the room. Her weight leaned in the opposite direction from the exit. "That door." She pointed to the far end of the corridor. "That way."

"No, the exit's this way, Ginny," Varun coaxed.

"That way," she pleaded, kicking hard against Varun. "That way!" Her voice rose to a scream.

Shouts of alarm came from doors along the corridor.

"Damn it," Jackson muttered. "We're out of time. Carry her."

Varun threw Ginny over his shoulder and followed Jackson down the corridor. Doors opened. The traps Jackson had wired across the doors snapped, and the room's occupants were driven back by loud explosions and brilliant flashes of light. "Go, go, go!" Jackson shouted.

"Will it hold them?" Varun shouted as he sprinted through the blur of smoke filling the corridor.

"No," Jackson grunted. "But I didn't think a real explosion underground would be a good idea."

Ginny continued to wail, the sound incoherent. Her fists pounded against Varun's back; her legs kicked against his chest. "It's that way! He's that way!"

Varun grimaced. Whatever Ginny thought was down that way, there was no going back for it. Men charged into the corridor, their hands shielding their noses and mouths from plumes of smoke. Jackson spun around and fired two shots past Varun's shoulders.

Two heavy thuds confirmed that Jackson had found his mark.

"No!" a familiar voice shouted.

Varun glanced over his shoulder. The man with wire-rimmed glasses stood in the corridor—the same man who had pursued and harassed Varun and Ashe in Baghdad as well as Mari. His expression livid, the man raced down the corridor even though the other cultists cowered in doorways.

Varun burst through the exit, and Jackson barreled in behind him, before slamming his weight back against the door. He cursed under his breath. "There's no lock. Go up the ladder. I'll be right behind you."

Carry Ginny, kicking and screaming, *up* the ladder? Varun grimaced. *Shit.* He set her down and grabbed her shoulders, squeezing them so hard her jaw dropped in shock. "Ginny, we've got to get out. You need to climb."

She stared at him as if recognizing him for the first time. "Varun?" She blinked. "But he's back there."

"Who's back there?"

Heavy fists pounded against the door. Jackson grunted, his feet braced hard to keep the door closed. "Move it, Varun!"

"He's..." She stared at the closed door. Her lips moved but no sound emerged. Ginny's brow furrowed. "I...don't know."

"Stockholm Syndrome," Jackson snarled. His muscles bunched, straining against the force pushing the door in. "Varun, go!"

Varun pushed Ginny up the ladder. "I'm right behind you. Go! Start climbing."

Trembling, Ginny started the climb. Varun scrambled a few feet up the ladder, then looked down. "Jackson, come on!"

Sweat beaded on Jackson's brow. "There's no lock. They'll be right on our tails. I gotta stay; buy you time."

Hell, no. Varun wasn't leaving Jackson behind. "You got my back; I got yours now." Varun scooted higher up the ladder to give Jackson enough space to maneuver, then pressed his hand against the earthen walls of the mining shaft. "On my mark, get up the ladder, fast as you can and hold tight."

Doubt flickered in Jackson's eyes, but he nodded.

"Ginny, stop climbing," Varun ordered. "Just hold tight."

A brief silence, then a frightened, "All right. I'm holding on."

It was going to be spectacular—either spectacularly awesome or spectacularly disastrous—but spectacular either way… Varun drew a deep breath. "Three. Two. One. Now!"

Jackson leaped forward and grabbed onto the ladder. The door burst open, and several men charged into the room, less than a foot or two behind him.

Varun's power surged out. The earth heaved—a sharp, jolting motion that flung the men off their feet.

Jackson's white-knuckled grip tightened on the rung of the ladder. "You should have warned me."

"I did," Varun snapped back. *Kind of.* Actually, he had more or less trusted the earth to come up with a plan to save his sorry ass. From experience he should have known that it was likely to involve a great deal of instability. "Up! Now!"

Jackson scrambled past Varun as the earth exploded beneath them. Mud and dirt poured out of the mine shaft walls, tumbling into the room like a deadly avalanche. The screams of men vanished beneath the torrent.

"Damn," Jackson muttered, his voice somewhat less-than-steady.

His chest still heaving from the potent combination of adrenaline and fear, Varun met Jackson's eyes. He said nothing; he did not know what to say.

"Are they gonna make it?" Jackson asked. "Can they dig themselves out?"

Varun looked down at the layer of dirt—who knew how thick it was—that now separated them from the Temple of Ishtar. "I don't know." He looked up at Ginny who clung to the ladder, her elbows hooked around a rung. He didn't know what he dreaded more—the disbelief or the horror in her eyes.

Her lips trembled. "Who…*what*…are you?"

"I'm Varun," he promised her. "The same Varun you've always known." He forced his grimace into a tight smile. "I'm still working on *what* I am."

CHAPTER 4

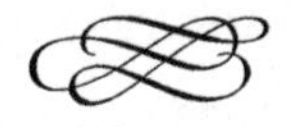

In Irkalla, the Sumerian underworld, gray was not just a color.

It was the weight in the unmoving air that filled the pause between breaths laden with despair. It slumbered in the sluggish flow of the stream; the bleakness of the unyielding earth; the absence of living flame.

In the underworld, color belonged only to those who were not dead.

Ashe stood in front of the river that flowed along the northern edges of Irkalla. Her blue and green hair streamed out in the dancing wind like a banner of war in the battle waged against death. She did not turn around as another slender figure joined her by the river.

Ninshubur. Handmaiden of Inanna, the goddess of heaven and earth.

For years, even decades, Ninshubur had concealed herself

within the form of a loquacious, foul-mouthed gray parrot. As Jinn, Ninshubur had served as Ashe's voice.

And as a spy for Inanna, Ashe thought sourly.

"Where is she?" Ashe spoke. Her voice sounded unfamiliar to her after nearly three centuries of silence.

"I do not know," Ninshubur replied. Her tone was sweet and mellow, unlike Jinn's raucous squawk.

Ashe, however, found herself missing her feathered fiend. "Inanna didn't tell you?" she demanded.

"I am only her handmaiden. The goddess does not disclose her mind to me."

Ashe scowled. "You've been here before."

"Many millennia before, when the goddess was, herself, trapped in the underworld. I came here to plead for her restoration and her freedom."

"Obviously, you succeeded. How did she get out?"

"Through the gates, but that is no longer an option," Ninshubur pointed out.

"I'm not hearing a great deal of panic in your voice."

"What need is there for a gate when there are no souls left on Earth that belong in here?"

Ashe squeezed her eyes shut against the sharp ache in her chest. "Not even Zamir's?"

"Zamir's consciousness is now bound to the First Commander. The First Commander did not belong in Irkalla, or he would never have passed through the gates as they collapsed."

"But Ereshkigal owned his soul."

Ninshubur shook her head. "Ereshkigal owns no souls. And the First Commander's soul was not bound here by necessity. He lingered by choice."

Ashe's eyes flashed opened. She exhaled, but the pain remained, embedded deep within, unshakeable. "Why?" she asked quietly.

"Because he loved her."

Ereshkigal? Ashe gritted her teeth. Ereshkigal had given to Zamir the soul of the man who had loved her? Why—if not to also bind Zamir to her? What was it with these blasted immortals who played it free and easy with lives and souls, destiny and eternity? Ashe wrenched her thoughts back to the problem at hand. "So, the fact that the gates have collapsed inconveniences no one?" *But me?*

"No line will form outside the shattered gates of Irkalla. There will be no terrifying onslaught of ghosts or zombies or creatures that humans fear."

"But there's no way out either."

Ninshubur spoke, her voice serene. "Souls were never intended to leave Irkalla."

Ashe turned to face the goddess's handmaiden, who was, in her own right, divine, or at least immortal. Ninshubur's beauty—like Ereshkigal's—was so ethereal as to be nearly blinding.

Ashe, however, settled for squinting. "I don't have a soul."

Ninshubur's shoulders moved in a gesture as graceful as it was dismissive.

Ashe glared at the handmaiden. "There cannot possibly be only one way in and out of the underworld. Humans would call that bad design."

"Design is a function of purpose. Irkalla contains. It does not release. Only the Illojim pass freely."

"The Illojim?"

"We are the Illojim—the descendants of An. Inanna, Enlil, Enki, Ereshkigal. Even Neti and I."

Ashe tilted her head. "You are…not gods, are you?"

Ninshubur shook her head. "We came from the heavens—from a planet the humans call Aldebaran. In the night sky, it is the eye of the Taurus constellation. A separatist movement broke out on Aldebaran, forcing out the ruling family—the An dynasty. The children of An and their servants—a lesser species—fled Aldebaran in their starships and made their way to Earth."

"The Beltiamatu myths say the Earth was uninhabitable when we arrived."

"The old stories are correct." Ninshubur's radiance was undimmed, but a sad smile touched her lips. "The servants of An, transformed by aether for their new lives, entered the ocean. They became the Beltiamatu, the merfolk."

"And the Illojim?"

"We lingered in our starships until the Earth was ready for life. When it was, we created another race to serve us."

"The humans?"

Ninshubur nodded. "For a time, all seemed well. Then the Beltiamatu discovered the humans."

"And so spawned Atlantis?"

"Only the ruling house of Atlantis could boast of Beltiamatu blood, but it was enough. The king was generous with his affections. The city prospered, until the war…" Ninshubur's breath whispered out of her in a sigh. "The war between the Atlanteans and the Beltiamatu. The war that destroyed Atlantis and drove Inanna, patron goddess of Atlantis, to her knees in grief."

"Yet it was Ereshkigal, the Beltiamatu patron goddess,

who ripped out our souls." If Ashe sounded bitter, it couldn't be helped.

"It was for love. She loved her sister, and that her people would have so hurt her sister, was unbearable to her. The punishment was more than your people deserved, but compelled by fury and sorrow, sometimes even the Illojim act irrationally. Ereshkigal tore the souls from the Beltiamatu, destroying their ability to touch eternity, to return to the stars, to Aldebaran." Ninshubur looked at Ashe, and Ashe was surprised to see tears brimming those golden eyes. "Inanna was horrified. The Beltiamatu, who had served *all* the Illojim so faithfully for so long—barring their war with Atlantis—had lost the only thing that mattered—their souls."

Ashe folded her arms across her chest. "And she thought attacking Ereshkigal and binding her beneath the earth was the solution?"

"Like I said…compelled by fury and sorrow, even the Illojim behave irrationally."

"That's a hell of an understatement for the chaos unleashed as a result. Shulim, the Beltiamatu capital is gone —melted to slag by the *Dirga Tiamatu*. Krakatoa erupted— twice! My son is dead, the ocean is poisoned, and now Nergal is out there, while I'm stuck in here! Where's Inanna? She's at the center of this. Why isn't she doing something?"

A delicate shudder shook Ninshubur's slender shoulders. "I…don't think she's ready."

"Ready for what?"

"To say she's sorry."

"It's been what? A millennium?" Ashe demanded.

"Several millennia," Ninshubur conceded.

Ashe rolled her eyes. "And I thought I was pathetically terrible at letting go and moving on."

"You are."

"I'm hardly as bad as the goddess."

"No one is ever as good as, or as bad as, the goddess. She could do it, though, if she chose."

"What could she do?"

"Rebuild the gate to Irkalla."

"She can? And why can't Ereshkigal?"

"The runes collapsed outward as Nergal burst through the gates. The gates can only be rebuilt from the outside. Any of the Illojim could possibly do it, but Inanna—she is perhaps the only one who would try."

"Why?"

"For love. For recompense. For reconciliation. After all, she sent me to be your companion, knowing that you were set on a head-on collision with the terrible consequences of the past."

"*Her* past," Ashe corrected testily.

Ninshubur peeked at Ashe through the seemingly endless fall of her silver hair. "You're angry."

"Angry's long in the past." Ashe clenched her teeth. Her stomach churned. "I'm furious. The problem is out there, and I'm stuck in here—and I'm not in even stuck in here with the people I can be legitimately and completely angry with."

"So, you acknowledge Ereshkigal is not to blame?"

Ashe sucked in a deep breath. "No one person is to blame for something so huge, so terrible, so out-of-control." She managed a self-mocking smile. "I certainly added more than my fair share to the chaos." Ashe shook her head. "But it doesn't change the fact that I'm stuck here, in the underworld, while all hell is breaking loose out there." She growled low in her throat. The wind skidded around her. "There has to be another way out of here."

"There isn't," Ninshubur said simply.

Ashe arched an eyebrow. "Have you tried?" She sat by the riverbank and slipped both feet into the water. For several moments, she wriggled her toes in the icy water. "Seems odd that the River of Death would encircle the Isle of the Blessed. Any halfway-decent marketing person would have pointed out to Ereshkigal that the concepts don't jive."

"It used to be the River of Life—until Nergal attacked Ereshkigal. She renamed the river on the day she married him. Many think it was to honor him as the god of pestilence."

Ashe shook her head. "I don't think so." Her gaze drifted toward the island, almost invisible behind the trees that surrounded the island like a mangrove swamp. Their branches and leaves were so tall as to be lost far above, beyond sight, but their gnarled trunks plunged deep into the water around the island, protecting the sacred fount of healing on the island.

"Then what do you think it is?" Ninshubur asked.

"I think she was trying to hide the truth from him. The Isle of the Blessed contains the Fount of Healing, which can bring even the dead back to life. The River of Life surrounds the island, drawing their waters from the fountain of eternal life." Her brow furrowed. "Those aren't trees…"

Ninshubur said nothing.

Her silence was the confirmation Ashe needed.

"They're the *roots* of the mythical Tree of Life. That's why there are no branches, no leaves. The roots draw water from the River of Life into the trunk of the Tree of Life, which rises somewhere far beyond Irkalla…on *Earth.*" Ashe's mind reeled from the possibilities.

"You are correct," Ninshubur said, "but I don't see how that information makes any difference—"

"It doesn't. Not yet…" Ashe pressed her heels together and pointed her toes. The astral energy holding her physical body together rippled its transformation through her. Her toes fused and elongated into diaphanous fins. Her legs melded together and thickened to a mermaid's tail. Scales emerged from her skin, overlapping into silver layers. The most profound changes were invisible; her lungs altering, greatly expanding her ability to process oxygen, her skin thinning and taking on a pale blue cast. Her fingernails elongated into curved talons, and her incisors into fangs.

Ninshubur smiled. "The Beltiamatu have always been the most beautiful of Illojim's creations."

Still a Daughter of Air, Ashe compacted air into the density of water so that her altered voice, now pitched at a higher frequency, could still be heard. "And the least tractable."

The goddess chuckled. "It's part of their charm."

Ashe flexed her hands, admiring the pearlescent sheen of her nails. Even in dreary Irkalla, her scales shone as if infused with their own light.

"Where are you going?" Ninshubur asked.

"I'm leaving Irkalla."

"Asherah, are you—?" Ninshubur shook her head. "Of course, you will not be talked out of it. No one could ever talk you out of anything. But you must know that what you hope to do is beyond reckless. No one—not even one of the Illojim —would dare it."

"But then again, none of the Illojim controls both water and air." She glanced over her shoulder. "Are you coming?"

Ninshubur stiffened. "You know I cannot."

Ashe smiled. "I'm going to miss you, Jinn." She dived into the water without waiting for a reply.

Scarcely fifty feet away, the water, polluted by Nergal's blood, had thickened into sludge. Nothing moved through it, yet where she had entered the water, the current was still strong, propelled by the overflowing from the fount of life. Crystal clear, the water poured from the island, filling the river, pushing toward the darkness.

At the intersection of life and death, the pure and poisoned water clashed, neither seeming to gain any advantage. When Nergal still ruled the underworld, death had the edge, but with his departure, life was holding its own once more and would do so indefinitely.

She, Varun, and Zamir had battled Nergal to a stalemate in the underworld.

Now, she had to defeat him on the surface.

But first, she had to get the hell out of the underworld.

Swimming in the effortless, sinuous way all mermaids did, she propelled herself through the water toward the Isle of the Blessed. She swam around the entire island—hardly more than a small patch of land—and ran her hand over the roots extending deep into the water. Did the roots eventually touch the Earth? She dived deep in search of the riverbed but did not find it. The depth of the river seemed to extend into forever—just as the fount of life on the island seemed to have no end. The roots, however, were finite, the gnarly thickness thinning until eventually they were as fine as hairs, trembling in the water every time she swam past.

Did she dare risk it?

Ninshubur's words came back to her. *No one—not even one of the Illojim—would dare it.*

She was an air sylph, but she was not air itself. She could be, though. After all, her physical body, such as it was, was theoretically a figment of the imagination, held together only by astral energy. As a Daughter of Air, she had reveled in being as unstoppable as a gust of wind. Invisible and malleable, she had squeezed her consciousness through impossibly small holes, and gone where only air could go.

In theory, she would will herself to be whatever she wanted to be.

Including air itself.

If her body scattered into air molecules small enough to be absorbed by the roots of the Tree of Life, would her consciousness eventually reform, or would she vanish forever?

Ashe trembled on the edge of indecision.

A face flashed through her mind. Zamir, her son, for whom she had once risked everything. She had bargained with sea witches. She had transformed from one species to another and gained two elemental powers in the process. She had broken into the underworld and challenged the goddess of the underworld and the god of pestilence.

All for her son.

She was not going to let one damned tree stop her from finding her way back to him.

Ashe stretched out beneath the hairlike roots. Like all her plans, it was either going to be utterly brilliant, or fail completely and cascade into horrific disaster. Actually, to be perfectly honest, most of her plans tended toward the latter instead of the former.

So what's another disaster? Varun and I will deal with it. We'll deal with whatever comes our way.

The astral energy peeled back from her fingertips, from her tail, from each strand of her hair. Her body dissipated slowly, bit by bit, as if dissolving in water, until there was nothing visible.

She was still there though—a Daughter of Air, not air itself.

That final step took one more act of letting go, with no guarantee that she would be able to pull her scattered consciousness back together.

Hold on tight. Hold on tight to something...someone who matters.

She fixed *one* face in her mind.

Then the astral energy blinked out, and all that was left was air.

CHAPTER 5

The first thing Ashe felt was the light, frantic slap of air against her cheek, then a gentle warmth kissing her skin. She blinked repeatedly before managing a narrow-eyed squint against the fading light of dusk.

The scents hit her then—the rich, heady musk of earth blending with the barely-there fragrance of the last summer flowers, and the deep scents of pine in the distance. Her head still spinning, her heart thudding erratically, she sat up slowly, and stared down at her silver mermaid's tail.

Confused, she looked around and confirmed that she was in pine forest.

Why did she have a tail?

She flipped the tip of her tail with some impatience as astral energy rippled through her, reshaping her tail into legs.

Ashe yanked in a deep breath as her full memories jolted into place. She scrambled onto her feet, her ankles wobbling, and looked around. Earth. She was back on Earth. Her absurd gamble to travel as air molecules through the roots of the Tree of Life, back to the surface, had paid off.

But…where was the mythical Tree of Life?

Heedless of her nudity, she walked through the pine forest. The wind curled around her, keeping her comfortably insulated from the rapidly dropping temperatures. She knew, from her innate alignment with the Earth, that she was in the Blue Mountains of Oregon.

She had honestly expected to show up somewhere in the Middle East. After all, wasn't that where life began?

Why would the Tree of Life be in the middle of a forest in North America?

The pines were tall but not extraordinary. Something niggled at her. There had to be something obvious she was missing.

She gestured, almost imperceptibly, with her fingers, and the wind, ever obedient, lifted her into the air. Her gaze swept around the landscape. Nothing remarkable attracted her attention beyond the arc of mountains dotted by pine trees as far as the eye could see.

A smile spread across her face. She had never thought she would be so happy just seeing trees again.

And color. The red and orange streaked the sky as the green of the trees faded to black.

Her eyes narrowed. When was black *not* black?

When it was streaked with vivid purple veins, writhing like living tentacles.

Far below, as dusk gave way to night, the forest lit as if it were a network of rivulets. Purple streaked through the deep black, and Ashe knew with absolute certainly, that no humans saw it the way she did.

In fact, until she passed through the roots of the Tree of Life, she was certain she would not have seen this purple phenomenon either.

Was *this* the Tree of Life?

The wind lowered her so that she could walk in the midst of the Tree of Life. But what was it? Certainly not the pines, but— She knelt to examine a purple-streaked mushroom.

Ashe inhaled sharply.

Fungus.

The Tree of Life was a gigantic fungus.

She darted into the air, rising high over the Blue Mountains. The patch of purple-streaked darkness stretched over thousands of acres, unspeakably vast. The Tree of Life was, without doubt, the world's largest living organism.

It was also—familiar.

Ashe tilted her head, trying to recall when she had last seen that image. Blackness, like an unformed cloud, shot through with streaks of violet and indigo, iridescent, like energy—

Energy!

Her breath caught. Her thoughts froze.

The aether core.

The aerial view of the Tree of Life was exactly like that of the aether cores that had powered Shulim and Atlantis for millennia. Except that it wasn't a ball of dark energy a mere four inches across.

It was *2,500 acres wide.*

Ashe's heartbeat stuttered.

The Tree of Life was an aether core—ridiculously, even impossibly large.

And it was growing.

From her vantage point, the purple veins extend like tentacles reaching forward in every direction. With the panic of a creature under attack, it was propagating desperately in an attempt to save itself.

But from what? The poison in the river of death was no longer spreading. The dark waters in the underworld would never reach the roots of the Tree of Life.

She lifted her face to the wind as the breeze carried to her the outpourings of the people—the soft sounds of weeping families, the sharp voices of emergency workers, the sterile scent of disinfectants, the stench of the dying. Panic and fear rode the wind like unbroken, fighting stallions, nostrils flaring, hooves striking, wild manes streaming out as they reared up, ready for battle, eager to kill.

The Earth, its people, were dying.

Ashe dragged in an unsteady, jagged breath of air. There was no curse word in any human language, Atlantean, or Beltiamatu large enough to encompass the careening disaster.

Nergal.

She had to stop him. Not just drive him from this realm, but defeat him completely, irrevocably.

And she could not do it alone.

Her astral energy relaxed, fading her body into invisibility. She had to find him—the man whose face was the last image that faded from her consciousness, and the first image that returned when she awoke, disoriented, in a pine forest.

Varun.

CHAPTER 6

Varun, lulled into drowsiness by the gentle rocking of the *Veritas* as it rode the waves, glanced up at the knock on the door. "Come in."

It opened, and Jackson looked in, his eyes meeting Varun's and Corey's in turn, before resting on Ginny, asleep beneath the covers. "How's our patient doing?"

"Nothing's physically wrong with her," Corey, the medic, confirmed. "It looks like they treated her well, for the most part. She does have a slight swelling on her head, where she probably fell and struck something, but nothing suggests a concussion of any sort. Her blood tests are coming back clean. They didn't drug her, or if they did, it was with something I don't have any tests for." He shrugged. "I really can't tell you why she's so disoriented." Corey stood and rolled his shoulders. "I'll be in the mess hall if you need anything else."

He let himself out, closing the door behind him.

Even with only two men in the room, it felt crowded, even

claustrophobic. The cabins on the *Veritas* were designed for utility, not comfort. Jackson studied Ginny for another moment before turning back to Varun. "Where to now?"

"I don't know." Varun winced at the querulous tone in his voice. "How soon do we have to make a decision?"

"When we run out of food," Jackson said. "We're about fifty miles offshore in international waters, and really well stocked. We're not going to run out of food any time soon. We're also close enough to reach a port within an hour in case of an emergency, but seeing how all the emergencies right now are happening on land, I'm not sure that's what we want to do."

Varun's gaze automatically turned in the direction of the North American coastline, even though, at fifty miles, it was not visible. Society was disintegrating at the edges, overwhelmed by fear of an unnamed disease that spread without vectors. How soon before whole nations—the entire world—descended into chaos? He expelled his breath. "I don't think—"

Ginny jerked upright, her eyes wide. Her trembling hands extended toward something only she could see. "No! Don't hurt him. Please don't hurt him anymore."

"Ginny, it's all right," Varun pleaded. He grasped her upper arms as Jackson sat behind Ginny to steady her. "You're safe now. No one's going to hurt you."

"Or him?" Ginny's terrified gaze fixed on Varun. "You saved him too?"

"Saved who?"

She blinked repeatedly as if Varun's question had woken her from a dream. "Him…"

"Who are you talking about, Ginny?"

She stared at Varun for a moment longer, then looked away. "I...don't know." Her shoulders sagged, and she buried her face in her hands. They muffled her voice. "I think I'm losing my mind."

"You were abducted. It's a traumatic experience—"

"My parents! Did you—?"

Varun nodded. "We called the police and told them we'd found you. We also called your parents—I tracked them down to their lake cabin—and told them you were all right. They'll let your dean know."

"I..." She frowned and twisted around in the bed to stare up at Jackson. Her brow furrowed. Clearly, she was unfazed by his proximity. "Who are you?"

Varun concealed a smile. Now *that* was the Ginny he knew. Pointed. Openly curious. Unafraid. Not the trembling, shaking woman, begging her captors to stop hurting *him*—whoever he was.

"Henry Jackson." The first mate extended his hand with as much grace as if they were meeting at a glitzy event.

They shook hands, and Ginny's eyes narrowed speculatively, before she looked around the room. Polished wood paneled walls and floors, and scarcely enough space for a bed. A night stand was mounted above the bed and a tiny closet stood on the far wall. "Not quite the Ritz."

"Didn't know you had expensive tastes," Varun said. He waved his hand at the open door on the other side of room, which led to an even tinier bathroom. "At least you have a private bathroom. Here, on the *Veritas*, only the captain's suite and the two guest suites do."

"We're on a boat?"

"Ship," Jackson corrected immediately, his tone so absent-minded that it was impossible to take offense.

"Where are we going?"

"That's what we need you to tell us."

Ginny touched her chest. "Me?"

Varun cleared his throat. "This is going to sound crazy, but just run with it for a moment. Ashe—"

"The woman who came to my office with you."

He nodded. "We went to Irkalla. The underworld." He paused for a moment. "You're not flipping out."

"You told me to run with it." Ginny shrugged. "I'm running hard here—and trying not to scream like an excited schoolgirl—but I'm running."

"Anyway…to skip straight to the end—" He paused as Ginny's eyes narrowed into dangerous slits. "I'll fill you in, I promise, but for now…just the end. I managed to get out before the gates collapsed. Ashe didn't."

"And now you need to find another way in, so that you can get her out?"

Varun nodded. "That's the gist of it." He sighed. "Is there another way into Irkalla?"

"Getting into Irkalla isn't quite like stepping around a shrub on the U.S.-Canadian border. If the myths are real—and I'm starting to suspect they are—there are many entrances to Irkalla, but all land up *outside* the first of seven gates. You still have to pass through the seven gates to enter the underworld."

"So, with the gates down, there's no way in and no way out?" The ache in Varun's chest hurt so much that he had to hunch to contain the pain. He shook his head. "I can't give up. Ashe is still in there. Without her, I just don't know how to even begin stopping all the shit that's going on."

Ginny sat up straight. "What shit?" She stared at him. "You're not the only thing that escaped from the underworld..."

Varun shook his head. "Nergal."

"The god of fire and pestilence?"

"It's just pestilence now," Varun said. He held out his hand, palm up. Heat burst into blue-tipped flame.

Ginny stared, wide-eyed. "But..."

Jackson broke in. "That's the homemade alternative to the Bunsen burner."

Ginny suddenly laughed. "Did he almost burn down your boat?"

"Ship. And yes, there was a recent accident requiring the use of a fire extinguisher."

She chuckled, but the sound faded as she stared down at her hands, as if expecting something to happen. Her fingers twitched, as if shaping around a ball—an invisible ball—then she brought her hands to her chest. Her breathing accelerated as her eyes closed. Her head tilted back, baring her throat in an oddly vulnerable yet sensual gesture. Beneath the covers, her hips rotated as if responding to sexual stimulus.

Varun and Jackson exchanged concerned glances. Ginny seemed all right, for the most part, but the all-too-frequent lapses more than implied that something was wrong, and it would not be easy to pin down. Jackson suddenly grimaced, and Varun followed the man's gaze to Ginny's chest.

Was it his imagination, or was there a faint dark glow—almost like a cloud—taking shape in Ginny's cupped hands?

Her chest heaved with each breath, as if that thing was drawing life out of her.

Jackson grasped her wrists, yanking them away from her body. That half-formed cloud of darkness vanished, and Ginny shuddered, as if emerging from a dream—or a nightmare. Her eyes fixed on the first mate. "Jackson?" She looked around. "What happened?"

"That's what we're trying to figure out." He flashed straight white teeth in a disarming grin, then looked at Varun. "Perhaps she needs to rest. I don't think she's ready for extended conversations."

"I want to hear about Irkalla," she insisted. "There's some evidence that the Isle of the Blessed inspired the early Jewish stories about the Garden of Eden." She stared at Varun's slow smile. "You saw it? The Isle of the Blessed?"

He nodded. "It's not much of an island. Patch of rock might be more accurate. There is a fountain, though, in its center—with healing water."

"The living water," Ginny mused. "It's said that it waters the Tree of Life."

"There were lots of trees in the water around the island, extending so high up I couldn't see any branches or leaves."

"So, you didn't know what kind of trees they were? Didn't they shed any leaves in the water or on the island? Was the bark rough or smooth?"

"Rough and twisted. Gnarled. Like roots, really…" His voice trailed off. "*Roots*?" Varun's eyes widened. "Could they have been the *roots* of the Tree of Life?"

"How large were they?"

"As large as tree trunks, and they surrounded the island, almost like a mangrove swamp protecting the island."

"They *were* protecting the island," Ginny insisted. "They were protecting the living waters." Her eyes shone. "I can't believe you saw the Tree of Life!"

"But if there's a tree, it's got to come out somewhere, right? Somewhere on Earth?"

Ginny stared at him. "If your plan is to dig through the roots to return to the underworld, I would put money on *that* plan not working."

"I don't know what the plan is, but it's the best lead we have right now. Where can I find the Tree of Life?"

Ginny shrugged. "It depends on who you ask. The oldest stories put it in the Garden of Eden."

"In the Middle East?"

"At the meeting of the four rivers. The Tigris and the Euphrates."

"That's just two."

Her shoulders moved in a shrug. "The other two—the Pishon and the Gihon—are believed to have gone underground."

"Just to make things difficult?" Varun asked.

Ginny laughed. "Sometimes, it seems that way."

Varun thought hard. "If we get close enough, I could probably find it."

"What do you mean—?" Ginny tilted her head. "It's that other thing you did—seeing buildings that existed before."

"That's part of the other thing that I can do," Varun confessed.

Ginny's fingers twisted into the sheets. The color slipped from her cheeks. "What else can you do, Varun?"

He sighed. "Maybe I should start at the beginning—"

Jackson stood up. "I'm going to set the new coordinates. I

reckon it'll take a few days to get where we need to be. Should we be expecting any trouble at sea?" he asked Varun pointedly.

"No more so than usual, although I wouldn't count on having favorable winds."

The first mate scowled. "Where's the captain when you need her?"

He shut the door behind him. Only then did Ginny speak. "The captain. Ashe. She's not normal either, is she?"

CHAPTER 7

The Garden of Eden was nothing like what Varun imagined it would be. He did not doubt that he was in the right place. The earth pulsed with energy. Ginny, who walked beside him, seemed entranced. Dreamlike, she drifted across the clearing, pausing often to touch the ground.

"What is she doing?" Jackson asked. His hands, shoved into his jacket pockets, were probably curled around handgun stocks. The passage out to Baghdad had been smooth enough. Negotiating a dock, however, proved impossible. All flights had been cancelled. Trains too. Ships lingered out at sea, desperately trying to conserve their resources. And the highways leading to the borders were littered with abandoned cars. Everyone was trying to flee the plague, but there was nowhere to go.

Jackson had finally abandoned the pretense at following the laws and instead sailed his ship up the Euphrates, as far as it could go. He, Varun, and Ginny continued the rest of the way in an exorbitantly priced rental car, but now that they were here, there was nothing to see.

An expensive journey—and for nothing.

Like Ginny, Varun pressed his hand to the ground. The architecture of ages past sprang up—buildings that seemed extraordinarily sophisticated, looking nothing like artist illustrations of the kinds of homes that must have existed at the time.

Even then though, there had been no tree larger than most. Certainly nothing protected by angels holding flaming swords.

And now, there was nothing. Not even ruins. Certainly no trees. They had retreated, as if pushed back by a repelling force. The clearing was stripped of grass, and covered with mushrooms sprouting from the dirt.

"Not much of a garden," Jackson commented.

Varun had to agree with him, yet Ginny walked through the clearing, carefully stepping around the mushrooms. That expression on her face was almost ecstatic.

But why?

Varun ran his hand over the mushrooms and jolted. The earth poured knowledge into him—knowledge he could not explain, and in fact, did not need to. The mushrooms were a single entity. A single root system, and not just here. There were colonies of mushrooms all around the world, all of them bound to one root system.

One massive root system.

He straightened, his breath catching in his lungs. "The Tree of Life..."

"Where?" Jackson demanded. He joined Varun. "That thing? It's a mushroom. Honey fungus. Damn near killed my mom's favorite oak. Took down a bunch of trees all across the neighborhood too."

"It's one living thing, Jackson," Varun said. "They share a common root system, which makes them a single organism."

"Maybe so, but how can that be the Tree of Life? It ain't even a tree."

"Hyperbole?"

Jackson glowered. "An awfully dangerous place for hyperbole. So, you're saying these mushrooms have roots that go all the way down into the underworld."

"It's like a river. The water in a tiny nameless creek in the Brazilian highlands eventually flows into the Amazon. Just one river pours into the Atlantic, but many—*countless*—rivers feed into it."

"Okay…" Jackson drew out the word. "How does this get us closer to Ashe?"

"I don't know." Varun dragged his fingers through his hair.

"You were going to cut up the damn tree, weren't you? Dig under its roots?"

"It crossed my mind," Varun admitted. "But this mushroom…I don't know. I need to think some more."

"Well, if you're done here, then maybe we should go." Jackson fixed his narrow-eyed gaze on Ginny who wandered through the clearing with a dreamy look on her face. "I'm not sure I like what it's doing to her."

Varun glanced at Ginny. "She's not going to hurt anything."

"It isn't natural, the way she's acting. I can't imagine what's going through her head. Makes me wonder what kind of undetectable shit those bastards put in her."

"Certainly not a tracking device of any sort; that much we know."

Jackson bared his teeth in a devilish grin. "We would have given them a hell of a reception if they'd tried to board the *Veritas*." His smile faded, and his shoulders slumped. "What now, Varun?"

"I...don't know." The admission was as painful as swallowing glass. "I..."

"You love her, don't you? The captain?"

Varun was grateful that Jackson chose instead to watch Ginny's flittering progress across the clearing instead of looking at him. "Guess I do."

"Crazy-ass choice. She'll keep you busy."

"If I can keep up." Varun was grateful for Jackson's choice of present-tense. The earth rolled beneath him, a slow, convulsing motion. "Something's..." A sensation of intense heat, of smoke and flames, of retching fear struck Varun. "This way!"

Jackson had the foresight to grab Ginny's arm. Together, they followed Varun as he sprinted across the clearing, away from their car. "Where are you going?" Jackson shouted.

"I don't know, but it's this way."

"Keep your head down." Jackson yanked Varun back before he charged out of the safety of the tree line. The three of them crouched behind shrubs to study the cluster of simple homes and the fire that blazed over a raised pyre. Lifeless bodies draped on the pyre, skin blackening from the intensity of the flames.

Ginny tilted her head, listening to the villagers' conversations. Her eyes were once again sharp and focused. "They're burning the diseased bodies. They think it will stop the spread of the sickness."

"Will it?" Jackson asked, his tone, like Ginny's, lowered to a whisper.

"I don't know, but they're desperate and out of ideas."

A loud, despairing shriek rent the air. Varun's attention jerked to one of the houses as a woman and her three children, the oldest not even a teenager, the youngest scarcely a toddler, were dragged out. The woman's heels dragged in the dirt as she fought the men, their noses and mouths covered behind cloths, who pulled her toward the pyre. Her children were hauled over broad shoulders. They kicked hard but could not free themselves. The youngest wailed, his arms outstretched to his mother.

"They're going to burn them alive?" Jackson asked incredulously.

Ginny leaned forward, listening hard, translating quickly. "They're not sick yet, but her husband died of the disease. Her mother and father too."

The villagers bound the woman and children's wrist and ankles, apparently deaf to the woman's pleas.

Ginny, her voice edged with tears, whispered, "She's asking them to let her children live..."

Jackson's grip tightened on his handgun. His gaze flicked across the clearing, counting heads, estimating casualties. He muttered softly, "If you've got a better idea than shooting our way through this, it's time to share it, because killing innocent lives to save innocent lives is just bad math."

Varun's heart thudded, its beat so loud he scarcely heard the woman and children screaming when the villagers tossed them onto the middle of the burning pyre. He shot to his feet, his hand extended. The flames leaped high then rushed across the clearing to pool around his wrist. Dirt and mud exploded out of the ground to blanket the extinguished pyre, quenching its heat in an instant.

Several stunned moments passed. Nothing moved, except for the fire dancing on Varun's open palm.

Then, on the pyre, the woman, covered in mud, sat up slowly. Her three children crawled toward her. Sobbing, she tried to wrap her bound arms around them. Jackson, his face set in a grim line, strode out from behind the trees. The woman cringed as he approached, but he held her wrists steady as he sliced through the ropes that bound them. Within moments, the woman and her three children had been freed, and he lifted them off the pyre.

Varun's gaze swept across the villagers. For now, everything seemed calm enough. The obedient fire seemed to keep things in check. They would not stay in check once he left. "Jackson, is there space in the car and on the *Veritas* for them?"

"We'll make the space," was Jackson's immediate reply.

Ginny walked up to the woman and murmured something to her. "I'll help her pack," she told Jackson, darting up a faint smile at him, before following the woman and her children back into their home.

One of the villagers, a stocky man, shouted something. It sounded angry, even hostile. Varun didn't understand a word of it, but Jackson yelled something back. The man's eyes flashed wide, and he retreated several steps.

Varun glanced at Jackson. "What was that about?"

"He said we were going to regret it. Seems he's the dead man's brother, her brother-in-law."

"What did you say to him?"

"Told him he was a chicken."

"That's it? And it made him retreat?"

"I added on a couple of profanities and threats for local flavor," Jackson admitted. "Hell, if your family can't count on you to have their back, then you're just a slug."

"I knew Ginny spoke Arabic. She spent a few years on archeological digs out here. I didn't know you did too."

"Yeah?" Jackson said. "The result of a misspent youth." He glanced at the flames, dancing and writhing on Varun's hand. "Neat trick. Definitely gets attention." His gaze flicked back to Ginny, the woman, and the children as they emerged from their home. They had washed off the mud, changed their clothes, and each carried a pillowcase stuffed with belongings. "They travel light. I like that."

"It's probably all they have."

Jackson's expression tightened. "That's not hard to fix."

Ginny must have overheard Jackson's passing comment. The smile she sent his way was radiant. "We're ready," was all she said, though.

"The car's this way." Jackson nudged his head back the way they had come. "Don't turn off that fire just yet, Varun."

Jackson led the way—just as well, considering Ginny's questionable sense of direction. Varun waited until the others had put some distance between themselves and the village before he turned his flaming wrist toward the pyre. The flames leaped forward, like race horses straining at the bit, and engulfed the wood. The heart of the fire burned incandescent blue, almost white. The villagers shied back from the flames, hotter than anything they had ever experienced.

The heat was a reflection of the heat within him—the

anger over stupidity, the fury over ignorance. The fire that now consumed the plague-stricken bodies was *Nergal's* fire.

Nergal—the source of the plague that was driving humans away from community, from decency, into self-inflicted terror.

Varun's stomach clenched. Nergal was *his* problem now—and with or without Ashe, he would have to find a way to defeat the god of pestilence.

CHAPTER 8

The sun-kissed, white-tipped waves and the clean ocean breeze enshrouded the *Veritas* in an illusion of paradise. Here, nothing seemed wrong with the world.

Varun knew better.

He sat on the deck, listening to the panicked voice on the satellite radio. Airports were closed, as were train terminals and ports. All official movement across borders had halted, but it did nothing to stem the tide of refugees trying to find safe places to hide. Rural communities built barricades, trying to keep what they thought were disease-ridden city folk from bringing the sickness with them, but death struck them anyway. Hospitals and morgues filled to overflowing. Research laboratories worked twenty-fours a day to identify the vector or the cure. They found neither.

On the opposite end of the deck, the three children, all wearing life vests, played beneath their mother's watchful eye. Ginny stood beside the woman, their conversations exchanged in lowered tones. The children were a favorite with the crew, but the woman, still wary, kept her distance from the all-male crew.

Ginny looked up, caught Varun's eye, and then crossed the deck to join him. "How are you doing?"

"Not great," he confessed. "We found lots of cool things—"

"Like how the Tree of Life is a stunted mushroom?"

"But none of it gets me closer to finding Ashe."

She slipped her arm through his. "We'll find her."

He shook his head. "I don't know if we can, and the problem won't wait. Nergal's not waiting. We have to stop him now."

"Where do we find him?"

Varun grunted. "I don't know. Maybe he's at the core of where the disease started."

"No one knows where. They haven't found patient zero."

"The portal out of the underworld dumped me near the Zagros Mountains. We'll start there—"

Ginny straightened and yanked her arm away from him. Varun followed her gaze across the deck. Jackson had stepped out from the bridge. Varun smothered a chuckle. So, *that* was how the wind was blowing…

Jackson was also looking at Ginny, but made it a point not to address her directly. "We've got to make a stop in a bit."

"Are we out of food?" Ginny asked.

He shook his head. "We're well-stocked, and the woman and kids don't eat that much. We need gas though. We have enough to get to most places from where we are, but not much beyond that. Given how things are falling apart, our best bet is to refuel as often as we possibly can. No telling when we might not be able to do so."

"Sounds right," Varun agreed. "What do you suggest?"

"Closest port is—" Jackson looked up as the wind accelerated to a howl, sending clouds scurrying across the sky. The waves tossed—higher, wilder. His eyes narrowed. "The forecast called for clear skies and seas all day today. This ain't natural."

"No, it's not," Varun agreed. He stepped away from Jackson and Ginny to peer over the railing. The water turned a threatening gray, the color of the cloud-covered sky. The wind coalesced, twisting into a visible spout.

"Damn it!" Jackson cursed, turning around. "I have to steer us out of this storm." Behind him, the woman called to her children, hurrying them back under shelter.

"No…wait." Varun said. The feeling in his chest was so sharp, so large, he thought it might burst out of him.

A child suddenly screamed, but it was a sound of amazement.

Varun looked up. Disbelief gave way to hope.

Hope escalated into joy as Ashe burst out of the water and soared over the *Veritas.* A flick of her silver mermaid's tail rained drops of water down on him. Her blue green hair streamed out like a cloak behind her. She was stunning.

Perfect.

Alive.

Waterspouts churned the ocean into a fury. The ship lurched over the crest of a wave at least twenty feet high. The wind screamed, and salt water swept over the bow of the *Veritas,* drenching the deck. Ashe made hardly a splash when she dived back into the water, but the exultant wind and waves confirmed that she had been there.

That she had returned.

Jackson's shock melted into grin. "Now, *that* is a mermaid with zero fucks left to give."

~

Ashe's second leap from the ocean positioned her directly over the center of the deck. She twisted into a midair somersault, flicking water off her tail. Her entire body blurred for a split second before she landed—on legs instead of a tail.

Varun offered her a towel and a smile. "Welcome back."

She stared at him as her heart did ridiculous things, its erratic beat thumping so loudly in her chest that she was almost certain he had to have heard it. Instead, she squared her shoulders as he wrapped the towel around her. His face was so close to hers that for several moments, they shared the same breath of air.

When her fingers brushed against his, he turned his wrist to clasp her fingers, squeezing tight as if he wanted to make sure she was real, was here. His eyes were moist; his smile charmingly crooked and more than just a little wobbly.

Maybe he had missed her too.

"Jackson. Ginny." Ashe acknowledged them with a glance and a nod of her head.

Jackson blinked. "You're…speaking. Where's Jinn?"

"Jinn—as it turns out—is a demigoddess. Her real name is Ninshubur; she's the handmaiden of the goddess, Inanna."

Ginny was practically bouncing on the deck. "Jinn…the

parrot…was not really a parrot? She was Ninshubur? Really? This is amazing! And she's—"

"Still in Irkalla, with Ereshkigal and Neti. No one's leaving until the gates are restored, and they can only be repaired from the outside. Ninshubur thinks that, of all the gods, only Inanna might care enough to do so—but that troublemaking goddess has been missing for millennia now, ever since her falling out with Ereshkigal over Atlantis and the Beltiamatu souls." Ashe glanced around. Her heartbeat stuttered, and she had to squeeze Varun's fingers for strength to ask the question stuck in her throat. "Where is Zamir?"

"I don't know," Varun said. "He vanished as he came through the portal. In Irkalla, he was the physical manifestation of a soul. He didn't really have a body, and when he returned to the real world…I'm sorry, Ashe." He drew her against his chest and stroked her trembling back. "I know you went through hell, literally, to get him back. We'll figure it out. We'll find him."

"He'll have to wait," Ashe forced out the words even though her voice shook. "Do you know what Nergal is doing?"

Varun nodded.

"Why haven't you done anything about it?"

"I was trying to get to you. How did you get out of Irkalla when no one else could?"

She shrugged. "I turned into air, dissolved into water, and was absorbed by the roots of the Tree of Life."

Varun's eyes narrowed. "Really?"

She nodded. "Landed up in Oregon."

"Oregon?"

"The Tree of Life is a mushroom patch—several hundred acres wide."

"I know. The patch, actually, has roots that go around the world. I saw part of it where the mythical Garden of Eden was supposed to be."

"The patch in Oregon is far larger. It may be the core of the Tree of Life."

"Is it still being poisoned?"

Ashe shook her head. "So far, it seems to be holding its own. The water from the Fount of Life can't seem to push back the waters polluted by Nergal's blood, but neither are the polluted waters making any headway. They're at an impasse for now, which buys us time to take down Nergal."

"We don't have much time. The world's in chaos. All public transportation has shut down. The hospitals and clinics are overloaded. No one knows how the disease is spreading. There's no classification, no name for it." Varun's breath escaped in a sigh. "Some people are calling it 'The One' as in *the one* that ends all life on Earth."

Ashe's brow furrowed. "Remember the Sphere of the Elements?"

"In Atlantis?"

"The inscription on it said, *'The sphere's light summons great protectors against humanity's ancient curse.'*"

"But the sphere is activated by five elements. You're only air and water."

"But you're earth and fire. The instructions didn't say that they had to be activated by one person."

"We're still an element short. What's the fifth?"

"I don't know," Ashe murmured. "But Medea might."

Jackson spoke up. "Is that our next stop?"

Ashe nodded. "The Levantine Sea, then back to Atlantis."

"We'll have to refuel and restock food. We could make it to the Levantine Sea, but Atlantis, way out in the middle of the Atlantic Ocean—that's too much of a stretch."

Ginny's eyes widened. In fact, they seemed almost perpetually wide. "Atlantis is in the middle of the Atlantic Ocean? Can I see it? Please?"

"Only if you like big cats," Jackson said with a straight face.

"I like cats," Ginny said.

"Then you'll love these." Jackson chuckled. He looked back at Ashe. "Should I head for the nearest port?"

"Pick a mid-sized port, one with easy access to local fuel supplies. If all international transportation has broken down, the ports could be running out of fuel."

"Aye, captain." Jackson touched his index and middle finger to his forehead in a quick salute, then headed in to the bridge.

"Now, Varun." Ashe turned to him. Her fingers were still entwined with his. She did not think she ever wanted to let go. "Tell me why there are children on my ship."

CHAPTER 9

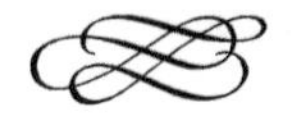

The exchange of stories lasted well into the night. In the crew's mess hall, emptied but for them, Ashe and Varun sat next to each other, hips and shoulders touching, knees frequently bumping, their fingers interlaced. Ginny sipped coffee and asked questions about Irkalla, Atlantis, the merfolk, and the ancient enmity that cascaded into present-day disaster.

"It's like a soap opera." Ginny sighed. "All those beautiful beings, and not a lick of sense among them."

"Do any of the myths offer any insight into where Inanna might be hiding?" Ashe asked.

Ginny shook her head. "To be honest, I'm surprised she's hiding at all. There is no supreme deity in Sumerian mythology, but if there were, it would be Inanna. She's the golden girl—the star of the cheerleading squad who also happens to be valedictorian. And prom queen. She's flashy. Over-the-top. Hiding isn't her thing, although—" Ginny frowned. "—getting twisted into a knot over the loss of the Atlanteans didn't seem like it would be a thing either or punishing her sister for stripping the souls from the merfolk."

Varun shrugged. "If soap operas were balanced, they wouldn't be interesting, but maybe there's more depth to Inanna than the stories suggest."

"What about Nergal?"

"Exactly as you described," Ginny said immediately. "Cynical, ruthless. A bit desperate. He doesn't really have a place of his own."

"What do you mean?"

"Inanna is the Queen of Heaven and Earth. Ereshkigal is the Queen of the Underworld. The other Sumerian deities, likewise have a place that belongs to them, be it the sky, the sea. Not Nergal, though. Neither pestilence nor fire is a place."

"Are you suggesting that he's a lost child trying to find a place to belong?" Varun asked incredulously.

"Hardly, but if he's a bit neurotic..." Ginny shrugged. She twisted the cup around on its coaster. "Actually, they're all highly neurotic, but if he's a touch more so than them, you could almost understand why. He's trying to secure his own place in their hierarchy." She looked at Ashe. "Did you say that he went after Inanna, but she spurned him?"

Ashe nodded.

"Sounds like he's trying to secure a place for himself on the ladder. Inanna was the perfect target, only she had better taste, and as the goddess of war, she could have kicked his ass without breaking stride. Ereshkigal was Nergal's backup plan, and he didn't even bother with trying to woo her."

Varun scowled. "He raped her and would have killed her if she hadn't offered herself in marriage to save her life."

Ginny rolled her eyes. "No soap opera writer could have come up with this storyline. The editor would have ripped it to shreds for 'lacking realism.' Well, Ereshkigal's better off now. She's rid of him."

"And we're stuck with him," Ashe murmured. "Any clues on how to defeat him, or any of the gods, for that matter? Can they be killed?"

"In theory, yes. Inanna once died and was brought back to life."

"She did?"

"Yes, in the underworld." Ginny pursed her lips. "She was a bit of a prick. Probably deserved it. Might even have stayed dead if Ninshubur hadn't gone down there and pleaded for her to be restored. All cultures have their winter-to-spring myths. This is the Sumerian version of it."

Varun sighed. "So, back to the characters in the soap opera. Some of them are stuck in the underworld. Inanna is missing. And Nergal is living up to his reputation as a pain in the ass. How do we stop him?"

"I don't know," Ginny admitted. "Apart from Inanna dying that one time, there's nothing in their myths about the Illojim dying. Obviously, they're immortal in the most basic definition of immortal—they do not age, nor do they get sick and die. Maybe they can still be killed in battle, but that's way out of my scope. I'm starting to realize how little the truth marries up to the myths."

"Really?" Varun asked. "Because I noticed quite the opposite. I noticed how the truth is perfectly obvious in the myth, if you looked at it from the right perspective."

"What do you mean?"

"Sometimes, it's in the words. Take them more literally, or less literally, and the meaning changes entirely. The truth finally makes sense."

"But which was is it—more or less literal?"

Varun laughed. "Depends on the myth and the truth."

Ginny huffed. "That's not helpful."

The intercom crackled. "Captain?"

Ashe straightened. "Yes, Jackson."

"Might want to come up here."

Ashe tugged her hand free from Varun's. Both Varun and Ginny rose to accompany her from the mess hall.

"Bad weather?" Ginny asked, her voice edging toward nerves.

"No." Ashe shook her head as she walked down the corridor and pushed open the door to the bridge. The first mate was in there with Meifeng, the navigator. The Chinese man darted a quick glance at Ashe. He, and all the other crew, had been on edge ever since Ashe's return, and the stunning revelation that she had once been a mermaid, who now controlled water and air. Jackson, however, kept the layer of normality in place with his easy communication style with both Ashe and the crew. "What is it, Jackson?"

He nudged his head toward the shore. "Take a chance, or go somewhere else?"

People swarmed the docks and quay, a crowd at least fifty people deep. All of them carried bags. Most of them waved wads of money. The clamoring made individual voices inaudible, but the desperation and despair shrieked louder than words. If a ship passed too close to the dock, even if it did not stop, people leaped into the water and tried to swim to the ship. A large yacht that docked was immediately swarmed. Its crew fired shots to keep the people away. Several bodies crumpled to the wooden dock, but mass hysteria overcame even the fear of getting shot. The crew was crushed and killed, and the people trampled over their bodies to rush onto the boat

Jackson grimaced. "Fools. How are they going to sail the ship if they kill the crew?"

"The yacht's not going anywhere," Ashe murmured.

Within moments, the boat tilted, listing sideways from all the weigh piling on to it, but people kept leaping onto the yacht. In slow motion, the side of the boat hit the water. Even from that distance, they heard the screams. The water thrashed with flailing limbs.

Not everyone made it back to the dock.

"Well, captain?" Jackson asked. "There's fuel, here. The port master confirmed it, but they can't run a line out to us. Nothing's getting through the people."

"Do we have enough to make it to another port?" Ashe asked.

"Possibly, but without any guarantee that it won't be the same exact situation meeting us there."

"We'll take our chances here, then."

"The crew's up for whatever it takes." Jackson wriggled his fingers in what he probably thought was some kind of mystical gesture. "And you do also have other resources at your fingertips."

"None that won't send the crowd into a panic."

He shrugged. "They already look plenty panicked to me."

"What's the port master's name? And where can I find him?"

Jackson pulled up a map of the Port of Alger on his computer. "The control building's right there." He jabbed at the screen. "It's a damn long ways through lots of people. The gas line is mostly underground, but it comes up here." He tapped a section about twenty feet away from the water. "Even if we manage to run a line out to it, we'll have to protect it if we want a shot at a getting any gas at all." He grimaced. "Twenty feet doesn't seem like much, but it's a lot to protect when the odds are about a hundred to one. Shooting people won't make us any friends." He looked at Varun. "Neither will setting them on fire. This plan to get gas could go perfectly sideways in less than a blink of an eye."

Ashe glanced at the yacht. The side of its hull was scarcely visible above the water. "Jackson, I want you with me. Meifeng, you have the bridge. Radio the port master. Tell him we're coming in, then bring in the ship about twenty feet from the dock. Do not extend the gangplank. We'll clear a path to the line and connect it. When we signal, turn it on."

"Got it." Meifeng took over Jackson's place at the controls.

Ashe turned toward the door. "Jackson, arm the crew and position them on deck. Ginny, make sure the woman and her children are in a cabin on the other side of the ship, and stay with them. No point alarming them any more than we have to."

Varun chuckled under his breath. "Are you sure you weren't a general at some point?"

"No, but I was a princess. Ordering people around comes naturally." She flashed him a faint smile. Their fingers entwined, and he gently squeezed her hand.

He glanced toward the dock as the *Veritas* slowed its

approach. "Short of sending an earthquake or a hurricane though this place, do you have any ideas?"

"Make a wall?"

Varun shook his head. "A large section of the dock is built over water. There's a thin layer of concrete over what looks like steel beams, but it'll fragment if I try to reshape it into a wall."

"How controlled is your fire?"

"It's not," Varun said flatly.

Ashe glanced up. Her power unfurled, stretching across the breadth of the sky and the depth of the sea.

The first few waves were small, their white caps slamming against the quay, spilling sea foam across the concrete. The crowd muttered, but did not move.

The ocean roiled, churning up higher waves. They rippled gently beneath the *Veritas* before swelling large, rising several feet high. Cries of alarm filled the air. The people closest to the edge tried to retreat, but there was no place to go. The crowd was too deep to easily move. Seawater crashed over the people, drenching them.

Varun squared his shoulders as the waves fell back and another assault upon the dock began. "I don't think they're going anywhere, but if the waves keep pounding them, sooner or later, they're going to get washed into the sea, and then we'll probably feel morally obliged to save them."

Ashe scowled. "So, we just do this the hard way, then?"

"I didn't know there was any other way but that." He chuckled when her scowl deepened. "You've got to acknowledge that the crisis has been continuously escalating—almost as if something or someone has it in for you."

Her scowl gave way to a thoughtful furrow between her eyes. "I wonder…"

"What is it?"

"Nothing." She shook her head. "It just *almost* made sense—except that this soap opera, as Ginny calls it, involves those melodramatic Sumerian gods. It has nothing to do with me."

"You're peripheral…except you're not," Varun pointed out. "You're the catalyst. The stalemate—Ereshkigal imprisoned, Inanna missing, and Nergal ruling the underworld—would have continued if you hadn't set off to find a soul for Zamir."

Ashe swallowed through the ache in her chest. "I…hope he's all right. I need him to be. After everything…"

Varun gripped her fingers, anchoring her. "I know. He's your son. He's everything to you."

"*Almost* everything," Ashe murmured. "But not the only thing." She kept her gaze out on the dock, swarming with clamoring people, but she scarcely saw anything beyond the rise of waves against the brilliant blue sky. "What happens…?" The question stuck in her throat. "How is Ondine?"

"You know this isn't about Ondine," Varun said quietly. "It's about us."

"You're human, Varun. I'm not."

"Funnily enough, I *did* notice that."

"Your elemental powers don't make you any more equipped to handle a world of gods and monsters."

Varun burst into laughter. "I don't think I will ever forget my encounter with Big Thing." His smile turned wry. "I think you're forgetting something, Ashe. Three hundred years ago, all of these would have been gods and monsters—creatures to fear and hate. But now, the gods are merely beings with cool, advanced technology—which humans desperately want to get their hands on, by the way—and the monsters are creatures the humans would be fighting to conserve—if only they knew about it." His hand tightened around hers. "Three hundred years ago, I wouldn't have been ready for you. God knows, my great-whatever-grandfather wasn't. But things change. Humanity grew up a little. We developed a smidgen of maturity and the semblance of an open mind. It's just as well you waited around for us to be halfway decent." His throat worked. "I'm glad you waited around for someone in my family to recognize what…*who* you really are."

"You were—"

An outcry rose from the dock as the *Veritas* cut its engines to idle in the water about twenty feet from the pier.

Ashe drew a deep breath and looked up at Varun. "You were worth the wait. Now, let's go. We have work to do."

"And we have a conversation to finish after that." The way he said it sounded more like a warning than a promise, but Ashe couldn't find it in herself to mind. If *she* had said it, it would have sounded like a threat instead of merely a warning.

Meifeng's voice came over the intercom. "Captain, the port master knows we're just offshore. He's ready to turn on the pump as soon as we're connected. I've unlocked the fuel door. The hose's unlatched, ready for you."

Ashe tugged her hand free from Varun's and strode toward the side of the ship.

"Is there a plan?" Varun asked.

"Connect the hose. Get gas."

His eyebrows shot up. "And…"

She shrugged. "That's it." Ashe waved her hand and the waves rose even higher, until it seemed like a wall of water, charging toward land. The water concealed her from the view of the people crowded on the pier. She stepped overboard onto a cushion of air, grabbed the heavy hose from behind the fuel compartment and walked unhurriedly toward the dock.

"Ashe!"

She glanced over her shoulder and beckoned to him.

Varun looked down at churning water, grimaced, and then stepped forward. His eyes widened as the wind sweeping beneath him kept his feet from hitting the water. He hurried toward her. The wind lifted them up, carrying them to the level of the pier, then swept forward like a battering ram, clearing a narrow path toward the pump head. A wall of rapidly spinning air rose up on both sides of the corridor, creating a tunnel.

The people, eyes bugging out of their heads, took a few steps back. The wind swept most of their voices away before Ashe could hear anything said, but the expressions on faces needed no translation. Shock gave way to desperate anger. The ship was too far to reach, and the warning shots Jackson fired into the water assured the people that it would be foolhardy to attempt a swim. The twenty-foot high waves deterred those would might have risked it anyway.

The rapid swirl of air blurred faces, turned smooth motions jerky. The buzz of voices—words inaudible—grew louder, angrier. Ashe attached the hose and turned to wave at the ship. A glance at the valve confirmed that gas was flowing. Her eyes met Varun's, and he nodded grimly. His gaze swept continuously over the crowd as desperation simmered into unthinking panic. Unable to see what was really happening near the pump, someone—or many people—in the back shoved forward. The momentum sent a man stumbling against the wind wall.

The lashes of whipping air, their edges as sharp as knives, flayed the man's skin off his face and hands. His scream was audible only for a moment. The wind slashed though his open mouth, ripping off his tongue. Crimson droplets, flung by the wind, sprayed across aghast faces.

"No!" Ashe gasped. The wall of wind collapsed as the man crumpled slowly, jerking spasmodically, to the ground.

Varun knelt by the man, searching for a pulse.

He found none.

Varun looked up and met Ashe's eyes, his own wide with shock.

A woman dropped to her knees beside the man, keening with anguish, her hands fluttering above the man's shredded skin and flesh. Terror escalated into outrage, and the crowd lunged at Ashe and Varun, their faces contorted with fury.

Varun slammed both fists into the concrete desk. The ground heaved, throwing the people backward, but only for an instant. They scrambled to their feet and surged forward, swinging their fists at Ashe and Varun.

The wind swept Ashe and Varun into the air, but they were chased by angry howls as the people on the dock turned to vent their fury on the hose connected to the pipe.

"They're going to rip out the hose!" Ashe shouted.

Flames flared to life on Varun's hands, but he folded his fingers into fists, extinguishing the fire. "I can't. Any hint of flame and the whole dock might blow up!"

On the *Veritas,* Jackson ordered his men to fire their handguns into the air, but the sound did not drive the people back.

Ginny, however, emerged from the bridge and raced across the deck to Jackson. From that distance, Ashe could see Jackson gesturing, but the situation hardly needed explaining. They were almost out of time and options.

Ashe hurled her power skyward, and the wind churned into a funnel.

"No!" Varun shouted. "You can't drop a tornado down on people."

"It'll catch them up. It won't fillet them."

"It'll kill them! Humans are fragile; you know that. We'll get oil somewhere else."

Ashe shook her head. "They're ripping the hose! If we lose that hose, we won't be able to get any oil, anywhere. It's over for the *Veritas*. We'll be stranded."

"You can't kill people, Ashe!"

"If we don't stop Nergal, they'll all die!"

More than forty feet away, Ginny crossed to the edge of the *Veritas*. The wind tugged at her hair and waves rocked the ship, as if the elements were instinctively rising to defend themselves.

Ginny cupped her hands in front of her, and a glowing blue-black cloud, streaked with purple slashes, emerged slowly from her chest to dance between the palms of her hands.

Varun's jaw dropped. "What's that?"

"Aether…" Ashe shook her head. "But it can't be."

Black energy crackled outward. Next to Ginny, a form took shape. Human. Male. The form raised its head. Its features were indistinguishable, but it seemed to Ashe that it met her eyes and inclined its head.

The grace of its acknowledgement.

The intimate connection—

Ashe's breath caught. *Zamir?*

Arcs of black and purple lightning streaked out from Ginny's fingertips and lanced across the pier along both sides of the hose. The terrified people leaped back.

The pier did not crack as much as dissolve—concrete disappearing, the steel beams beneath them vanishing—until there was a five-foot gap on either side of the hose.

The people pushed away from the gap, their feet scrambling along the edge.

They twisted around to stare at the *Veritas* and at the small-framed, blond-haired woman who stood beside the rail.

Seemingly ordinary.

Anything but.

The lightning vanished. On the ship, Ginny reeled and crumpled to the deck, but Jackson caught her before she hit the wooden planks. The vanished sections of the pier, however, did not reappear. They were not illusions. The changes wrought by aether weren't just real. They were permanent.

Ashe gestured, and the wind swept into the five-foot gap and pushed outward, creating a steady pressure that made it impossible for anyone to leap over the distance.

Varun studied the valve, rattling beneath the pressure of flowing gas. "How much longer?" he demanded.

Meifeng gesticulated wildly from the bridge. *Done. Cut it off.*

A tendril of wind flipped the valve on the hose, loosened the screws, and then tugged the hose free, winding it up beyond the reach of the shouting crowd. The wind carrying her and Varun aloft, Ashe returned the hose to the fuel chamber then locked the door before vaulting back onto the ship. "We're clear, Meifeng. Get us out of here."

The engines of the *Veritas* throbbed to life, and the ship pulled out of the harbor.

Ashe walked up to Ginny. Both Jackson and Varun were already bending over her. Corey, the medic, scurried past Ashe and knelt to examine Ginny.

"Is she all right?" Ashe asked.

"Unconscious, but her vitals are stable," Corey said, his voice brisk, although there was a worried furrow on his brow. "Let's get her back to her cabin so she can rest."

"I've got her," Jackson said, lifting Ginny easily. Varun went on ahead, opening the doors, and tugging back the covers on the bed in Ginny's cabin.

Corey lingered by the door, a frown on his face. "What was that thing she did?"

"It's aether," Varun said quietly, stepping back as Jackson smoothed the covers around Ginny's shoulders. "I don't know what she did, but aether is the energy source that powered both Shulim and Atlantis. I saw it—at both places—but how did it get in her?"

"Only she can answer that," Ashe said. "But why didn't she tell us earlier?"

"Maybe she doesn't know. Maybe she doesn't remember. Her memory of her abduction is hazy," Corey said. "I'll be in my clinic. I want to do a bit more reading and see if there's anything else we can do for her."

Jackson waited until the door closed behind Corey. He frowned. "She's not showing any signs of post-traumatic stress disorder, except for those fuzzy memories. Don't think I've met anyone more balanced and levelheaded than she is, except for all that gushing about ruins and ancient civilizations."

"What happened when she came on the deck?" Varun asked.

"I told her what was happening, then she walked to the rail and just...did that thing." Jackson's voice sounded hollow. "Did the pier really vanish?"

Varun nodded.

"Not just invisible, but *gone?*"

He nodded again.

Jackson waved his hands, the gesture frustrated, perplexed. "How does that even happen? It crumbled? Melted?"

"No. It just vanished. I don't know how."

The first mate shook his head. "That's not...possible." He looked at Ashe. "What the hell is aether?"

"Dark energy. The most abundant form of energy in the universe. But it's also here on Earth now."

Varun's head snapped up. "In Shulim. In Atlantis."

"No. Those were small aether cores—scarcely larger than a human head—but they powered the cities for thousands of years."

"And you saw more aether?"

She nodded. "The Tree of Life. It's an aether core."

Varun shook his head. "No, that's not possible. The Tree of Life is a *fungus*."

"With roots sprouting into vast colonies all around the world. The largest colony is in the Blue Mountains of Oregon—hundreds of thousands of acres."

"What is it *doing* there?" Varun demanded.

Ashe shrugged. "Nothing. It's just there."

"That's crazy..." Varun frowned suddenly. "It must have happened at the Garden of Eden. Ginny was walking among the fungus, as if in a daze. Somehow, it got into her."

"We were there too. Why didn't it affect you or me?" Jackson asked. "Hell, there are villages within spitting distance of the garden. Why isn't everyone there spewing aether magic?"

"I don't know."

Ashe drew a deep breath. "Could it be the fifth?"

"The fifth what?" Varun's eyes widened. "The fifth element needed to trigger the Sphere of the Elements? You think that's it?"

"Why not? The sphere is at Atlantis, and we know the Atlanteans used aether. It's a guess, but it's the best one we've got. We could trigger the sphere and free humanity's protector to stop Nergal."

Varun cleared his throat. His shoulders were stiff. "Ashe, I saw something else when Ginny used aether to make the pier vanish. Next to her—"

Ashe nodded. "I saw him too. Zamir. He's here."

CHAPTER 10

"Who the hell is Zamir, and why is he here?" Jackson demanded.

Varun glanced at Ashe, then replied for her. "Zamir is Ashe's son."

The first mate jerked his startled gaze to Ashe. "You have a son?"

"He was the mer-king. He gained a soul, died, escaped from the underworld with me, but doesn't have a body." Varun's shoulders sagged on a sigh. "I couldn't see him. I didn't know what had become of him, but clearly, he's still here—following us."

"Is he biding his time? Is he going to hurt Ginny?" Jackson demanded.

"Why would he? The thing she did—with aether—made him visible, at least for a moment. I don't know what we can do, but at least we know he's not just gone."

"I knew he wasn't," Ashe murmured. "I felt him, even though I couldn't see him."

Jackson looked grim. "So, he's like a ghost? Are you sure we have nothing to fear from Zamir?"

"No, I don't think so," Varun said. "We're all trying to stop Nergal."

Jackson glanced at Ginny. "So, she's the key? We'll have to keep her safe, then."

Varun concealed a smile. "You got it?"

"I'm on it," Jackson promised.

Varun ushered Ashe out of the room before him, then closed the door. "I think he's falling hard."

"Who?"

"Didn't you see? Jackson's falling for Ginny."

"He is?"

Varun shook his head. "You really don't get this, do you? Don't the Beltiamatu have courting rituals or some such?"

"They did. I didn't. I told you—I selected my mate…and he was ritually sacrificed after Zamir was born."

"No wonder you have so much trouble with the concept of love." He chuckled suddenly. "No wonder the thought of everyone believing that you went up on land because you loved my whatever-great-grandfather drives you crazy. I would be grumpy too." His smile faded. "Ashe. The rules have changed."

"Have they?" She walked onto the deck. The sky was steel gray, the sea choppy. The wind tugged at her hair. "The world is in crisis, but that's no reason for the elementals to display the powers they've spent thousands of years hiding. It was one thing to strike at Ondine, who was perfectly capable of flinging out flames in response, but these people out there—

they were afraid and desperate for their lives. They shouldn't have died."

"I know."

"There may not be rules, Varun, but the universe exists in balance. Sooner or later, there will be an accounting." Ashe's eyes squeezed shut against the future. "I'm afraid of what it might be. I don't have anything else that I can afford to give up."

He gripped her hand. "Denying what I know you feel for me isn't going to change the accounting, or the aftermath. I don't think the universe is fooled by facades or charades, so let's not waste what time we have."

"Captain," Meifeng's voice crackled over the intercom. "We're coming up on the Levantine Sea. Do you want me to head to a port, or drop sea anchor?"

Varun and Ashe exchanged glances. "I should check on my parents," Varun said.

Ashe nodded. "If they want to come on board, we'll make space for them." She raised her voice. "Meifeng, we'll stop at Kalymnos. Anchor her at sea and send the speedboat in. Jackson?"

"Yes, captain?" Jackson's deeper voice answered.

"You have the bridge."

"Yes, captain," Jackson replied. He asked no further questions. Varun did not doubt that the first mate was burning up with questions, but he was too much a stickler for protocol to openly challenge the captain of the *Veritas*.

Varun and Ashe walked toward to the section of the deck concealed from the view of security cameras. "You're going to talk to Medea?" he asked her.

She nodded as she tugged her dress over her head. Varun

sucked in a breath. Ashe was casual about nudity. It probably went with not really having a body to begin with.

What have I fallen in love with?

"You'll be careful, won't you?" was all he said as she climbed onto the rail. The waves tossed, rising to welcome her.

She glanced over her shoulder and flashed him a smile. The wind swept her hair away from her face as she leaped high, somersaulting in midair before cutting into the water without a single splash. The water shimmered. It could have been sunlight reflecting off the waves, but somehow, Varun did not think so.

The surface of the sea trembled, then split apart, as Ashe leaped high out of the ocean. Perfectly graceful. Flawlessly svelte. A powerful flick of her silver tail sprayed water over him.

The intercom crackled. "Whoo! Go, captain!"

Varun chuckled. Had he ever doubted that the crew of the *Veritas* would not follow their captain? "Go, captain," he murmured. *And come home safely.*

I'm waiting.

~

The ruins of Shulim, the capital city of the Beltiamatu, no longer blew dark plumes of smoke into the sky. The waters around it no longer bubbled and boiled, but the temperatures were still high and the seafloor, where Shulim had once rested was a black, cratered wound in the Earth. Its core oozed gray molten iron and silver-hued platinum.

Ashe paused in the water, her gaze sweeping over the

devastated seascape. Other than the melted slags of metal, there was no hint that a city had ever stood in that place. The rocky overhang, with a hole blasted through its center, bore testimony to the savagery of the *Dirga Tiamatu*. Nothing had ever survived its blast.

Nothing ever would.

Not that it mattered anymore. The controls for the *Dirga Tiamatu*, the weapon that harnessed the heat from the planet's core, had been destroyed with Shulim.

Earth's greatest weapon had been rendered inaccessible. Powerless.

And it was for the best.

Quick motions darted through the shadows beneath the rocky sea shelf. Ashe frowned and swam through the uncomfortably warm water. Whatever it was, it cowered by the stones that littered the seafloor, just beyond Ashe's sight.

Something flickered in her peripheral motion. Water rippled behind her.

The currents trembled with the low, haunting war chants of the Beltiamatu.

Ashe twisted around. Faint shafts of sunlight glinted off multiple bright streaks flashing toward her. She flung out her hands. Air pushed water into a powerful surge. The spears racing toward her wobbled to a stop, as if striking a wall.

From the deep water beyond the rock shelf, more than a score of Beltiamatu swam into view, their long tails swaying in sinuous curves. Their skin was gray, leeched of the pale blue tints of a healthy Beltiamatu, and the luster had faded from their aqua, teal, and violet hair.

Diseased Beltiamatu.

Apparently, not all of them had been destroyed in the devastation of Shulim.

Ashe's eyes narrowed. She waved her hand and the current shifted, swinging around to carry the Beltiamatu spears to her.

The merfolk exchanged glances, and one of them swam forward. "You control the currents? Where is the trident of the mer-king?"

Ashe shrugged. The words of the ancient Beltiamatu language came easily to her. "The aether core is gone. The technology that allowed the mer-king to control the currents has been destroyed."

"Then how are you doing it? Where is our king? Where is Zamir?"

"Zamir is gone. I rule the Beltiamatu now."

The merman snarled, baring fangs. "The Beltiamatu honor none but the royal family."

"I am Asherah, Zamir's mother. I am of the royal family, and I now rule the Beltiamatu."

"Impossible. Asherah abandoned the ocean. Some say she became a Daughter of Air, but regardless she is long gone." He gestured the others forward. "Kill the poseur!"

Ashe flicked her tail. The water twisted into a spiral, churning into a waterspout that blocked their view of her. The underwater tornado sliced over the seabed, carving swirls into the sand. The merfolk stared at death barreling down on them, and scattered out of its path.

The merman, his bravado fading, was the first to dart away. He stared, wide-eyed, safely—or so he thought—from the side, away from the churning waterspout.

He stiffened when Ashe's voice came from behind him. "Perhaps you should have paid attention to the old stories."

He twisted around in the water and found himself face-to-face with Ashe. He stared into Ashe's blue-green eyes, flecked with the gold stamp of royalty. "You…*my lady*…"

"It's too late for your homage," Ashe murmured.

The air in the water danced at her command, molecules scattering from the water around the Beltiamatu. The water pressure altered, just enough to squeeze in upon the merman's lungs. Air leaked out, altering the water pressure further.

With each escaping gasp of air, the water pressure increased, crushing the merman's lungs. Horror filled his eyes. His hands reached out imploringly to Ashe. His long tail flailed in the water as all his air vanished. The pressure against his chest was too heavy to allow him to draw another breath. His eyes went blank an instant before the water pressure cracked his ribs, puncturing his lungs, killing him without spilling his blood.

The waterspout twisted next to Ashe like an obedient pet, seemingly alive, swirling to intercept all the Beltiamatu who would have charged in to save their leader.

"My lady…" one of the diseased Beltiamatu stammered. He and the others exchanged glances. With rapid flicks of their tails, they darted away.

Teeth gritted, Ashe let them go. Perhaps she should not have, but in her heart, she could not see how the Beltiamatu—diseased—were any more to blame than the humans on Earth, now likewise afflicted. If she could stop Nergal, if she could find a cure for the humans, was there also a cure for the merfolk?

Without turning, she said, "You can come out now."

After a silent moment, the water rippled with movement. Only then did Ashe turn slowly to see a small cluster of Nereids and Oceanids. The nymphs, daughters of Poseidon, looked like small-framed human women, except that they breathed under water and swam as swiftly as mermaids. Behind them, mermaids and mermen emerged from a cave concealed behind the rocks. Their healthy skin and hair tone confirmed they were not diseased, although all seemed too thin, as if they were slowly starving to death.

"The ocean is dying," a blue-haired Nereid confessed. "The disease has taken all the reefs, the fish."

"Are the diseased Beltiamatu spreading it with their spilled blood?"

The Nereid shook her head. "They come here, trying to get their fellow merfolk to join them, but they have spilled no blood—not yet. The disease spreads itself. We thought we had it under control, but then about a week ago, it exploded, as if something had set it free from all constraints. It unleashed death within hours. Reefs died. Massive schools of fish died. The bloated carcasses of whales will soon sink and poison the seabed. Entire communities of Beltiamatu vanished in a night of terror.

Nergal.

The sea was waging a battle for survival as desperate as the one waged on land.

"The diseased merfolk—what are they trying to do?"

"We don't know." A mermaid swam forward. She stared at Ashe, then bowed her head. "You really are of the royal family. Are you truly Asherah, the lost princess of the Beltiamatu?"

"I am."

"And our king, Zamir?"

Ashe swallowed hard. "He is gone."

"And Kai? His grandson, who would have been our king?"

"I don't know where he is."

The mermaid had noticed Ashe's choice of words. She looked up sharply. "But he is alive?"

Ashe hesitated. "I hope so."

The mermaid's shoulders shuddered. "We need him. We don't know what to do. There is little…no food, and the others—the ones who are sick—are trying to compel us to fight their war."

"What war?"

"To aid the diseased one."

"The diseased one?" Ashe's eyes narrowed. "Nergal?"

"Is that his name?"

"Where is he?"

The mermaid shook her head. "We have seen him a few times from a distance, but we do not know where he conceals himself. Blackness oozes out of him. It melts into the currents, leeches into the coral."

"Why would the Beltiamatu aid him?"

"Because it is better than dying." The mermaid's voice was bitter. "We are running out of time, my lady. If you would stop Nergal, tell us what we can do." The mermaid glanced around at the small cluster of survivors, and at the nymphs who surrounded the merfolk, as if to protect them. "We will do everything we can, whatever it takes."

"How many Beltiamatu communities still survive?"

The mermaid glanced around. "Less than a quarter of

them. The most isolated ones. Should we gather them for war?"

Ashe shook her head. "Not yet, but be prepared to make the journey at my command. We cannot allow Nergal to gather strength."

"Even if it means killing our own."

Ashe straightened her shoulders. Was it the fate of rulers to make terrible decisions with hundreds, thousands of lives at stake? "Yes. Nergal cannot win. The ocean cannot die. But for now, protect what is left." She glanced at the Nereids and Oceanids. "You will help them?"

The nymphs nodded. "We are all that's left. We cannot win this on our own. We will join together, or we will all die. We will herd the healthy fish shoals this way to feed this Beltiamatu community until you return with fresh commands."

Ashe swam away, and only one of the mermaids—the one who had spoken to her—followed. "Will you permit me news of Kai, if you have it?"

Ashe tilted her head. "Who is he to you?"

The mermaid lowered her head. "I am no one to him."

Ashe smiled faintly. "That's not the question I asked."

The mermaid's shoulders slumped. "I was offered to him, to be his mate. He refused."

"You know the Beltiamatu traditions."

"Yes, I would have been sacrificed after the birth of our child. I was willing, my lady, to bear this great responsibility and this great honor."

"Perhaps Kai chose not to ask it of you—not because you were worthy, but because he did not count the loss of your life worth the gain."

The mermaid shook her head. Her violet hair swayed. "I don't understand."

"Sometimes, it takes more love to let go than to hold on."

Ashe left the mermaid alone in the currents. Kai, when she found him, would have someone to return to. There was no need for the archaic traditions put in place to protect the royal family from external influences. The Beltiamatu could start fresh, their lives and fates no longer bound to immortal star voyagers from a distant planet.

But first, Ashe had to stop Nergal.

The ocean was familiar, yet it was not. Water surrounded and caressed her, clinging to her, as if afraid. The sparse air molecules in the water hovered around her, edgy, wary, waiting for only the slightest provocation and her murmured order to spin into battle. Sunlight faded the deeper she dove. She had not seen a single fish since entering the water. Crabs and crustaceans no longer scurried along the seabed. The plants that once nestled among the rocks had faded into brown strands, skeletons of life.

Huge swaths of black covered the seabed like patches of oil. Beneath the black, she caught glimpses of rotting corpses —fish, eels, marine mammals. The seawater was cloudy, foul with decay.

The quality of water turned putrid the deeper she swam, and when she entered the cave where Medea made her home behind the coils of Big Thing, the water was rank with death.

She stared at the cave walls. They oozed, as if melting beneath its own weight, to puddle upon the cave floor. Beneath the melting gray walls, she caught glimpses of white. The Big Thing—the sea monster feared by the Beltiamatu, utterly magnificent in all its vortex-churning glory—was dead too.

The phosphorescence that used to light the way had faded into deep shadow. "Medea?" Ashe called softly. She swam around the last curve of the tunnel into the alcove where Medea had made her home. The glowing crystals that filled the cave with light were dark—so dark that Ashe had to sweep tiny tendrils of air around the cave to feel her way forward.

She held her breath as she reached out, tracing the outlines, then the seat of Medea's throne.

It was empty.

Relief flooded her. What had she expected? A rotting corpse?

The ancient sea witch, wise and wily, would not be so easily trapped or killed, not even by a god like Nergal.

But where was Medea now when Ashe needed guidance more than ever?

CHAPTER 11

The Greek island of Kalymnos, although edged by pristine white sand beaches, was too far off the beaten track to be a popular holiday destination.

Just as well. The locals did not want tourists bringing disease and death with them. The port was closed—any attempt to dock a ship would have been met by angry fishermen and sponge divers wielding crude, homemade weapons—but Varun knew his way around the island and directed his speedboat to a quiet stretch of beach on the far side of the island. His family home, which had stood for centuries, loomed high on the cliff overlooking that lonely beach.

His parents were already waiting for him, their arms linked, as they stood several feet from the white-capped waves lapping ashore.

They did not have any bags with them.

Varun cursed under his breath. He had called ahead.

Hadn't his instructions been clear enough? He steered the speedboat as close to the shore as he could without scraping the bottom, anchored it, then leaped overboard and waded the rest of the way.

"Varun!" His mother, Marina, threw her arms around him. Her slender body shuddered with pent-up tears. "I was so worried for you."

"I called, Ma," he murmured softly, stroking her back.

"Not often enough." She pulled back as Paulos, Varun's father, strode up.

The thin man beamed at his son. His clap on Varun's back was hearty, but his unsteady smile belied the warm welcome, as did the deep furrows on his brow. "We heard about Ondine." His gaze flicked toward the *Veritas,* anchored in deep water. "What's happening out there? Is the captain—?"

"About the captain…" Varun grimaced. How was he supposed to tell his parents?

Marina clasped his hands in between hers. "She's not… normal, is she?"

"Ah…" Varun drew a deep breath. "Remember those old family stories?"

"The ones you scoffed at and didn't believe?" Paulos asked.

Varun winced. "Yes, those. Well, you see…"

Marina stiffened. "Ashe, the captain of the *Veritas,* is a mermaid?"

His mother had always been more intuitive than he had given her credit for. Varun nodded. His attention darted between his mother and his father, studying their reactions.

Marina's eyes were narrow slits. "The dead spots in the ocean. The underwater volcanic eruption. The pandemic that's breaking out all around the world—it's all related, isn't it? And it has something to do with her."

"In a roundabout way, yes," Varun admitted. "We're trying to stop it."

"You?" Paulos cut in. "You're not..." He squinted at Varun's legs.

What was his father expecting? Fins and a tail? "No, I'm still me." *With the powers of an earth and fire elemental...*But his parents didn't need to know that part. "Come back with me to the *Veritas.* Let's get you away from here."

"No, Varun." Marina shook her head. "This is our home. We're related to half the island through blood or marriage. Centuries ago, your father's family ruled the island. Even now, the people look to us. We cannot leave."

"And we've closed the port," Paulos added. "We'll be safe."

"A closed port isn't going to keep the disease away," Varun said. "No one has figured out how it's spreading. As far as they can tell, it just appears."

"Then how would being on the *Veritas* at sea be any safer than staying home?" Paulos countered. "No, my son—"

"I'm trying to save you."

"Then do what you need to do to fix what's happening. We will be safe here." Marina looked at Paulos who nodded. "We'll be safe as anyone anywhere can be amid this madness. But we cannot go with you. This is home."

Varun growled under his breath. Did they know what they were saying? His gaze snapped across the beach—the beach where he, as a teenager, had left his toddler sister asleep under a tree while he went diving. He had returned in time to scoop up her lifeless body, floating facedown in the surf.

Home was where his selfishness had killed his sister. Devastated, Varun had left home, seeking refuge in a boarding school in Athens, burying his love for the ocean—the love that had killed his sister.

Yet home—this very stretch of beach—was where he had returned, decades later. It was where he had finally come to peace with what he had done. If any place embodied his love for the ocean, it was right here. If any place embodied his family's love for him, it was also *right here.* He swallowed hard through the lump in his throat, before looking at his father first, and then his mother. "Is there anything I can say that will convince you to come with me?"

His mother placed her hand gently against his cheek. "No, Varun, although we are grateful you thought of us and came back to check on us. You will call often, won't you?"

"As often as I can."

She stared up at him, and her throat worked too. "It's changed, hasn't it?"

Somehow, he was certain she wasn't talking about the world, but him. He nodded. "Yes, Ma." He glanced over his shoulder as the wind picked up, its snap brisk and irritable. Ashe was nearby; he was certain of it. "I should get back to the *Veritas.*"

Paulos nodded. "This captain, Ashe—have you told her? Does she know those old stories too, about the mermaid who visited our family? Who gave up her tail for love?"

Varun huffed out his breath. "It wasn't quite like that."

"Says who?"

"Says the mermaid who visited our family."

His father's eyes went blank with shock. After a silent, stunned moment, he gasped, "Ashe?"

Varun nodded.

Paulos stuttered. "But she…she's…and that parrot!"

Marina burst out laughing. "That's wonderful. She is nothing like the stories say she is."

"No." Varun smiled slowly. "She's far more exasperating…and amazing than all the stories."

His mother searched his face, her eyes widening. "You love her."

"I do." He nodded. "I have, for a long time. Ever since stepping onto her ship."

"Does she love you?"

"She has, I think, for a long time. She's only just barely begun to admit it, and grudgingly—like it's my fault."

Marina's chuckle was warm and wry. "It probably is." She smiled again. "I am so happy for you, Varun, and for her."

"The mermaid tail could make a wedding tricky, though," Paulos rumbled.

"I'll think about putting it on the to-do list, after we save the world." *If we save the world.* "I have to go—"

The sea tossed up white-capped waves, washing sea foam over the sand. Then the surface of the water split, and a mermaid leaped over the speedboat, the opalescent spread of her diaphanous tail fins glittering in the sunlight.

His parents gasped, jaws slack.

Varun chuckled, hurling his thought out at Ashe. *Were you eavesdropping?*

I was nearby, and you think very loudly.

Eavesdropping isn't a thing in polite society.

He could almost see her shrug. *Good thing I'm not human, then. Do you want me to come up and say hi?*

You could shift forms, but then you wouldn't be wearing clothes.

I'd forgotten about that tiresome human custom.

Yes, we have lots of customs in polite society; clothes are one of those things. Wait for me. I'll say goodbye then be on my way.

Ashe's mermaid's tail broke the surface of the water and waved a polite farewell. Varun glanced at his parents. Marina's eyes were wide with delight, her hands clasped under her chin like an eager child on Christmas morning. His father, however, was possibly moments from passing out.

"Hey, breathe, Dad." Varun shook his father's arm.

The older man blinked hard. "I never believed I would ever…" His voice was thick with emotion. "I believed, but now I know." His teary gaze focused on Varun. "It's different."

If only you knew how different. Varun embraced his parents before wading back to the speedboat. With Ashe darting alongside, easily keeping up, he glanced back often, until his family, and his home, was finally out of sight.

~

Bolstered by favorable winds and easy seas, the crowded island cluster of Greece gave way to the breadth of the Atlantic. They were in the middle of nowhere—closing in on a nameless rocky atoll.

Atlantis.

Ashe was on the deck when Varun joined her out there, late one night.

She glanced over her shoulder. "Did you call your parents to check on them?"

"Every day since leaving them on Kalymnos. They're all right, but yesterday, one of women in the village started coughing." His jaw tightened. "We went to school together. She has two little boys." He was silent for a moment. "Nergal's destroying everything that means something to me. I know it's not personal, but damn if it doesn't feel like it."

"At least Ginny's doing better."

Varun's chuckle sounded rueful, but it was not forced. "She and Jackson have really hit it off. I didn't see that coming."

"You haven't spoken to her about that aether incident, have you?"

"Jackson's had a ton of experience with PTSD cases. He insists that the best thing is to let her recover her memories naturally." Varun studied Ashe's face. "You agree, obviously, or you would have ordered him down."

"I don't know anything about this trauma disorder, but you humans act like it's a big thing."

"I really wish you'd stop saying 'you humans' like we're an interesting rodent species in the lab."

Ashe burst into laughter. "That's a fascinating comment, considering it's coming from a marine scientist."

Varun chuckled and reached for her hand. He did that a great deal, almost absentmindedly, as if unconsciously seeking physical contact with her. "Are we close to Atlantis?"

"We'll be there within an hour. I'll have Jackson prepare the speedboat—"

"We're not waiting until morning?"

"Why should we?"

Varun sighed. "Because not everyone uses air to navigate, unlike you. *We* humans use our eyes, and it's easier to avoid walking into a tree if there's some light by which to see."

She hesitated.

"There's no point in getting Ginny killed. We need her to activate the sphere, remember?"

"Fine," Ashe conceded Varun's point with a wave of her hand. The wind grumbled against her ear, and tugged at Varun's hair, before settling into a light breeze skimming over the waves.

"While we're waiting for light, I do have a question for you."

"Hmm?" She turned to face him.

"Can you teach me how to use elemental magic? Earth's less of a problem. It's like a happy puppy who wants to play, who wants to please. But fire magic—it's almost as if it hates me and cooperates only when it can show off or hurt someone in the process."

"That's because it's not *just* fire magic."

Varun conjured up a glowing red flame on the palm of his hand. "Then what is it?"

"It's *Nergal's* fire magic. He's left his mark on it."

"Can it be undone?"

Ashe shrugged. "With time and patience, anything can be undone, but it could be nerve-wracking for a while."

"Should I just *not* use it?"

"Elemental magic is a relationship, Varun. How do you think it'll fare if you ignore it?"

"Do you know anyone who can teach me?"

"I've never been on a good relationship with the fire imps."

"Why is that?"

Her shrug was purest grace in motion. "Probably because I control water—their opposite element."

Varun frowned. "And you control air, earth's opposite element."

She nodded.

"So, what does that make us? You—the air and water elemental. And me with earth and fire?"

"Natural opposites, doubly so."

"A double negative is a positive." Varun grinned.

Ashe tilted her head. "What?"

He waved it away. "Don't worry about it. It's math, one of those human things. Just take my word for it." He drew a deep breath and his grip tightened around her fingers. "Can we do it, Ashe? Are the two of us—and Ginny—enough to stop Nergal?"

"If the inscriptions on the sphere are correct, we're enough to bring forth a power great enough to save the Earth. We're just the conduits for a greater power. But if we were to try take on Nergal—" Ashe shook her head. "I don't know. He holds all lives hostage. And I don't even know how to find him."

"He knows we are trying to stop him." Varun allowed himself a grim smile. "I suspect he'll find us."

~

Within the belly of the *Veritas,* Ginny sighed and flung the bedcovers aside. Her legs wobbled slightly as she stepped out of the narrow bed. She scowled. No wonder. She hadn't been using them for days. The *Veritas* hardly rocked—thank God for that—and she couldn't blame the ship for the hours she spent in bed.

The blur of confused impressions that assaulted her each time she opened her eyes kept her vision swimming in a kaleidoscope of colors and overlapping images. Something flickered in the corner of her eye. She turned her head to look directly at it, and unlike the other gyrating images, this one did not disappear under the focus of her full attention.

A man—or at least the glimmering outline of a man—stared back at her. He was tall and clean-shaven, with an unusual blend of features that did not belong to any distinct racial group. His shirt and pants were of a sleek design that draped elegantly over his lean, muscled body.

She tilted her head.

His lips quirked in a smile, as if she were a curious, bewildered puppy.

"I see you," Ginny murmured. She extended her fingers, but they passed through the man's ghostly figure. The man's eyelashes dipped, the motion slow, sorrowful. Disappointment knotted in Ginny's chest. Was he real or was he not?

If he wasn't real, what about the other images quavering around her? She squinted at the shelf above the bed—a simple plank of polished wood resting on two notched pegs. For an instant, it seemed perfectly whole, then it flashed into an ornately carved pattern, then into jigsaw puzzle pieces—as if it could not decide what to be.

But what was it, really?

Ginny reached out and stiffened as a purple-tinted black lightning arced from her fingertips. There was no heat, no sound as it struck the wooden shelf, but the shelf broke into pieces and tumbled off the wall. The books resting on it hit the cabin floor.

"Ginny?" Jackson's voice came from outside the door. "Are you all right?"

"Yes, yes," she lied as she scrambled to pick up the books. She had gathered most of them up in her arms as the door opened. Jackson's shadow loomed over her, then lowered as he squatted beside her.

Carefully, he picked up one of the jigsaw puzzle pieces, then looked up at where the shelf had been. "Neat."

She stared at him. "*Neat*? Is that all you can say?" She stared at her fingertips, but they seemed perfectly ordinary. No crazy black and purple lightning. Had she imagined it? She glanced at the silent ghost who stood beside the bed, watching her. "The shelf just became that…literally." Her voice wobbled. "I…don't know what's happening to me."

Jackson took her hands in his. No hesitation. No fear. "You don't have to figure it out now."

"I don't even know what's real anymore. It's like I see the world in overlapping layers—variations of what things could be. I'm not sure what *is*, anymore."

"Can you put that shelf back together?"

"I don't know."

"Can you try?" Jackson gathered the pieces of the puzzle and arranged them back into the shape of the rectangular plank.

Ginny looked at him, then at the ghost. If her silent companion had answers, he certainly was not offering them. "What am I supposed to do?"

"I don't know," Jackson said. "Imagine what you want it to be and let loose."

Ginny squinted at the transformed plank. It was pretty—that smooth polished wood—but a little dull—

Black and purple lightning arced from her fingertips and struck the puzzle pieces.

Jackson burst out laughing. "Definitely an improvement."

Ginny picked up one of the pieces. "Is it…a rainbow?"

"You didn't just magically paint on a rainbow. It's a swirly rainbow with sparkly glitter. And this…" He held up another piece to her. "What does it look like to you?"

"A unicorn…with wings." Ginny grimaced. "What the hell is wrong with me? It's bad enough that I can do magical transformations, but it's worse when it looks like I have no taste." She shook her head. "How did I get this, Jackson?"

"I don't know. Ashe and Varun think it's aether."

"Aether?"

"Some kind of space energy. I don't know. I live in the real world, where mermaids are fairy tales, but here I am, first mate on a ship captained by a former mermaid, and we're on our way to Atlantis."

The ghostly figure stiffened at Jackson's words. Ginny's eyes widened. "We are going to Atlantis?"

"There's something on the island that apparently will help battle the disease that's taking over the world, or at least Ashe thinks so." Jackson nodded down at Ginny's hands. "And the power you have inside you may be part of the key in unlocking it."

"But how did I get it?" Ginny demanded. "It wasn't like this before...before…"

"Varun thinks you may have picked it up when you were walking through the mushroom grove."

"At the Garden of Eden?"

Jackson nodded. "Right. The Tree of Life—"

"The mushrooms?"

"That link to a common root system that goes all around the world. Yes, *that* Tree of Life. Ashe says it's an aether core."

Ginny shook her head. "If it's an energy core of some type —a *vast* energy core—how does it pass unnoticed?"

"Probably because we're not looking for it, or because we don't have instruments that can track it."

Ginny stared down at her fingertips. They looked perfectly ordinary—except that they were not. "I wasn't the only one walking through the mushroom grove."

"No."

"So…Varun? You?"

Jackson shook his head. "Looks like you were the only lucky one."

"Lucky?" Her voice cracked. "My vision is a psychedelic nightmare, and I don't know what's real." *And I have a ghost no one else can see.* "What's so lucky about any of this?"

"The world is dying, Ginny, as much from disease as from despair. We're lucky to have a plan," Jackson said quietly. "We're lucky to have hope."

Ginny drew a deep breath as Jackson's words settled over her. "Hope…" She curled her fingers into a fist. Energy pulsed in the palm of her hand. "Is it enough?" she whispered.

But not even Jackson had an answer for her.

CHAPTER 12

The next morning, the rising sun had burned all the fog from the sky by the time the speedboat pulled away from the *Veritas.* Ginny stood at the stern of the ship, shading her eyes from the glare as the speedboat darted through the circle of rocks that surrounded the islet, where the center of Atlantis had once stood. "It doesn't make sense," Ginny murmured. "I get how the outer edges might have survived the blast. But if the weapon, this…"

"*Dirga Tiamatu,*" Varun supplied.

"Was directed at the center of Atlantis. How could the middle of the island survive the blast?"

Ashe spoke up. "The earth elementals protected the aether core from detonation. If it had been destroyed, the blast radius would have been far greater."

Ginny frowned. "I guess that means hurling a nuclear bomb at the Garden of Eden would be a really bad idea."

"More than likely," Varun agreed. "Is there a plan, Ashe?"

Ashe shrugged.

"Remember, plans come about through conversation."

The former mermaid chuckled. She glanced over her shoulder, met Varun's gaze, and winked.

Ginny found herself smiling. "Is this an inside joke?"

Varun nodded. "Communication apparently wasn't one of the core subjects in mermaid school. Ashe seems to think plans magically come together whenever she says, 'Anytime now.'"

"When was the last time one of our plans worked?" Ashe asked.

"I don't know. Could it be because we've never really had a plan that extended beyond 'go in and do something about it'? The only time we had a plan was when we battled Nergal —and that was Zamir's plan."

Zamir. Ginny frowned, trying to recall—Ashe's son. Varun's passing comment about Zamir not having a body. *Like...like a ghost?* She studied the ghostly figure who had accompanied her onto the speedboat and who stood next to Ashe at the bow. If there was any resemblance between them, she could not see it. Besides, he didn't have a tail.

But then again, neither did Ashe.

"Ashe..." Ginny turned to face the captain. "I was—" She stared into Ashe's eyes and her focus flittered away, like the howling wind tearing a delicate leaf from her fingertips.

An intoxicating swirl of blue and green.

Flecks of gold like sunlight dancing upon the water.

She had seen those eyes before.

But where?

A graceful flick of a dark-scaled mermaid tail.

Spears slashing.

Blood in the water—

She shuddered.

There was an instant of blackness, then she heard someone screaming. Surely that high-pitched, terror-filled scream could not possibly be her voice—

"Ginny!" Jackson's voice cut into her bemused state.

She blinked hard and shook her head sharply, to find Ashe, Varun, and Jackson staring at her. Even her ghostly friend was looking at her like she had lost her mind. Jackson had his arms around her, holding tight. She sagged against his chest. Her breaths hitched in her throat for several moments. Only after they steadied did she raise her head to look up into his brown eyes. "What…what happened?"

"I don't know. You just stared at Ashe and froze. Then you started screaming. What happened?"

"I don't know…" Ginny pressed her hand against her forehead. "I thought I saw…but it doesn't matter. I see things that aren't real." Except for the ghost. That ghost was real. Ginny's laugh was bitter in spite of her best efforts. She sank down on a seat near the stern and stared at the water. The sunlight over the water—gold over blue.

Black scales thrashing.

Spears cutting into flesh.

Crimson trails in the water.

Ginny pressed the heels of her hands against her eyes, but even with her eyes closed, the images refused to retreat.

What the hell was wrong with her?

Jackson's presence beside her anchored her. Solid. Unshakeable. He did not touch her, but he did not need to. It was enough to know that he stood behind her, ready to catch her if she needed support. Ready to push her forward if she needed encouragement.

She winced when she thought of the rainbow-colored jigsaw puzzle pieces in her cabin, but it was accompanied by a rueful smile.

Ginny glanced up as the cliffs of the islet came into view. It was at least fifty feet above the ground, and there was no beach or landing point that she could see. "How are we going to get up there?"

The wind darting around the speedboat tugged at her ponytail before racing ahead, kicking up the waves.

Of course. The wind…

Ginny glanced around, her gaze resting briefly on Ashe and Varun. The air and water elemental. The earth and fire elemental.

They had powers no one else did. They were going to be all right, weren't they?

So why did Ashe and Varun both look so grim, and so uncertain.

~

Jackson anchored the boat at the base of the cliffs. "It's gonna be all right," he assured her, his smile tight.

"Then why do you have your hand around your gun?" Ginny shot back.

Jackson jerked a guilty gaze down at the bulge in his coat pocket. "Ashe doesn't do plans; Varun doesn't do backup plans; but someone has to."

Ginny drew a deep breath. She glanced at the ghost. Even *his* expression was grim. Her breath shuddered out, a tremulous sound. "What do we need a backup plan for? What's up there, Jackson?"

"Never been up there." Jackson shrugged. "But the last time I was here, a panther and a warrior came down."

"A *panther*?"

"Big one too, although reportedly not nearly as big as the one that almost mauled Varun."

Ginny's jaw dropped. "Almost...mauled...?"

Varun glanced over his shoulder. "I'll show you the scars later." He moved toward the stern of the speedboat. "I'll go first."

Ashe looked at him as if he were speaking a foreign language. The wind came at her bidding and swept her—not Varun—up.

Varun grimaced. "How do you protect someone who's better at life than you?" he mused.

Jackson shrugged. "I've never tried to tell the captain what to do. Usually, she comes out okay anyway."

Varun's shoulders stiffened. "That's because you didn't lose her."

Ginny stared at him. "You...lost her." She glanced up at the cliff, but Ashe had already vanished from view. A shimmer moved through the air; her ghost had accompanied Ashe. "How did she...how does an air elemental even die? She said her body was astral energy, held together—"

"Nergal has weapons that don't obey human laws." A muscle ticked in Varun's cheek. "Don't get hit."

"How did she come back?"

"We put her in the fountain of life."

"But the water..." Ginny frowned, then shook her head. "Never mind. They were all just stories anyway."

"What stories?"

"That the water of life grants eternal life."

Jackson frowned. "Isn't that in the Bible too?"

Ginny nodded. "Recycling is what religions do best. The best way to shove something down someone's unwilling throat is to make it look vaguely like the familiar thing that came before it."

The wind swept in and seized Varun, before snatching Jackson and Ginny a moment later.

Ginny giggled, wriggling her shoes in the air, and looking down at the ever-growing space under her feet. Jackson made a strangled sound in his throat, and she looked at him. "Are you all right?"

"Never been this high up with nothing below, and without a harness attaching me to something," Jackson said.

"You're attached to me," Ashe's voice cut in as the wind set down all three of them on the top of the cliffs. Her hair swayed in the breeze. Ginny studied her and wondered how she had ever thought of Ashe as human. The dead giveaway wasn't the fact that the wind danced like a living thing around her, or that her eyes were distinctly not normal.

The dead giveaway was her otherworldly elegance, the sinuous unthinking grace of a mermaid. Even when she was moving quickly, her body seemed to flow as if through water. What did she look like underwater, her tail undulating with the current?

Was there anything more beautiful than she?

Ginny stiffened and blinked hard against the sudden vision of deep blue-black scales—a mermaid's tail, lashing furiously, helplessly against the piercing spears.

"Ginny?" Jackson's hand gripped her elbow. "Are you all right?"

"I'm fine." She shook the vision off, although even she realized the motion was closer to a shudder. She looked up into Jackson's concerned gaze.

"This isn't a place to get distracted," Jackson warned her. "There's nothing normal about it."

Ginny looked around and suddenly realized what Jackson was saying. Everything seemed larger. The leaves hanging from the trees. The branching ferns on the ground. Even the clusters of mushrooms at the base of the trees. Not enough for her to feel like she had suddenly found her way into a Jurassic forest, but just enough so to make her feel disproportionately smaller.

"I think it's the exposed aether core," Varun said. "It changes things."

Just like she changed things—the concrete and steel pier, the wooden shelf.

It looked like magic, but Ashe had said that aether was *energy*. Energy was subject to physics, to scientific laws, wasn't it? There were rules, something understandable about it. If she could get a handle on aether, perhaps she could find a way to get rid of it.

The wind darted around them, brisk and chill. Ginny frowned. She could almost—but not quite—hear something, as if the wind were murmuring words in a language that skimmed just beyond her understanding.

Ashe suddenly stiffened. "This way, and keep down."

Really, Ginny mused. Ashe would make an amazing spymaster. Just send a little breeze in to listen to conversations and come back to report to her.

They crept through the bushes—Ashe in the lead and Jackson bringing up the rear. Ginny brushed away the fronds of a fern dangling beside her face as she pressed herself flat to the ground. Several men and women gathered in the clearing. Ginny frowned, studying them intently. They looked human, but their skin seemed lightly tinged blue. They were speaking to each other in a language that sounded vaguely familiar. She closed her eyes and listened.

It was *almost* Sumerian, but not entirely. It was close enough for her to make out most of it. Context allowed her to guess at the rest of it. A man stood in front of the others, a leader of sorts. Ginny whispered, her voice carrying no farther than Ashe, Varun, and Jackson. "He's saying they're the chosen ones. The ones destined to rule the Earth. And they will, when the humans are all gone…"

A woman gesticulated furiously. Her voice was loud but stately even in her anger. "Don't trust him, she says. He lies. He uses us to spread the madness—"

The man cut in with a flurry of words. Ginny frowned, translating quickly. "We are the only ones who can spread it. We are the warriors, the bearers of death."

The woman interjected. "There is no honor in carrying death in our veins, expelling it in the air we breathe—"

Ginny stiffened. "They're the *vectors*?"

Varun glanced at Ashe. "It almost makes sense. The Beltiamatu were the vectors in the ocean, and the Atlanteans are genetically related to the Beltiamatu. Maybe something about them genetically allows them to carry the disease that is Nergal's blood, and spread it without actually dying from it."

"But the Atlanteans are here—on this island. It's the rest of the world out there that's dying."

"They're not the only Atlanteans," Varun said grimly. "The Temple of Ishtar. They claim to be descended from Atlanteans. What if it's true? What if there are Atlanteans, living among humans, indistinguishable in every way, but genetically different enough to carry and spread Nergal's pestilence?"

Jackson grimaced and cursed under his breath. "You're all missing the point."

"And what is the point?" Varun asked.

"If they're this far along in the plot to kill humans, they know who Nergal is, and there's a good chance they know *where* Nergal is."

"And even if they don't, I found others who might know," Ashe murmured.

"Others? Who?" Varun asked.

Ashe nudged her chin at the flames dancing on the torches the Atlanteans carried. "Why do you need torches in broad daylight?"

Ginny frowned and took a closer look at the flames. For a moment, she could almost make out a face in the flames. The tongues of fire swayed like hair—burnished red, glistening gold.

Varun sounded incredulous. "Are those…?"

"Imps," Ashe said. "Fire elementals."

"Why would they obey Nergal?"

"He was the god of fire, although he obviously did not tell the imps that he lost his fire powers to you."

"Are they going to be a problem?" Jackson asked.

Ashe grimaced, nodding. "They're temperamental, and prone to melodramatics—and that's on a good day."

A deep, melodic voice cut in from behind them. "Are you looking for me?"

Ginny twisted around and found herself staring at a man as tall as Jackson, with a lean, muscular build. His skin was a light bronze, as smooth and flawless as a sheet of metal. His angular features did not seem to belong to any distinct racial group. He might have been handsome if not for the petulant frown that seemed permanently pressed into his generous lips.

Ashe, eyes narrowed, stepped forward, setting herself between Nergal and her friends. The ghost was a glowing presence by her side, his hands clenched, shoulders squared, as if for battle.

Ginny glanced around as Varun stepped away, deliberately turning his back on Nergal so that he could focus his attention on the closing circle of Atlanteans and fire imps.

Jackson took his gun from his pocket and racked the slide back. He stepped closer to Ginny to protect her.

Ginny's heartbeat skittered. What was *she* supposed to do?

What could she do?

Nergal spoke first. "As always, Inanna, you surprise me—coming back from the dead, and then escaping from Irkalla. You were never one to let rules or gates stop you."

Inanna! Ginny stared at Ashe. Was Ashe *Inanna,* the Sumerian goddess of heaven and earth?

Nergal continued. "What a fantastic ploy you played in Irkalla. How canny of you to unveil Ninshubur, to explain away your presence. I fell for it too, and then, I see you—out *here*. No one, but you, Inanna, could have escaped from Irkalla in absolute defiance of the laws of the underworld."

Ashe did not deny or confirm it. Instead, she said, "Stop what you're doing to the people of Earth. Go back to Irkalla."

"I can't." Nergal smirked. "The gates have collapsed. No one can go in and out, but you already know that. Besides—" His expression hardened. "You turned Ereshkigal against me."

"I think you did that a long time ago when you raped her, then threatened her with death so that she would marry you instead and make you coruler of the underworld. Oh, and then you schemed to take her kingdom from her."

Nergal smirked. "If all I wanted was Irkalla, I would have killed Ereshkigal. She was always only a means to…*you*."

"Me?" Ashe shrugged, the fluid motion as graceful as it was dismissive. "Why didn't you try sending flowers instead?"

The god of fire and pestilence snarled. "Don't mock me, Inanna. There is no love, no gentleness in you. You were the goddess of war long before you extended your rule over heaven and earth, even love."

"A lost cause, as you say." The wind howling around Ashe was as cold as winter, its bite as vicious and as real as a snapping wolf. "Why did you bother, then? Why spend millennia plotting revenge?"

"Revenge?" Nergal's eyebrows shot up. "Is that what you think this is? I'm courting you, Inanna—not with flowers—but by restoring your people to their birthright."

"How? By destroying the Earth?"

"The humans have to go. There are too many of them. Even the Atlanteans, with their genetic superiority, will never be able to rule, as outnumbered as they are."

"And the merfolk?"

"They will die when their ocean dies. They were fools to seek souls. No one will mourn them but Ereshkigal. She never stopped loving them, even when she stripped their souls from them as punishment for their crimes against Atlantis, and against you."

Ashe shook her head. "Really, Nergal. You need to learn how to let go of things in the past. If we're always trying to justify the things we do based on something that happened millennia ago, we'll always be fighting the same battles, with the same lousy reasons, and I'm tired of that."

The wind screamed down and slammed into Nergal, flinging him back.

"Run!" Ashe shouted. "To the aether well!" The wind blasted ahead of her, scooping Jackson and Ginny up.

Ginny shrieked. Her feet scarcely touched the ground.

"Just relax!" Jackson shouted over the scream of the racing air.

She glanced back. Ashe and Varun were battling the Atlanteans. Fire arced through the air, swirling and spinning into maddened patterns. "We have to go back and help them!" Ginny shouted.

"Just as soon you tell the wind to let us down," Jackson snapped back.

Ginny wriggled, but the wind was a great deal stronger and did not let her go.

Heat and light whizzed past her. "Jackson!" she shouted a warning.

Jackson twisted around and fired his handgun. The bullet passed right through the dancing flame, no larger than a fist. The fire suddenly swelled until it was the size of a football. Indentations appeared on its glowing surface. The dents deepened, then eyes popped out. Cheekbones emerged, then a nose, and a mouth.

The lower half of the football elongated into a skinny torso. Arms squeezed out of the tiny frame, then legs. They looked no thicker than chopsticks, but glowed like molten living flame.

The creature—a fire imp—stared at Ginny. Whatever magic it used, it kept up easily alongside Ginny's wind-propelled pace. It tilted its head in a quizzical expression then extended a scrawny finger toward Ginny.

"Watch out!" Jackson fired another bullet. It punched through the fire imp, leaving a small hole in its body. The imp stared down at its chest as the hole slowly shrank until it vanished. The curious expression on its face tensed into a scowl. Its fingertips, which looked like sticks dipped in lava, burst into flame. It drew its hand back over its shoulder and hurled it forward.

Fire rushed out. Straight at Jackson.

"No!" Ginny shrieked.

Black and purple lightning arced from her fingers to pierce the hurtling ball of fire.

The flame vanished in a deafening boom and a blinding flash of light.

The concussive impact knocked Jackson and Ginny off their wind-driven course. The fire imp was also sent flying through the air in the opposite direction.

Ginny hit the ground with a loud thump. She shook her head groggily as the world twisted and gyrated around her.

"You okay?" Jackson was suddenly next to her. His grip on her arm steadied her. He stiffened. "It's coming back. And it looks pissed."

Ginny blinked then squinted at the glow of fire weaving around the trees toward her and Jackson.

"Let's go." He pulled her to her feet, and pushed her on to the nearly invisible path.

Ginny sprinted forward. Jackson's footsteps thudded behind hers. The undergrowth, almost as tall as she, slapped her in the face as she pushed past fern fronds and squeezed around bushes. "Are we going the right way?" she shouted over her shoulder.

"Damned if I know," Jackson yelled back. "Ashe put us on this path. It's—"

The ground suddenly vanished beneath Ginny's feet. Her scream became a panicked wail.

"Ginny!" Jackson's voice sounded far away, farther with every second.

Do something! Save yourself!

But what?

The glimmer of light at the top of the tunnel shrank. The darkness below seemed to have no end.

If there was something around her, she could not see it.

If the bottom of the tunnel was racing up toward her, she had no idea where it was.

Damn it! She twisted so that she faced the bottom, then flung her fingers out.

Nothing happened.

"What the—?" Ginny wriggled her fingers.

Still nothing.

"Oh, come on!" Of all the times for her newfound aether powers to break—

Not that she knew what it did. Throwing it out there and

letting it do its thing, whatever it was had worked well, at least so far.

Ginny clenched and unclenched her fist, as if it would warm up her powers.

"Come on!" She extended her hands again.

Nothing. *Still* nothing.

Did her aether powers only work on the surface of the Earth?

What if it did…?

And what if she had picked the worst possible way to find out?

CHAPTER 13

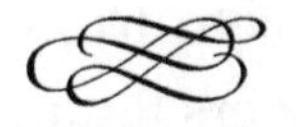

"Try not to hurt them."

Ashe's jaw dropped. She stared at Varun. "Are you really still saying that after all this time?"

"You can't win the fight by hitting the wrong people," Varun said, his back to Ashe as they surveyed the noose of Atlanteans tightening around them.

"Maybe they should have chosen their allies better."

Nergal's voice rose mockingly above the low mutters of the Atlanteans. "Who's going to argue with a god? *Their* god." He strode forward as the Atlanteans folded back to give him a wide berth. "Your mistake, Inanna, like Ereshkigal's, was in abandoning your people. You wanted to give them self-governance—a way to make mistakes and to save themselves from their own mistakes. But they are little different from humans. They crave meaning. They believe in something more than themselves. If you do not give it to them, they will make it up—and it will not be good."

Ginny's scream sounded thin in the distance, panic ringing through her voice.

Damn it.

Ashe extended her arms, her fingers stretched out, beckoning.

The air moved sluggishly.

Varun looked around, alarmed, as Nergal laughed. "What is it, Inanna? Are your powers fading?"

Ashe's eyes narrowed. Varun's breathing labored as the air grew heavier, so thick it seemed to clog every breath.

"What's going on?" Varun reached back with his hand to grasp hers. Their fingers entwined.

The circle of Atlanteans closed. The flames on their torches wriggled and writhed as if alive, and reshaped into thin bodies with spindly arms and legs.

"How much damage can the fire imps do?" Varun asked grimly.

"That depends," Ashe said, her voice calm.

"Depends on what?"

"How much energy they can muster in the face of a hurricane."

The slow-moving air dropped to a dead calm.

The Atlanteans turned their attention to the heavy clouds in the sky. Even Nergal's gaze darted up, alarm in his eyes.

Above the clouds, air and water churned, spun by raw elemental power, until the laws of physics took over.

"I need some steam, Varun," Ashe said.

He flung his hand out. Flame—not red but dazzling blue—scalded a path through the trees to plunge into the sea. The Atlanteans leaped back. The red flames on their torches quivered.

Water sizzled into plumes of steam and wafted up.

Heat poured into the infant hurricane, feeding it, strengthening it. It twisted around its eye, its titanic power held in place only by Ashe's whim.

When Ashe tore the clouds apart, a category five hurricane dropped down on Atlantis. Its tiny eye—only ten feet across—centered on Ashe.

On the periphery of the storm, the ocean lashed up in waves thirty feet high, battering the cliffs and flooding the forest. The bands of the hurricane ripped ancient trees from the ground. Marble blocks, covered with ivy, the last remnants of Atlantis, were flung into the air. The Atlanteans were caught up. Their bodies swirled around the hurricane's vortex. The wind swallowed their screams, their terror soundless. Flickers of living flame also swirled around the vortex, like lights on an inverted Christmas tree.

"What are you doing?" Varun screamed.

"Hitting the right person."

"What are you talking about?" Varun flung his arm out at Nergal, who stood alone, amid the swirling madness. The hurricane lashed at him, but could not move him. "He's still there. He's the only one out there!"

"And he's alone." Ashe's power wound around the hurricane, directing its bands. A small nudge of energy yanked at a huge marble column. It hurtled out of the hurricane and smashed into Nergal.

The god staggered back—more likely from the shock than from the impact. He straightened, his stunned gaze fixed on Ashe—but the hurricane flung more pieces of large debris. An uprooted oak tree. A broken temple cornice. A massive elm. A marble statue.

Each attack drove Nergal back.

"Come on." Ashe squeezed Varun's fingers. "Let's get to Ginny and Jackson."

"How long is the hurricane going to keep doing that?"

"Until it runs out of things to throw, or until they lose interest, whichever comes sooner."

"They?"

Ashe looked up and smiled. The whipping wind briefly coalesced into the faint outline of a face with delicate features and a hesitant smile. Then another appeared, and a third.

"Daughters of Air. Young ones, enjoying their first hurricane."

Varun glanced toward the ocean and caught a glimpse of ripples in the water, of heads bobbing above the surface. Their hands waved, and in perfect obedience, the ocean churned into waves, the rising water feeding the hurricane's violence. "The ocean nymphs. They're also here."

"This battle can't be won alone." Ashe looked at Varun. She did not need to speak it aloud. She could see it in the hesitation in his eyes. He was not sure how it could be won at all. All they were doing was buying time.

But time—precious moments, priceless seconds—was their real advantage. They had to activate the Sphere of the Elements. The great protector of the Earth—whatever it was—would win the battle and the war against Nergal.

Hands linked, Ashe and Varun raced toward the well that led to the aether core. The eye of the hurricane hovered over them—a tiny space of utter calm. She saw the path that Ginny and Jackson had trod into the undergrowth, then the dark hole up ahead. The core…

And there was no sign of either Ginny or Jackson.

~

"Ginny!"

Jackson's voice. The thin edge of pain. The fact that it sounded closer than it had earlier—

He had fallen into the hole too.

Damn it! Come it! Ginny shook out her fingers and pointed them down as she tumbled through the darkness. *Do something!*

Lightning arced out, the purple slashes vivid in the darkness.

"Yes!" she squealed.

Then she landed in something soft, gooey, and sweet smelling.

"Aargh!" Jackson tumbled down beside her. He flailed wildly. "What the hell is it?" He brought his arm up to his nose and sniffed hard. "Is this…strawberry Jell-O?"

"Is it?" Ginny tried to suppress a giggle, but it came out as a squeak instead. "It…smells like it, but I'm afraid to taste it."

"I wouldn't. Not after landing in it."

"Did you fall down too?" Ginny asked.

"No, I jumped when the hurricane dropped out of the sky."

"The…hurricane?"

"The captain might be a little bit irritated."

"Ashe made a hurricane?" Ginny echoed, feeling rather like a slow child.

Jackson nodded. Standing in the huge pile of Jell-O was an impossible physical feat, so he rolled to the side and spilled off the Jell-O heap. "I'm going to smell like strawberry for days."

Ginny's mouth twitched as she grasped Jackson's extended hand and rolled off too.

"Why strawberry?" Jackson asked. "Why not lime?"

"Strawberry was my favorite. Mom used to make it for me, and serve it up with gallops of whipped cream."

A strong gust of wind whooshed past them. Ginny glanced up as familiar shapes appeared out of the darkness. "That's a much better way of falling down a rabbit hole," she said as Varun and Ashe landed soundlessly beside the quivering mound of Jell-O. A shimmer of light accompanied them down. The ghost was obviously intent on sticking around. His gaze flicked to Ginny, and he inclined his head. It almost seemed like an apology for not having been with her, for having chosen to stay—however briefly—with Ashe instead.

"What is this?" Varun asked, staring at the red goo on the ground.

"Strawberry Jell-O," Jackson said. "It's what happens when you give magic to a woman who has happy childhood memories to draw on. You get strawberry Jell-O and sparkly rainbows. Where's Nergal?"

"Still dealing with the hurricane," Ashe said. "We've got a few minutes on him. Let's get to the sphere."

"Let me go ahead," Varun said. "I'll deal with the golem."

Ginny's heart stuttered. "What…golem?"

She followed Jackson and Varun while Ashe brought up the rear. Varun led the way toward an opening that glowed faintly. He jerked to a stop and cursed under his breath. Ginny peeked around Varun's shoulder. "What's wrong?"

"It's not here."

"What's not here? The golem?" Ginny squinted at what

seemed like a blocky tumble of buildings in the corner of the cavern. "Is that…?"

"The golem." Varun grimaced. He strode over to it and walked around its crumpled body.

Ginny hesitantly touched it. "It looks like my mom's granite kitchen countertop, but it's burnt. I didn't even know stone could burn."

"If the fire's hot enough, anything will burn," Jackson said softly. "Looks like the fire imps got down here first."

"The sanctuary!" Varun sprinted through the cavern and into a narrow passageway that opened into an even larger space.

Ginny gaped, turning in a slow circle to take in the ruined wonder of her surroundings. It had once been a garden, but the trees were reduced to burnt stumps, and the ground had been razed to barrenness. "What is this place?" she asked, but the question faded as her gaze fell upon a glowing black and purple cloud, hovering above a pedestal.

"It was a grove. A holy place," Varun murmured.

Ginny heard his voice like through a dream as she walked toward the swirling aether cloud. Images flashed through her mind.

A merman with an iridescent black tail, his hands cupped in front of his chest.

An aether cloud slowly emerging from his muscled torso. The living black cloud rippled like alien tentacles oozing out. It hovered in the palm of his hand as he extended it up to her.

She reached out but did not actually make contact with his fingers. Steel bars separated them.

Ginny's brow furrowed as she mused over that stray image.

Why had there been bars over the merman's tank?

Why would she have imagined such a thing?

The slashes of purple lightning in the aether cloud drew her attention back to the pedestal.

"Is that what I think it is?" Jackson's voice alone anchored it.

"It's an aether cloud."

"Is it supposed to be in people and plants, or just left out like that?"

"In Shulim, the mer-city, it was in the center of a room almost like this—hard to get to, but filled with technology instead of plants." Varun kicked at the dry soil. "Damn it." His eyes squeezed shut briefly, and his hands clenched into fists. "This place was the most amazing place I'd ever seen. If there ever was a Garden of Eden the way most people imagine it, this would have been it."

Ashe laid her hand over Varun's fist. Some of the tightness around his shoulders seemed to loosen and his chest heaved as he released a sigh. "The Sphere of Elements." His eyes met Ashe. "It's time to set all this madness to right."

Ginny, Ashe, and Varun stood in front of the pedestal. It was a shiny gold-colored material, but even brighter. "Is this gold?" Ginny asked.

Ashe shook her head. "Adamantine."

"And this?" Ginny pointed to a large colorless sphere embedded in the middle of the pedestal. Thin trenches, like transparent veins, connected the sphere to five smaller spheres around it. Each sphere had a pattern engraved upon it—three wavy vertical lines; three wavy horizontal lines; a circle with a straight vertical line through it; a triangle pointed up; and an inverted triangle.

"Air. Water. Earth. Fire." Ashe glanced at Ginny. "And aether."

The inverted triangle. Ginny inhaled sharply. Of course. Hands cupped at chest level, carrying the aether core, looked just like an inverted triangle.

Below each of the small etched spheres was the imprint of a hand.

Ashe's gaze rested on Varun and Ginny. "Let's do it."

They arrayed themselves around the pedestal, in front of the elemental spheres.

"We're running out of time," Jackson warned.

Ginny glanced over her shoulder. Jackson aimed his handgun at the entrance, which glowed brightly, as if fire were washing toward them.

Ashe drew a deep breath. "Now."

Ginny placed her right hand upon the hand imprint beneath the aether sphere in the same moment Varun set his beneath earth and fire, and Ashe beneath air and water. Purple and blue mist filled the air and water spheres before surging into the trench and pouring into the large sphere, blending with the green and red mist pouring from the earth and fire spheres.

But nothing filled the aether sphere. It remained gray and colorless.

Ginny's panicked gaze flicked between Varun and Ashe. "What did you do? What am I supposed to do?"

"Just put your hand on it."

"I am! But nothing's happening."

"It had to!" Varun insisted. He looked at Ashe. "Aether's the fifth element, isn't it?"

Ashe stared back at him. "Isn't it?"

Ginny's eyes goggled. "You don't know?"

"No. I went to ask Medea but she wasn't there. We don't know what the fifth element is, but we thought—we hoped—"

"Guys," Jackson growled through clenched teeth. The heat pouring into the room was palpable now. "What the hell are you all doing back there?"

"The fifth element." Varun scowled. "What is the fifth element?" His head snapped up. "It's love."

"What?" Jackson asked.

"That movie—hell, it was even called The Fifth Element."

Jackson glared at him. "It was a girl. Some weird mystical woman cloned from an ancient thing was the Fifth Element."

Varun shook his head. "Yes, but in the end, love saved the planet—not some mystical energy from space." Varun yanked his hand off the fire imprint and set it on the imprint below the fifth sphere. His eyes met Ashe's. Instantly, the sphere filled with mist the color of a sunset. The color surged through the trench, but the red of fire had faded from the large sphere."

"Damn it," Varun cursed. "I'd need another hand to make all this work."

"Move over." Jackson sprinted toward the pedestal and shoved at Varun with his shoulder, sending him back to the earth and fire spheres. He took a deep breath, and with his gaze fixed firmly on Ginny, set his hand upon the imprint of the fifth element.

For a single breath-holding instant, nothing happened.

Then the air within the fifth sphere swirled faintly, color leeching into the translucent gray. Less than the brilliant sunset that Varun summoned. More like a tentative watercolor. The first blush of something that could be, given enough time and nurturing, swell into the deep and gorgeous color Varun had created.

Ginny swallowed hard. *Almost love.*

Jackson.

Maybe she hadn't imagined the flutters after all.

Vivid swaths of purple, blue, green and red, and the blended hues of a hesitant sunset surged into the Sphere of the Elements. The colors in the large sphere swirled, twisting together into a cloud. A black cloud with slashes of purple arcing through its depths. It looked exactly like the aether core above the pedestal. It looked exactly like the thing she kept seeing in her fractured visions of a black-tailed merman.

"What is this, Ashe?" Varun sounded perplexed. "It's just another aether core. It's summoning an aether core to save us from Nergal. How?"

A female voice resonated around them—quiet, yet it seemed to fill the vast chamber. "Because aether—dark energy—is the most abundant and powerful force in the universe." The voice, vibrant with infinite power, seemed to sink into their bodies until they heard, not just with their ears but with each beat of their heart.

A golden light descended over the pedestal, its glow condensing into a woman's body. The glow faded from the feet first before rippling up her body, revealing gem-studded sandals, then a pleated robe gathered around her waist with a flowing belt.

Ginny followed the fading progression of the blinding glow. A heavy necklace that shrieked of wealth and status, a slender neck, and then a face upon which perched an elaborate headdress—slanted back, like the carvings of the Illojim.

The woman's features emerged last as the glow finally faded. It was the face of absolute, prime beauty, yet racially unspecific. It seemed to combine every good thing—almond shaped eyes, straight nose, generous lips, high cheekbones, and skin the color of sun-kissed honey.

Inanna.

This could not be anyone but Inanna—the goddess of love and war, the Queen of Heaven and Earth.

But Ashe's jaw dropped. She surged into the air, flying straight at the woman. Fury transformed her cry into banshee's shriek. "Medea!"

CHAPTER 14

The wind hurled Ashe forward. The force of the air and her trajectory should have taken Medea down, but the sea witch simply slipped to one side. Ashe twisted around. The breeze swirled around her, keeping her aloft—at the perfect height to glare at the goddess.

"You're *Inanna,*" Ashe snarled. It was not a question. "You—as Medea—you *lied* to me. You sent me to the humans in search of a soul for Zamir. You set off the entire chain of events—events that cascaded into absolute disaster. Events that led to *this*! My son is dead. Shulim is destroyed. All of this! Because of you!" Ashe's voice shook. Her hands trembled. Her mind stuttered around scattered thoughts and whirling emotions. No start. No end. Just a horrific, tangled mess.

The dying seas. The dying planet.

The goddess spoke, her voice like the chime of silver bells. "I couldn't fix it alone."

There was a hint of a plea in Inanna's voice, but it was too much to take, too much to process. Ashe swept her hand across the charred remains of the garden paradise that had once surrounded the Sphere of the Elements. "*This* is fixing it?"

"Guys..." Jackson's voice sounded terse.

Out of the corner of her eye, Ashe saw Jackson, Varun, and Ginny line up to face the entrance. It was more than glowing hot now. Flames licked around the corners of it.

"I've never lied to you, Asherah," Inanna murmured. "I warned you of the dangers. I told you that you might have been asking the wrong questions. And...I needed you. I needed someone to be the words I could not speak, the acts I could not do—"

"Guys..."

Ashe ignored Jackson. The entirety of her attention focused on Inanna. "You're a goddess! And this family drama that began with war between the Atlanteans and the merfolk—"

Inanna shook her head. "It started long before that. Nergal—"

"Captain!" Jackson shouted. "Incoming!

Ashe snarled. She flung her hand down at a patch of dry earth. Air sharpened into a spear, cutting into the ground, slicing a perfect square ten feet across. Then, the wind reshaped into a wedge, lifting up an edge of the square before hurling it across the room.

Seawater sloshed over the rim of that perfect square. "Hold tight," Ashe ordered. The breeze swept around, widening its breadth to seize Jackson, Varun, and Ginny, lifting them off the ground and carrying them into the uppermost reaches of the cavern, a hundred feet in the air.

Fire burst through the entrance, tongues of flame fanning out.

The sea roared through the hole in the ground. Water surged into the cavern. Neither Ashe nor Inanna moved as the cavern flooded around them, the water rushing up to their feet, their bodies, over their heads, then rising even higher, even faster.

Water smashed into fire.

Water *drowned* fire.

The flames vanished as if they had never been there. Heat flowed across the water, spreading out until there was nothing left of it.

The dark shadow of a man appeared by the flooded cavern entrance.

Astral energy rippled through Ashe's body. Her legs fused and elongated into a silvery mermaid's tail. Her nails elongated into talons, her incisors into fangs. Her tail slammed against the water. Air raced behind her, propelling her forward faster than any mermaid could swim.

Nergal stepped into the cavern. He yanked in a sharp breath and flung his hands over his face in a feeble defense against the swirl of water and the spike of air, the slap of a mermaid's tail and the slash of curved talons. "No!" he gasped, then his eyes widened, fixed on Inanna, standing over the pedestal. "You…" His gaze flicked back to Ashe. "Then you're not—"

Ashe extended her arms. Air coiled around her right wrist; water swirled around her left. Her eyes narrowed. "I am a Daughter of Air, and the Lady of the Ocean. I am a creature of this world. I serve this planet—the Great Mother of life —and I will not rest until all you damned aliens are banished, together with the curses you have unleashed on this planet."

"Inanna!" Nergal extended his arm to the goddess, but Ashe's talons slashed down, ripping gashes in his flesh. He yanked his arm back, cradling it against his chest. He glared at Ashe. "The curse is too deeply embedded in your planet, and your planet's pulsing heartbeat will spell its own doom. You cannot stop it!"

Ashe lunged forward to rip out his throat, but Nergal vanished.

There was nothing but water and air, Ashe and Inanna... and Nergal's promise of absolute, unstoppable destruction.

~

"Got a bit dicey up there," Varun said after the water subsided, obediently rushing back out through the hole Ashe had carved in the ground. "We were so high up our heads were touching the ceiling, but our feet still got wet." He stared at the tiny ripples sloshing up against the square rim. "Not obeying the laws of physics, are we?"

Ashe glowered at him. She was once again in her human form. "I'm not in the mood for it today."

Varun slid his hand into hers and gently squeezed her fingers. "Listen first."

"But—"

"Zamir is dead. Shulim is destroyed. We can't change the past, but we can stop the Earth from heading down that same path. *You* can stop the Earth from dying. Don't let your anger, or the past, get in the way."

"I can't stand how you're so rational."

"I'm not. I'm trying not to panic and rush out and do something, anything, but panic isn't a strategy, and right now, we need to know what we're up against. We need to know what to do. And Inanna, who knows Nergal—"

"Who set me on a collision path with him," Ashe added tartly.

Varun turned to look at Inanna. His arm slipped around Ashe's back to rest against her hip, steadying her, holding her. Even so, her body trembled—from fury, not fear. And from grief. He was certain of it, and his heart ached for her. He gazed up at the goddess who still hovered above the pedestal. "You're the power concealed within the Sphere of the Elements, right? You're what's going to save the world—"

"No." Inanna shook her head. "It is the coming together of your power that will save your planet. The sphere was merely a gateway to bring together the four elements and to unite them in common purpose—hence the fifth sphere. If you—all of you were powerful enough to activate the Sphere of the Elements—then the task of saving the Earth is yours."

Varun scowled. "Why didn't you just use an application form? And why us? Surely the goddess of heaven and earth is up to fixing things."

Inanna, golden and beautiful, glanced away. "I didn't know how to do it alone."

"But you're you, and Ashe—back then—was just a mermaid. How did you expect her to be able to make *any* difference?"

"Because she loved deeply and utterly." Inanna gestured

at the pedestal. "And spirit—*love*—is the fifth element. This began with the Beltiamatu—"

Ashe's eyes narrowed into slits.

Varun tightened his grip on her.

"—and it will end with the Beltiamatu."

"It began with the destruction of Atlantis, and it ends with the destruction of Shulim?" Ashe demanded. Beneath the anger, her voice cracked.

Inanna shook her head. "However poetic the justice, no. It began with an Atlantean king who damned his people and his children to expand his kingdom. It will end with a Beltiamatu princess who gave up her kingdom for love of her child. The story has to end *in* love, *with* love, or the disaster will cascade—vengeance building upon vengeance until no one remembers how it began." Inanna's gaze rested on each in turn—Ginny, Jackson, Varun, then Ashe.

Inanna's golden eyes met Ashe's blue-green, gold-flecked eyes. "Do you know why the eyes of the Beltiamatu royal family is dusted with gold?" She paused for a breath. "They are the gold of Ereshkigal's eyes, of mine—of the An royal dynasty." She extended her arms to Ashe.

To Varun, the gestured seemed almost imploring.

Ashe's eyes were still narrow slits, almost spitting fire.

Varun hoped the goddess was patient. A reconciliation would be a long time in coming.

"I acted rashly, cruelly, against my sister," Inanna murmured. "But simply freeing her would not have fixed anything between us, or between her and the Beltiamatu people she had wronged so deeply. A Beltiamatu had to free her." Inanna looked at Ashe. "And so I set you on that path."

"What if I had killed the prince with the *Isriq Genii*? This path would never have unfolded the way you envisioned."

Inanna's shrug was dismissive. "You had higher standards." Her gaze flicked to Varun. "You still do."

"Your plan could have unraveled at any step along the way if I, or Zamir, had made different choices."

"But I was there," Inanna said. "You and Zamir kept asking the wrong questions—and I kept giving you the answers you needed to accomplish what I needed. And so you have. My sister is free. She was freed from her imprisonment beneath Krakatoa by a Beltiamatu king, and then from Nergal's abuse by a Beltiamatu princess. Her story, the story of Ereshkigal and the Beltiamatu, can end in love, instead of perpetuate in hate."

"Your sister isn't free. She's trapped in the underworld."

"And that is for me to attend. I can rebuild the gates of the underworld, but it will leave me with nothing to battle Nergal." Inanna drew a deep breath. "I hadn't planned for Nergal."

"What do you mean?" Ashe demanded.

"I set out to reconcile the Beltiamatu with my sister, and me with my sister. I hadn't accounted for Nergal's actions, his interference."

Varun stared at Inanna. "So, now, this part's not in the plan."

Inanna shook her head.

"You do know that Nergal is obsessed with you," Varun said. "Is this part of the story supposed to end in love too?"

"Stories end in two ways, Varun. With love, or in death." Inanna's eyes hardened. "Nergal's story must end in his death or the world will perish."

Ashe and Varun exchanged glances. Then Ashe spoke, "All right. How do we kill him?"

"He is an Illojim. Weapons, made here on Earth, cannot hurt him. Only weapons from Aldebaran can."

"From your home planet?" Ashe asked. "And where can we find such a weapon?"

"You've held it."

Her eyes widened. "The *Isriq Genii.*"

"The dagger was forged from the metal in Aldebaran's core. I forged it myself while we were on our starship, leaving Aldebaran forever. It is the only weapon from my home planet—the only weapon that can kill Nergal."

"Well..." Varun looked at Ashe. "Damn."

Jackson cut in. "What do you mean by damn? This weapon—you do have it, don't you?"

"No." Varun grimaced. "It's buried somewhere on Krakatoa."

Jackson shook his head. "But there isn't a Krakatoa anymore—not after the second explosion. It's just a red-hot boiling mess in the ocean—a slowly building mound of superheated rock."

Varun nodded slowly. "That's where the *Isriq Genii* is..."

CHAPTER 15

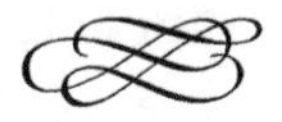

Krakatoa was no more welcoming the second time around, Ashe mused. It was, however, a great deal flatter. The top of the mountain had melted into the sea, and only an islet, still glowing red, was visible above the surface of the water.

Ashe's eyes narrowed. Frustration was a tight knot in her chest. Why, in the name of all the blasted Illojim, had she left the *Isriq Genii* behind? Burrowing through a still-live volcano —the ultimate amalgamation of earth and fire—was the last thing an air and water elemental needed.

Varun stepped onto the deck. "We've got a problem."

She turned to face him. "Tell me something I don't already know."

"It's a new problem."

"I don't need another one."

"It keeps us from getting bored." Varun held out his tablet. "Pierce Laurent called. Ondine's missing. She apparently woke from her coma and walked out of the hospital room sometime in the night."

"And no one noticed?"

"The hospital's shorthanded because of the pandemic, but the security cameras were running." He tapped the tablet screen, and it played a recording of a hospital corridor. The images were crisp and the colors clear, but then the middle of the screen blurred, and a moment later, there stood a man who had seemingly appeared out of nowhere.

Ashe leaned in for a closer look. "Is that…Nergal?"

Varun nodded grimly as the recording showed the man entering one of the hospital rooms. Several moments later, Ondine emerged, wearing only a hospital gown, trailing IV tubes. Her hair was in disarray and her face expressionless, but her gait was purposeful and steady despite having spent at least the past week unconscious and bedridden.

Ondine strode out of the camera range.

Nergal never emerged from the hospital room.

Varun continued. "Her parents are looking for her, but they're not getting much help from the authorities. Apparently, money can't buy you attention when the rest of the world is going to hell."

Ashe looked at Varun. "She's a threat."

"I know." Varun grimaced. "If Nergal's infected her—"

"Or possessed her."

The bleak expression on Varun's face confirmed that the thought had occurred to him too. "We'll have to track her down after we find the dagger. Whether she's infected or possessed, she could be the key to finding Nergal."

The volcano rumbled, the earth's upheavals sloshing water over the deck of the *Veritas* as Jackson and Ginny walked up to join Ashe and Varun. Ginny staggered and would have lost her balance if Jackson had not caught and steadied her. Both of them peered at the remains of Krakatoa. "How bad is it going to be?" Jackson asked quietly.

Ashe shrugged as the waves swept higher around the ship. A head broke the surface of the sea. She looked like a small female human, with flowing blue hair that blended into the water. She looked at Ashe, then glanced nervously at Varun, Jackson, and Ginny.

"It's all right," Ashe told the Oceanid. "They're with me. Tell me what's happening down there."

The Oceanid spoke in Beltiamatu—the *lingua franca* of the ocean's humanoid beings. "The earth is still broken, far worse here than at Shulim. It was torn apart once before, and now, shattered again, it bleeds lava, unable to close, unable to heal."

Varun frowned when Ashe translated the Oceanid's words. "Aren't any earth elementals working to close the wound?"

The Oceanid shook her head. The ocean's embrace swayed around her; her hair drifted on the waves. "They cannot come. They have to prevent the spread of the disease through the plants and soil. They cannot allow the black blood to weaken the Tree of Life."

"Wait..." Varun said. "What do you mean—the disease doesn't just affect people now? It's also in the Earth itself?"

"Pestilence affects all living things. Humans and animals are dying. Trees are dying—"

"We're out of time," Ashe snapped. "We have to find that dagger and kill Nergal." She vanished and her clothes dropped to the deck of the *Veritas*.

Varun cursed. "Damn it, Ashe!"

The sea trembled, the waves parting as air speared into it. A moment later, Ashe arced out of the ocean, drops of water dripping off her silver tail.

"Vanishing and dropping her clothes in front of people might be an improvement on stripping them off, but not by much," Varun muttered. He grabbed several bang sticks and a WASP knife before shrugging off the T-shirt he wore over his dive suit.

"Wait," Jackson said as Varun stood on the edge of the ship. "Your oxygen tanks—"

"Don't need them. They'll only slow me down."

"But—"

Varun dived off the ship. The water was warmer than he expected, and murky, marred by dirt-like particles twisting with the current. He hovered in the water but saw no sign of Ashe. He could hold his breath and dive deep, but not indefinitely.

Wherever she was, he had to get close to Krakatoa. The ocean was an old and familiar friend, but it did not seem as welcoming that day. Angry riptides forced him away from the tortured land mass, and he had to dive deep to get around them.

Something swift darted out of the murky water. Varun twisted aside, but not quickly enough. The shark's rough skin scrapped along his side, tearing through the thin layer of his diving suit and slashing his skin. Blood oozed out of that tiny wound, dark brown against the cloudy water.

More sleek shapes emerged from the distance. Their sinuous, leisurely glide through the water accelerated into bursts of speed, weaving around each other, circling him. He pulled out his knife, and drove the blade down as a shark darted past him. The knife nicked the shark, and it thrashed, its jaws snapping, its tail slapping sideways against Varun's stomach.

The impact punched the breath out of his lungs. His vision blurred for an instant. He barely managed to evade a second shark's lunge, but the motion set him right in front of the gaping jaws of another. Varun brought his arms up in front of his face in an instinctively defensive gesture. The shark's jaws yawned apart, displaying its double rows of teeth, then slammed down.

The serrated teeth slapped together a fraction of an inch from Varun's face.

He blinked in disbelief as the shark was yanked backward. The large predator thrashed, trying to break away from the unyielding grip on its tail.

Ashe. Her hands were wrapped around the narrow part of the shark's tail, but not even she was physically strong enough to hold a creature more than ten times her weight.

But then again, Ashe was a Daughter of Air and the Lady of the Ocean. Physical strength was optional.

The current changed—visibly, suddenly—moving with her as she twisted, flinging the shark away from her. The shark flailed against the current for several moments before righting itself and swimming away.

Ashe spread her arms. The current rippled outward, away from her, making it impossible for any shark, however powerful, to approach. She swam up to Varun. Even in the dark, deep water, her tail was iridescent silver and possessed its own radiance, casting off light that caught the highlights in her blue and green hair.

Damn, you're beautiful. Varun threw out his thought.

Nice try, Ashe snapped back. *Not working. I'm still irritated.*

You're always irritated.

You were supposed to stay on the ship until I made sure the ocean was safe enough for you to enter.

Then say so. Don't just vanish and expect me to read your mind. Speaking of which—so that you don't have to read my mind —I could use some air.

Ashe glowered at him, then waved her fingers in front of his face.

A large bubble of air formed in front of his nose and mouth.

He shook his head. *Is that it? I hoped for something more personal.*

Personal like this? Ashe closed the distance. Her tail brushed against his legs. Her body pressed up to him, her arms wrapping around him. The air that flooded his lungs was like mountain air, so fresh he could almost taste it.

It was not the first time she had kissed him. It was not the first time she had given him air to breathe underwater. But the other times had never been quite like this. This was different. It was real.

She was real.

He ran her hands along the smooth skin of her back and traced, along her hip bones, the subtle transition to scales. Her bone structure was more delicate than any woman he had ever embraced in his bed, yet he knew that a solid flick of that tail would slam him unconscious. Fragile, yet strong. Opinionated, with a tendency to ignore facts and a compulsion to take on too much of the responsibility and blame. Powerful, headstrong, and possessed of more love than she dared to admit or display.

Except that he knew her better than perhaps she even knew herself.

How had he fallen in love with a mermaid, with a Daughter of Air?

How could any man be so lucky?

Varun angled his head. Their kiss deepened until they shared the same breath. His world condensed into the mermaid in his arms. Her long hair swirled on the currents, brushing against his cheek. The swish of her tail fins stirred the water. In the ocean, she was, without question, the more powerful, yet she trembled in his arms—like an innocent virgin, or like a woman finding love after an impossibly long time.

He never wanted to let her go.

The cocoon of air vibrated, the motion jolting through his bones. With slow reluctance, he broke the kiss and glanced at the circle of sharks slamming their blunt noses against the sphere of air Ashe had erected around them.

They've changed, Varun said quietly. *These reef sharks are not normally aggressive.* He approached the edge to observe the shark's gums. They were as black as Nergal's blood. Varun studied the violent swish of the shark's lean body and the whip of its tail. *They're diseased, and in a frenzy. I don't think we can scare them away.*

But spilling its blood will pollute the ocean further.

Right. Varun grimaced. He glanced beyond the circle of sharks, at the molten rock still bubbling out of the savage wound in the earth. A slight furrow touched his brow as he extended his hand toward the glowing red stones.

The sensation that followed was not something that could be put into words. Power did not flow out of him. Neither did it flow into him. Yet something connected him, resonating within him, out of him.

The lava bubbled out, oozing down the growing ridge of stone. The motion quickened, intensified.

Varun glanced at Ashe. *Are you ready to get us out of here?*

She wrapped her arms around him. *What are you doing?*

The kind of thing you usually do—proceed without a plan.

The earth erupted, flinging out boulder-sized rocks. One hurled toward the sharks with such force that its speed was hardly slowed by the density of water. Others followed, each pummeling into the frenzy of sharks around them—both stunning and wounding the creatures, pinning them to the molten seabed.

The sharks thrashed, their writhing growing feebler as their skin cooked and burned, their blood sizzling before it could be spilled.

The shafts of pale light from the surface vanished as a massive boulder hurled directly at them. Ashe's swirling cocoon of air would never be able to stand against it—

The sphere of air vanished. Ashe, her grip tight around Varun's waist, darted forward, directly at the approaching boulder. She skimmed under it, so close that Varun could feel its heat almost scald his skin. She darted through what felt like an endless onslaught of boulders, twisting to the right of one, then to the left of another. Ducking beneath one before swimming over another.

Almost like the Millennium Falcon flying through an asteroid field, Varun mused.

Is that another movie reference?

It certainly is. He glanced over his shoulder as a boulder slammed a shark into the rocky bed. Varun could even hear the sizzle of the shark's flesh burning, cooking. He winced. It was like an asteroid field, except that he had started it—with his earth elemental powers.

Ashe's voice murmured through his head. *One day, you shall have to show me all these movies you talk about.*

We'll start with Star Wars. It's something to look forward to after saving the world, right?

Ashe stopped close to the wound in the earth. Boulders flew over their heads, thudding as they hit the seabed. She stared at the split in the seabed, like a gaping cut, oozing blood. *The* Isriq Genii *is somewhere in there—damn it.*

Next time, we'll just have to be more careful about not leaving anything else behind. Varun frowned. *There's got to be a way to get to it.* He touched his hand to the ground. *There's a network of tunnels leading down, probably to where Ereshkigal was actually imprisoned. Something's there—*

What do you mean something's there?

Exactly what it sounds like. There's something there that shouldn't be there. I can't get a clear picture of it, but the earth is roiling around it, leaving a void.

The Isriq Genii*? If it's from the stars—if it's made from materials not found here on Earth—it might explain the void. How do we get to it?* Ashe asked.

Varun drew a deep breath. *I think I finally understand how you feel about someone looking to you as if you have all the answers. It's infuriating.*

Ashe's lips quirked up in a half-smile. *Glad to return the favor.*

How insulating is air?

Insulating enough, especially when layered with water, but it won't last forever—not against such extreme heat.

Varun nodded. *We better move quickly, then.* He stood still as air, then water, then air layered around him. He met Ashe's eyes. *Ready?*

She nodded.

This way. He instinctively held his breath as he plunged into the broken earth. He could not tell where rock ended and fire begin. The water, which had been hot, seemed almost cool in contrast to the extreme heat around him. The earth around the void pulsed like a beacon, aching like an open wound, but all around, Varun saw only glowing red stone walls.

There was no way out of the pit…but down.

The heat intensified until it seemed as if the air were evaporating, the water boiling around him.

We're running…out of time. Ashe's voice was faint.

Almost there, Varun whispered, although his vision seemed trapped in a world of glowing red and melting orange. *It's close…*

And it was close. Tantalizingly close. He could almost feel it a mere heartbeat away. He blinked hard and almost screamed as his inner eyelids scraped against his eyes. He was dying, the moisture evaporating from his body. He looked over his shoulder. His heart thudding so loudly that it seemed to echo through his head, he twisted around and caught Ashe as she crumpled. Her breath was so faint he could not even see her chest rise and fall. Sweat plastered her long hair to her skull, and her skin was so dry that it cracked like desert sands. The silver scales on her tail turned black from the heat.

Their eyes seemed to meet, but her gaze was so unfocused, she could not have seen him.

She was dying—air and water, surrounded by earth and fire, weakening. Dying.

But I am earth and fire.

They mold to me, respond to me. He extended an arm toward a wall of glowing red rock. The earth churned, rocks sliding against each other, melting away to reveal an opening in the earth. It was only marginally less hot in there, but he slung Ashe over his shoulder and dashed into the tunnel.

The remnants of the armor of water and air clinging to him started to mold around Ashe, perhaps instinctively attempting to save her life. Which left him with nothing.

He dropped to his knees, screaming as his skin cracked then peeled. Ashe toppled off his shoulder. She lay unconscious on the ground. What little air and water she had taken from him would burn through within moments.

Varun stared down at his hands as blackened flesh smoked off to reveal bone. *I am…*

His thoughts stuttered. His heart skipped a beat, then another, failing.

He stared at Ashe.

If he died, so would she.

Astral energy. All she is is astral energy—her form is almost a figment of imagination.

And mine…can be a figment of imagination.

Because…I am…

Varun gritted his teeth and flung out his consciousness.

Fire!

He exploded.

CHAPTER 16

Varun's skin and flesh burned away. His bones splintered into dust and sprayed out. His internal organs melted into nothing.

There was a single terrifying moment of emptiness when only his consciousness hovered where his body had once been.

The words, his thoughts, expanded outward.

I am earth and fire.

His consciousness coiled like a living thing, a graceful thing.

And I am alive!

Power rushed inward, layering over his consciousness a body that seemed like him—only it was not the body he had been born with. Varun stared down at his reformed body. It appeared entirely human, completely physical, but he knew it was astral energy, held together by his will.

He was changed—no longer human, but an elemental. A *true* elemental. And he was in control.

Varun straightened. Vast power unfurled without moving a muscle. *Enough.*

The red heat of the rock flickered before fading to a pale orange, then cooling into black. The murderous heat melted into a gentle warmth as air returned, no longer consumed by the endless burning.

Ashe stirred, her eyes slowly opening. She stared at Varun. "Something happened…"

He nodded. "How did you know?"

"You're not wearing any clothes."

He looked down. "I'd forgotten about that little inconvenience when shifting forms."

"Shifting forms…" Ashe's body—the mermaid's body—vanished and reformed as a human, skin unblemished, as perfect as he remembered her, and she remembered herself to be. Ashe reached out and laid her hand on Varun's arm.

Varun grimaced. "If astral energy can form a body, there's no logical reason why it can't form clothes as well, right?" He squeezed his eyes shut, blocking out all around him so that he could focus. He could almost feel the drawing in of energy all around him, layering and building into something. He opened his eyes and looked down, grateful to see his body clad in a plain white T-shirt, denim jeans, and black boots. Standard wear. His body, it seemed, had opted for the familiar.

He looked at Ashe. "Clothes don't have to be optional anymore."

"You humans have such quaint hang-ups." She waved his statement away. "What happened?" Ashe asked.

"I died. Just like you died as a mermaid before you became a Daughter of Air."

She paled. "But it was…excruciating. Dying. I melted into sea foam. My tail, my body…it all dissolved until there were nothing left."

Varun stared down at his hands, remembering the blackened skin, the melting flesh, the white of his bones charring. "Yes. It was excruciating. I don't think…" He hesitated. "I don't think I'm human now."

Ashe shook her head. "Humans cannot be elementals. The power of the elements is too great to contain."

"So what am I now, Ashe?"

"Perhaps, like me, you are astral energy held together by your consciousness."

"And this astral energy? Is it dark energy?"

"Aether?" Ashe shook her head. "I do not know. There is so much I do not know about the energy in the universe—aether least of all."

"You can't help Ginny understand it, or control it, can you?"

"No, but we can stop Nergal and buy Ginny the time she needs to figure it out."

Varun nodded. "The *Isriq Genii*. I can feel the void it leaves in a way I never could—not when I was human. It's down this way." He held out his hand. Without hesitation, she slipped her hand into his.

His breath caught. Her hand felt as real in his as it had when he had been human.

"How much has changed?" Varun asked quietly.

Ashe looked up and met his gaze. Her eyes were blue and

green, flecked with gold—the eyes of a mermaid, the eyes of royalty. "Nothing that matters has changed."

She made it sound simple.

He knew it was anything but.

They traveled through the cavern together. The void in the earth pulsed like a homing beacon—an anomaly that screamed to be righted. Varun frowned as they hit a dead end. He pressed his hand against the cavern wall. "It's here. Through this way."

The stone wall crumbled into dust at his feet. Varun walked through and looked around. He frowned. "It's where Ereshkigal was imprisoned. Look—the well with the inscriptions. The iron golems." He glanced to his left, expecting to see a heap of stones—a burial mound for Zamir.

The pile of rock was there. Ashe was looking at it, too.

Varun inhaled sharply. His orientation perfect, he strode along the curve of the wall.

The gnome, Duggae, had left no body behind, but Varun saw his final imprint, his little boots pressed into the ground where he had flung himself in front of Varun. The *Isriq Genii* had struck the gnome first, then Varun.

The dagger lay right where it had fallen. Its hilt was deceptively plain; its blade curved and inscribed with runes.

The *Isriq Genii*. According to the myths of the merfolk, it was forged in a demon's heart from the core of a fallen star. It was true, in a way. Medea had said that the dagger was forged from rare metals in Aldebaran's core. Myths had a way of expanding, one layer building upon another until it was no longer clear where the truth ended and the lies began.

"Is the dagger still bound to Zamir?" Varun asked. "Will it deliver the next soul it kills to Zamir?"

"How can it?" Ashe replied. "Zamir's dead." Her glance flicked to his burial mound—worthy of a king. "Besides, he already has a soul. Ereshkigal gave him the soul of the First Commander."

"The dagger still steals souls, though." Varun knelt to retrieve it. He was no expert on weapons, but its grip felt natural in his hand; the dagger was both light and balanced. "Let's not lose track of this thing again."

A voice boomed around them, echoing through the cavern. "And who do you intend to kill with the *Isriq Genii*?"

Varun and Ashe immediately shifted to stand back-to-back as pinpricks of light appeared in the cavern. They swirled together, dancing into a humanoid shape, solidifying as features took shape. "Nergal," Varun growled. If Nergal was here, where was Ondine? Hope flickered through Varun. Perhaps Ondine wasn't possessed after all. "You get around, don't you?"

The god strode out of the darkness. "Inanna forged that dagger—a last memento from Aldebaran. Did she tell you what's in it?"

"She said it's the only weapon that can kill you."

"And she is correct. It is the only weapon that can kill the Illojim—but there's no magic in it. The particular alloy of metals Inanna forged into the *Isriq Genii* severs the connection between our consciousness and astral energy. It prevents the Illojim from reforming their bodies. Just as it would stop an elemental—like you—from reforming her body." Nergal chuckled, the sound cold. "She did not tell you that, did she? Of course, she didn't. No one has lied to you or misled you as much as Inanna. How do you still trust her?"

"I don't," Ashe replied. "But I'll fight one enemy at a

time." The wind swept her into the air as tiny sparks of flame appeared. The fire imps still fought for Nergal—but why? Ashe snarled. The why didn't matter. The only thing that mattered was stopping Nergal. She flung her arms out at the tiny flickers of flame skittering toward Nergal.

The flames shook and quivered, but did not go out. They darted into the four inert iron golems slumped against the cave wall. An instant later, the eyes of the golems glowed, and the four behemoths straightened and lumbered toward Varun.

"Ashe!" Varun shouted.

She darted back down to him.

"We don't have to fight them." He glanced around the enclosed chamber. None of the openings were big enough to let a golem through. "Let's just get out of here."

"But we can kill Nergal here! We can't let him get out—there's too much out there that won't survive an encounter with him."

"We're outnumbered." Varun raised his hands, and rocks broke off from the wall to tumble down in an avalanche. The closest golem looked up, and the light blinked out of its eyes as the fire imps abandoned that shell to hop into another. The rocks smashed the golem into the ground, burying it.

"We're not outnumbered now!" Ashe shouted.

Varun still counted three golems. And not forgetting Nergal— Varun scowled. "Math isn't your strong point, is it?"

The wind twisted around one of the golems and wound its way into the mechanical creatures through its entry points, many of them as tiny as hinge points in the joints. Ashe's eyes narrowed. The golem stiffened, then the light in its eyes vanished. It toppled sideways slowly.

"What did you do?" Varun asked.

"Forced air into the golem, then separated the air molecules."

"What do you mean?"

"I forced out all the oxygen. Fire does not burn without oxygen."

"You killed the fire imps?"

"I put out their fire. It'll be a few minutes before they regain enough strength to light up again." Ashe looked at Varun as the remaining two golems lumbered toward them. "Two on two. See? I can do math."

Varun's head snapped up, and he pushed her to one side before leaping to the other. A black spear struck the ground between them. For an instant, it quivered in the ground, as real as a physical weapon, and then vanished, evaporating like mist in the sun. The ground where it had struck remained black, as if it had absorbed the darkness.

Varun glanced up at Nergal who stood on a ledge, another dark spear in his hand. A mocking smile touched the god's lips as he dragged the tip of the spear across the palm of his hand, staining the spear with his blood.

"Don't let it hit you," Varun warned. "Can you handle the golems? I'll take Nergal."

Ashe nodded, then took to the air. The wind carried her in dizzying loops around the golems. They twisted like marionettes, trying to keep her within sight, as she led them farther and farther away from Nergal.

Varun tapped on the ground, and it rose beneath him, stones shaping into steps curving along the wall of the cave.

He walked up, his pace steady, until he stood several steps away from Nergal.

The god of pestilence studied Varun as if he were a curious lab specimen, before saying quietly, "This isn't your fight. This war began aeons ago on Aldebaran."

"But you chose to bring it here. This is my planet—my ocean, my land. When you poisoned it, you made it my fight."

"It can be undone," Nergal said casually.

"Will you undo it?"

"For a price, of course."

"Is it a woman?"

Nergal shrugged. "Isn't it always?"

"And you want Inanna?"

Nergal's gaze flicked briefly to Ashe—darting between the golems, which lumbered like drunken fools attempting to catch the wind. "I thought she was Inanna. She mirrors Inanna as I remembered her—her boldness, her audacity, her verve. I understand now why Inanna chose her. The mermaid loves powerfully enough to challenge destiny, even reality—and that love anchors her through life, through death, through transformations. The core of her is untouchable, unchangeable." Nergal smiled. "Not many can claim that power and that privilege."

Dread inched into Varun's heart.

Nergal's smile thinned. "I want her. I want the Little Mermaid."

CHAPTER 17

"There is something I don't think you understand about women." Varun forced casualness into his tone even though his heart skittered with near panic. "You won't win them just by saying you want them."

"I'm not interested in winning her. I only want to claim her." Nergal's gaze fixed on Varun. "From you."

"That's the other thing about women. You don't own them. I love Ashe, but she isn't mine. The only person she belongs to is herself."

"That flawed perspective is the fallacy of a selfish society that pretends to be enlightened." Nergal shook his head. "Love guides our actions, determines our path, selects our sacrifices. We belong to the ones we choose to love. That has always been the truth of all ages." He smirked. "Inanna belongs only to herself, for she loves no one. But not the Little Mermaid. She loves, in fact, too deeply. If she hadn't, we would not be here today."

Varun winced. "She didn't start this on-going saga among you, Ereshkigal, and Inanna."

"That saga has never been settled to my satisfaction. But now, finally, it may be." Nergal hurled out a dark spear.

Varun twisted aside. The tip of the spear struck the rock behind him. The haft of the spear was still quivering when Varun wrapped his hand around it to yank it out of the rock, but it vanished the instant he touched it.

"You cannot win this battle, Varun," Nergal said. He did not sneer. He simply said it as if it were matter of fact. The Illojim are greater than the Beltiamatu; the Beltiamatu greater than the Atlanteans; the Atlanteans greater than humans. It is simply the way of things."

"Is it?" Varun hurled the dagger at Nergal.

Then Varun vanished.

Nergal was still blinking when Varun reappeared right in front of him. Varun's fingers folded over the hilt of the flying dagger and slammed it down into the tender junction where Nergal's neck touched his collarbone.

Nergal stiffened and staggered back as Varun jerked the dagger out. Nergal's hand pressed against the wound in his neck. Black blood oozed out from between his fingers. His eyes were wide, his mouth gaped like a perplexed flounder. "You...you're not human."

Varun gritted out the words. "Where do elementals sit in that hierarchy of power?"

"Not high enough." Nergal sneered, but there was fear in his eyes. "You will die—all of you. Death is already pulsing beneath you—a mere trigger for the curse that sprawls across the Earth's surface. Nothing can stop it."

He extended his arm to the sliver of daylight high above, then vanished into pinpricks of light that swirled up.

"Ashe!" Varun shouted. "Nergal's getting away!"

She swung around a golem so sharply that it reeled off balance and stumbled into the remaining golem. "I thought you were going to kill him!"

"I stabbed him in the neck," Varun snarled. "There's a jugular there, right? Usually people die." He stared down at the dagger, its blade stained black with Nergal's blood. "Is there a trick to this?"

"If Inanna made it, there's probably a trick to it." Ashe snatched Varun up, and they chased the pinpricks of light that were Nergal. Her eyes narrowed. "That hole is too narrow to let us through."

"Will the dagger fit?"

"It might scrape off some of its nice paint work, but yes, it will."

Their eyes met. "Together, then," Varun said. "It's the only way to do this." Their fingers entwined briefly as he handed the dagger to her. The tiny hole was close now. The pinpricks of light squeezed through the opening.

Varun nodded. The wind coiled beneath him and flung him up. He transformed into pure astral energy and raced through the opening, before shifting back into human form. The dagger slid through the opening a second later. He snatched it out of the air as Ashe's astral consciousness squeezed out of the hole after the dagger. Ashe reappeared in front of him and glanced around. They stood together on the remains of Krakatoa. "Where is Nergal?" Ashe asked.

Nowhere that Varun could see. He frowned and looked around. The *Veritas* was anchored about ten miles away. The

Indonesian islands of Java and Sumatra were even farther. He had wounded Nergal, hadn't he? Where would the god go to recover?

And Nergal's words...*Death pulsing beneath, a trigger for the curse that sprawls over the Earth's surface.* Hadn't Nergal said something like that to Ashe and Inanna? "What did Nergal say to you?" Varun asked.

"He didn't say anything to me."

"Back at Atlantis. What did he say to you and Inanna before he vanished?"

Ashe frowned. "The curse is too deeply embedded in your planet, and your planet's pulsing heartbeat will spell its own doom."

"Pulse...in the planet. The Earth's core." The words rushed out of Varun. "And the sprawling curse...the Tree of Life. What will happen if the Tree of Life—the aether core that is spread out all over the planet—is struck by the energy from the Earth's core?"

"It will destroy the Earth, but it can't happen. There is nothing that can tap the energy from the Earth's core."

"The *Dirga Tiamatu* did."

"But the controls for the *Dirga Tiamatu* were destroyed at Shulim."

"Are those the *only* controls for the *Dirga Tiamatu*?"

"Yes, of course!" Ashe insisted. "Did you think the mer-king would let the controls of so powerful a weapon extend beyond its most protected, most secured area?"

"But it's not a Beltiamatu weapon, is it? It's technology the merfolk inherited. It's Illojim technology." The words raced out of Varun, the facts as plain as day. "That's what Nergal's going to do. He's going to activate the *Dirga Tiamatu* and turn it on the Tree of Life. The explosion of that massive aether core will turn the Earth into an asteroid field."

Ashe paled. "So…there's another control panel for the *Dirga Tiamatu*?"

"Yes," Varun said. "And we have to find it before Nergal."

"But where?"

"The Illojim starship, obviously, the one that came from Aldebaran."

"It's destroyed, isn't it?"

"We don't know that, but—" Varun straightened. "Zamir would."

"Zamir?"

"He has the First Commander's soul—the one who commanded the Illojim starship. He would know, wouldn't he, where that ship is?"

"But Zamir…"

"He's here. We know it. You've sensed him. I have too."

"But we cannot see him. He cannot make himself heard."

Varun grimaced. "We'll add one more thing to that never-ending to-do list—"

An explosion rocked the *Veritas*. Plumes of dark smoke rose into the air.

Ashe's jaw dropped. "Nergal!"

CHAPTER 18

Ginny loved the sound of the *Veritas* engines, a low bass that hummed in her ear whatever the time of day or night. It anchored her, however high the waves rose or loudly the wind screamed. The *Veritas* was where she had regained consciousness after her kidnapping, and it was, in some odd way, her sanctuary amid the unleashed plague and the unfurling elemental war.

During the day, while the ship bustled with activity, the crew mess hall would have lapsed into silence, if not for the Iraqi woman and children they had rescued. If the weather was too hot or too cold, the children used the mess hall as a playroom while their mother and Ginny sat and talked. Ginny liked to think of herself as the woman's entry point into a kinder world—a world where family and friends stuck by you, even if everything else was falling apart.

That day, Ginny tried to tell herself, was no different from any other. Both Ashe and Varun—and her ghost—had left the ship to search the islet that used to be Krakatoa. They had not yet returned, but that was not unusual, right? Ginny wiped the damp palms of her hands on her denim jeans, and tried to breathe in a calm and measured way. There was no reason to panic—

The *Veritas* jolted. Ginny looked up sharply, and the woman across from her cried out in Arabic. "What was that?"

Ginny stood and listened as the ship's engines ground down to silence. "Stay here," she told the woman, who beckoned to her children and wrapped her arms around them. The little girl clutched a toy penguin to her chest. "I'm going to see what's happening."

She walked to the door, and the ship jolted again, so violently it threw her off her feet. What the hell was going on? She yanked open the door.

The heat and black plumes drove her back.

The engine room was ablaze.

"Out! Get out!" Ginny shouted. "Get up onto the deck." The woman and her children scurried from the room and ran toward the stairs. Ginny yanked the fire extinguisher off the corridor wall and sprinted to the engine room. She sprayed the foam into the room, but it seemed to have as much effect as a bucket of water on a forest fire. She held her arms over her eyes. "Is anyone in there? Mitch?" She called the engineer's name.

Ginny squinted as something dark on the floor crawled toward her. "Mitch?" She sprayed the entirety of the fire extinguisher's contents, then flung the empty canister aside. The man's low moans were barely audible over the crackle of the flames.

There was another fire extinguisher in the mess hall! She

spun around and bumped into Corey, the medic. His eyes were wide with fear, but he aimed his fire extinguisher into the engine room and sprayed it down.

"Mitch's in there."

"I know." Corey sounded anguished. "We got to—"

Another explosion from the back of the engine room rocked the *Veritas*. Black smoke rolled out of the room. Ginny's eyes watered. Her lung choked up.

"Seal the fire door!" Jackson's voice shouted from behind her.

He pulled her back, his brown eyes flicking over her, making sure she was all right, then reached over Corey's shoulder to slide the door over the threshold.

"Mitch's still in here!" Corey shouted up at Jackson. His face was streaked with soot.

Jackson looked into the room, his hand held over his nose to protect him from the poisonous fumes. The dark figure on the ground no longer moved. A muscle twitched in Jackson's jaw, and he yanked the door close. "We'll get him when it's over. If we still have a ship. Now, get up on deck. Corey, make sure Ginny, the woman, and the kids are in a lifeboat. You get them off the *Veritas*."

"Wait! What happened?" Ginny grabbed Jackson's arm. "How did the engines explode?"

"I don't know what happened, but they didn't explode for no reason," Jackson said grimly. "Now get off—"

"No, I can help—"

"You're getting off." Jackson gripped her arm and pushed her, ahead of him, toward the steps leading to the deck.

Ginny hacked out a cough and stretched out her arms in front of her to feel her way through the corridor. She stumbled over something soft and small. One of the toys the children had dropped—

Something thudded behind her.

Jackson turned too.

Corey lay unconscious on the ground, his chest hardly moving. His soot-covered face dripped sweat, streaking clear lines through the black. Jackson combat-rolled over Corey, and staggered up, with Corey slung over his back. "Keep going," he ordered Ginny, his voice a wheeze.

Ginny found the staircase by tripping over it and almost hitting her chin on a higher step. It was narrow; how was Jackson going to manage while carrying Corey's dead weight across his shoulders?

Only the steady huff of Jackson's breath behind her allowed her to keep moving in spite of the panic that made it hard to think clearly. Ginny pushed her weight against the fire door at the top of the steps, and blinked hard, shying away from the sunlight. "Hey!" she shouted at the other crew members. "We need some help here."

Two men hurried over as Jackson emerged and collapsed slowly to his knees. The men tugged Corey off and started CPR. Jackson watched them for a moment, then looked at Ginny. "You okay?"

She stared back at him. Beneath the soot, their faces were flushed from the heat, and their clothes were streaked gray and black. "I…" Her heart wrenched when she thought of Mitch. Ginny glanced around. The woman and her children huddled by the door of the bridge. Ginny stared down at the stuffed penguin in her hand, then held it out to the little girl.

With a sequel of delight, the girl raced forward and

snatched the toy out of Ginny's hand before flinging her arms around Ginny's neck and pressing a kiss to her cheek.

Ginny blinked back her tears. She had not been ready for the girl's effusive gratitude. It had been a long time since her problems could be solved as something as simple as a stuffed toy.

Ginny glanced back at Jackson, but he was looking past her shoulder.

When Ashe and Varun left the ship hours earlier, the seismic activity around the volcano was a steady wisp of gray smoke.

Not anymore.

Fire and magma roiled off the top of the islet that was now Krakatoa.

"It's the captain," Jackson muttered. "Wherever she goes, it's on fire."

"But she's there, and we're here. So why is the ship on fire?" Ginny asked. "Engines don't just randomly explode."

"No, they don't." Jackson stood. His broad shoulders straightened, and his hand went into his jacket pocket.

Was he gripping his handgun? Ginny drew a tremulous breath. "Do you think it's…Nergal?"

"If it is, he won't take this ship easily from us. You stay with the family. Don't let them panic. It's easier to keep people safe if you're all together."

Ginny nodded, then went over to join the Iraqi family. The little girl, holding her penguin, wrapped her arm around Ginny's leg and leaned close.

"What's going on?" the woman asked, her voice scarcely audible above Jackson's shouted orders. "Are we being attacked?"

"I don't know," Ginny murmured. "Just stay with me. Jackson and the men will keep us safe." She glanced up at the sky, her attention drawn to something that looked like a streak of purple across the bright blue. "Up there." She pointed to it. "Do you see it?"

The woman's gaze searched the breadth of the sky. "What are you looking at?"

"The swirling lights—like a galaxy. It's coming closer."

"I don't see anything," the woman insisted, her voice edging toward fear—not of Ginny, but of what Ginny saw. "Is it going to hurt us?"

"Jackson!" Ginny shouted. "Up there!"

He spun around. She didn't think he actually saw anything, but he yanked out his handgun and fired two shots at the area she pointed at.

The lights dropped onto the deck of the ship, piling on top of each other to take on the form of a man. Ginny shoved the woman and children behind her. A flicker of motion beside her caught her eye. Her ghost! He stood next to her, like a warrior braced for battle. If he had left Ashe and returned to her side, all hell was probably about to break loose. Ginny's fingertips tingled, the dark, purple-streaked aether cloud taking shape between her cupped hands.

The column of light faded as Nergal's aquiline features emerged—his piercing eyes, the slash of his cheekbones, the thin press of his lips. The bullets Jackson fired struck Nergal's chest, but the god did not even seem to realize that he had been hit.

Nergal's gaze swept dismissively over everyone on the ship to focus on Ginny. His eyes narrowed. "An aether core. A *living* aether core. How remarkable." His chin lifted. "Do you have any idea how much destructive power you carry in you? Do you know what happens when aether explodes?"

Light shimmered in Nergal's hand, taking on the shape of a spear. He drew the tip across the palm of his hand, staining the gleaming edge with black blood. With a smile and a careless flick of his wrist, he hurled the spear at Ginny.

"No!" Jackson leaped in front of Ginny.

The spear pierced Jackson. The uncanny force of the blow hurled him back. His body slumped over the weapon as the spear raced through the air, toward Ginny.

The shimmering presence of the ghost hovering beside Ginny hurled itself in front of her. The spear plunged through the ghost.

And kept moving.

Ginny stared, wordlessly, at impending death. The aether cloud at her fingertips flickered and flared but nothing happened.

Behind her, the waves roared, and a mermaid leaped out of the water, arcing through the air. The air around Ashe trembled as she landed on human feet. She held out her hand, and the spear stopped, quivering in midair as if it had struck a steel wall.

Ginny's breath whooshed out of her. Suddenly, Varun was beside her, pulling her, the women, and children away before setting himself in front of them.

Nergal chuckled, the sound low and amused. He looked at Ashe. "How desperate you must be to dabble with dark energy—to hope that the power which will destroy the Earth might, somehow, be able to save it. Third time lucky…" He laughed. "The Earth escaped destruction at Atlantis and at

Shulim. There is nothing that can stop it this time." He faded, evaporating into pinpricks of light.

Ashe snarled. The wind swept in, scattering the light, but it regathered high up in the air and swirled away.

"Jackson…" Ginny dropped to her knees beside Jackson. Her hand fumbled on the spear.

"No, don't pull it out," Varun said. He pressed his fingers to Jackson's throat, to his wrist, then his shoulders sagged. "He's…gone." Varun drew his hand over Jackson's eyes, closing them. "We're too late." Pain infused his voice.

Ashe's eyes were dangerous, narrow slits. She gripped the spear and drew it out slowly.

Ginny's mouth dropped as the ghost, pinned on the spear behind Jackson's body, was drawn forward into Jackson's body. "Wait—" She blinked hard and shook her head. The ghost was gone. The shimmering outline of his body had vanished.

"What is it?" Varun asked.

Ginny looked away. "I don't know." Her voice cracked. She had crazy visions and fantasies. She saw things that weren't there. A merman trapped in a narrow, vertical tank. The ghost of a man who said nothing, but who knew that she saw him.

Ashe laid her hand on Jackson's body then rose to stare out at the ocean. She said nothing, but her eyes were moist. Her shoulders trembled from silent tears.

"Captain," Meifeng said quietly. "Engine room's on fire."

She nodded. "Stay here. I'll handle it." Ashe turned toward the crew quarters, but in that instant, Jackson's chest heaved.

Ginny gasped. She and Varun supported Jackson as he

rolled over and tried to rise. His head hung low, the muscles in his shoulders and back shaking hard. The crew members exchanged uncertain glances.

"Jackson?" Ginny called softly. She gaped as the spear wound in his back slowly closed as if he had never been injured.

Jackson raised his head. Ginny stared at him. His eyes were no longer brown but a swirl of blue and green, dusted with gold.

Just like Ashe's eyes.

Just like the merman's eyes—the one she saw every night in her blur of memories and dreams.

Across from her, Varun stiffened. He had noticed the change too.

Jackson's gaze fixed on her for a moment, before sweeping across the deck to focus on Ashe. His lips trembled. *"Ummum..."*

Ginny's thoughts immediately skidded through an automatic translation of the sound. *Ummum* was the Sumerian word for "Mother."

CHAPTER 19

"The engine fire's out but we're dead in the water," Ashe confirmed when she returned to the bridge. "The ship will have to be towed to port for repairs, and considering the chaos on land, I wouldn't take this ship anywhere near a port." She looked at Zamir, who huddled beneath a heavy blanket. "How are you feeling?"

Jackson's face turned toward her. Zamir's eyes fixed on her. "I…don't know."

Varun sat across from Zamir. "I know this is a big shock—to everyone, but we need answers, and we don't have much time. Are you ready to talk?"

Zamir turned the cup of hot tea he held between his hands. "Yes."

"How long have you been here?" Varun asked.

Zamir shook his head. "I never left. When we passed through the portal, first you, then I, I realized that you could not see me, that I was a soul without a body. I could see you and hear you, though, and I knew you were trying to find a way back into the underworld to release my mother, so I stayed with you. Then you found her." Zamir glanced at Ginny. "And she could see me."

Varun's jaw dropped "You could…what? Why didn't you tell us?"

Ginny shook her head. "I don't know what's real. Ever since…*that*…I see all kinds of things, imagine all kinds of things."

"I realized she couldn't hear me," Zamir continued, "but it was enough to be seen. Enough to keep hoping. And then you came back." He looked at Ashe. "I've been here all this time. Listening. Watching." He gritted his teeth. "Helpless."

"But how did you get into Jackson's body?" Varun asked.

"They were protecting me." Ginny's voice cracked. "They were both protecting me. Jackson stepped in front of the spear, and Zamir did too. The spear pierced both of them, and when Ashe pulled it out, Zamir's ghost vanished. It melted into Jackson's body."

Ashe stared at Zamir. "So, Jackson's dead, and you're in his body?"

Zamir drew a deep breath. He did not nod; neither did he shake his head.

"And your soul. Is it still the First Commander's soul?"

Zamir nodded.

Ginny's jaw dropped. "Wait, what's going on?"

"Merfolk do not have souls, at least not normally," Varun said. "Ereshkigal gifted Zamir the soul of the First Commander, but then Zamir died, and somehow, his consciousness remained fused with that of the First Commander's soul."

"So now there are two people in Jackson's body?"

Zamir shook his head. "No. It's...hard to explain. I have fragments of his memories, but I am still me."

"And you are Ashe's son," Ginny said slowly. "You were once a merman."

"I was the mer-king." Zamir shrugged off the towel and rose to his feet. "Then many things went wrong. And now, we are no more."

Ginny frowned. Had she only imagined that black-tailed merman in the tank? Possibly. More than likely. Who knew what craziness she was cooking up in that overheated brain of hers?

Except that she hadn't imagined the ghost man. *Zamir.*

It was no longer Jackson, of that much she was certain. They even stood differently. Both men were given to standing still for long periods, but Jackson's stillness was the watchfulness of a trained soldier; Zamir's was the aloofness of a king.

Jackson was quick to retort and quick to laughter. Not Zamir, who weighed his words and actions as if they carried life and death implications.

As indeed they probably had.

Varun and Ashe exchanged glances, then Varun spoke. "Zamir, we believe that Nergal is going to use the *Dirga Tiamatu* to destroy the Tree of Life. That aether core is infinitely larger than the ones at Atlantis and Shulim, both of which escaped destruction. If the aether core at the Tree of Life explodes, it will destroy the Earth." He drew a deep breath. "Do you know if there are any other controls for the *Dirga Tiamatu*?"

Zamir shook his head. "The *Dirga Tiamatu* was controlled only from Shulim, and that city was destroyed. The Illojim though..." He frowned and the color of his eyes changed, the flecks of gold expanding until his eyes were as golden as Inanna's. Varun, Ginny, and Ashe exchanged glances but said nothing.

Zamir's gaze fixed on the far wall, but Ginny did not think he actually saw anything. His lips moved as if in a trance. "The *Dalkhu Libbu*. The controls for the *Dirga Tiamatu* are on the *Dalkhu Libbu*."

Ginny frowned. "The Demon's Heart."

Varun stiffened. "The what?"

"In Sumerian, *Dalkhu* means demon, and *Libbu* means heart. The *Dalkhu Libbu* is the demon's heart."

Varun glanced down at the plain-looking curved dagger he had set down on the table. "Forged in a demon's heart from the core of a fallen star," he murmured. "The Illojim are surprisingly literal. Maybe our problem was simply not taking their words seriously enough. Zamir, where or what is the *Dalkhu Libbu*?"

"It is the Illojim starship. The one I piloted in our escape from Aldebaran."

"The one that carried Inanna, Ereshkigal, and Nergal, among others, to Earth."

Zamir, his golden eyes gleaming, nodded.

"We have to get to it before Nergal does. Where is the *Dalkhu Libbu*?" Varun asked.

Zamir looked up, meeting Varun's eyes. "I buried it in hell."

CHAPTER 20

Hell was a three-night journey from the waters of the Sunda Straits to the middle of the Karakum Desert, in Turkmenistan. Society, driven to the brink by a global pandemic, hovered on anarchy, but some things—like flying through the air in broad daylight—was just not done, whatever the state of society. Furthermore, Ginny and Zamir's still-human bodies forced Ashe to coast at low speeds and low altitudes.

Varun chafed at the slow progress—who knew what Nergal was doing?—but there was a difference between saving the world and attempting to save the world while accidentally destroying it. The last thing anyone needed was generalized panic. Let the people of Earth imagine they were alone in the universe and that the plague was their problem to solve. It kept them focused on their hospitals and morgues instead of chasing Ashe to the Gates of Hell.

Varun grimaced. As a fire elemental, he—technically—

controlled flames, small and large, natural or otherwise. The byproducts of fire, like heat and soot, was par for the course. *Supposedly.*

In reality, he was still mentally bound by physical laws and human customs, and standing at the edge of all that fire —all that unchecked fire—really bothered him.

He inhaled deeply and with effort, modulated his tone. "So, this is hell..." Varun stood beside Ashe and peered down at the Darvaza gas crater. The hole in the ground, seventy meters across, bubbled boiling mud and spewed orange flames. "I don't understand. This area collapsed into a crater in 1971 after drilling for oil. A natural gas pocket—"

Zamir shook his head as he walked up to stand beside Varun. "It wasn't a natural gas pocket. It was the hole left by the *Dalkhu Libbu.* The excavations in the area disturbed it, and the ship settled deeper in the ground, leaving the gas pocket, which caused the ground to collapse."

"But the fire—it's recent, right? Those geologists set the gas on fire."

"This fire is recent," Zamir agreed. "But the fire from the *Dalkhu Libbu*'s crash lasted for hundreds of years before it was finally extinguished and covered by the earth."

"There must always have been gas pockets in the area," Varun murmured. "Why did your ship crash?"

Zamir's brow furrowed, and confusion lodged in his gaze, as if the memories were too tangled or too cloudy to draw out. "I battled...with a dragon..."

Dragon? Varun's eyes narrowed. He glanced at Ashe, who shrugged. Apparently, she didn't know anything about dragons either.

And probably just as well.

Mermaids and elementals were problematic enough. The world didn't need a dragon on top of that. Varun refocused the conversation on the problem at hand. "So where is the ship now?"

"Beneath the crater," Zamir said.

"Underneath all that fire?" Varun asked. "But wouldn't it have been destroyed by the heat?"

"The *Dalkhu Libbu* is made from the same alloy used in the *Dirga Tiamatu* to channel the heat of the Earth's core. It can survive far more extreme temperatures than this." Zamir waved his hand at the crater." His eye color shifted without warning to match his mother's, as he glanced over his shoulder at Ginny, who stood a slight distance away from the three of them. "She does not look at me. Does not talk to me." He shook his head. "I did not ask to be in this body. I would not have chosen his body even if it were the only path left to me. I saw how much he cared for her, and how she was coming to care for him." Zamir squeezed his eyes shut and a muscle ticked in his jaw. "I would not have come between them."

"This…wasn't your fault," Varun said. "Ashe pulled out that spear, and she didn't know you were there."

"No one knew—I never even imagined that I could take over a dead body. Yet, here I am." Zamir stared down at his hands. "A merman, in a human body." He looked up and met Ashe's eyes. A slight smile quirked his lips. "Our family seems destined to repeat its mistakes, one generation after another."

Ashe shrugged, graceful in spite of the taint of anguish on her face. "At least you're not mute or lame." Her voice quavered. "And you're back. Whatever form you wear, you are my son. I can see you, hear you, touch you." Her hand extended toward Zamir, but she did not make contact. "I never thought I would—"

Zamir closed the distance and drew Ashe into his arms. "I'm here now." He leaned his cheek against his mother's hair. "We can still get this right."

Varun's throat tightened, and he stepped back to give Ashe and Zamir some privacy. He shoved his hands into the pocket of his jeans and walked over to rejoin Ginny. For several moments, they stood next to each other, staring out at the gaping crater maw. "Are you okay?" Varun asked finally.

Ginny was silent for a while. "I'm alive," she murmured.

"It's a good start," Varun said. "Can't do anything if you're not alive."

Ginny swallowed hard. "He's really gone, isn't he?"

"Jackson?" Varun drew a deep breath and nodded slowly. "Yes, he's gone. He was a good man. Hell of a first mate; put up with Ashe and had her back the entire way."

"We never really..." Ginny's voice cracked. "I miss him, but I don't even feel like I really had a right—"

Varun took Ginny's hands in his. They were cold, trembling. "Hey, you always have a right to miss someone, especially a good friend. I miss him too, but it's confusing. His body is still here, and Zamir's in it—"

"But I don't know Zamir," Ginny said flatly.

"Grief, for you, is less complicated. You're mourning the death of one person, and not simultaneously celebrating the return of the other." Varun pressed his hand against the ache in his chest. "I don't know what I feel. My emotions can't seem to get a fix on true north. And Ashe is probably even more conflicted than I am. Jackson was one of the few humans she considered a friend, and yet…"

"And yet, her son has returned." Ginny's shoulders sagged as she sighed. "I don't think there's a true north, not where emotions are concerned. I shouldn't be feeling this way; I hardly knew him. Just over a week." She squeezed her eyes shut. "I was kidnapped ten days ago, and now, I don't recognize my life. I don't recognize me. And I don't recognize the Earth. How could it go to hell in just ten days?"

"Hell was a long time in building up. It was just waiting for a chance to be let loose."

She shrugged. "I could have used a bit more warning, especially if I was going to be sucked into the mess." The purple-tinged black cloud took shape between her cupped hands. "It's dark energy. I looked it up after Inanna's passing comment on aether."

"What is dark energy?"

"It is the largest source of energy in the universe—almost 70 percent of the total energy in the universe today. It's believed to be power behind the accelerating expansion of the universe."

"And it's in you."

"A portion of it."

Varun shook his head. "I still don't understand how you managed to pick it up just walking through the mushroom grove in the Garden of Eden."

Ginny frowned. Her thoughts seemed elsewhere, her gaze distant. "I don't either." She drew a breath and expelled it in a sigh. "Varun, if Nergal is trying to blow up the Tree of Life because aether is explosive, does it mean that I'm explosive too?"

Varun winced. He had hoped that he would not have to break it to Ginny, but Ginny was too logical and too pragmatic not to have come to that conclusion on her own. "Yes. I guess so."

"I guess that's why Nergal was trying to kill me. We probably have Jackson and..." She glanced over at Zamir. "And Zamir to thank for saving my life. The *Veritas* might have left a hole in the ocean otherwise." She laughed, but the sound wobbled. "I'll have to make it a point not to get hit by a nuclear weapon."

"Stick close. We'll do our best to protect you."

"I...I want to help. I just don't know how." She stared down at the living cloud in her hands. "Aether—dark energy—changes things, but I can't seem to direct it. It does its own thing."

Varun frowned. "Elemental energy does its own thing too, even though it may seem like Ashe has air and water perfectly under control. There are no rules, no magic words. It's a relationship. Ashe has cultivated her relationship over hundreds of years. I've had weeks. And you've had even less than that. It's not going to develop overnight."

"Unfortunately, I don't think you and I have the luxury of centuries. The Earth is falling apart *now.*"

"And that's what Nergal was counting on. The air, water, and earth elementals are too busy running around trying to contain the spread of the disease. The fire elementals are still on Nergal's side. That leaves Ashe and I to counter Nergal. And we have you now. The winning card."

Ginny shook her head. "The wild card. When Nergal hurled that spear at me, I couldn't get any of this power to save me. I don't know what good I am, Varun, or worse, if

I'm a walking time bomb—an accident that could wipe out everyone and everything around me."

"We'll take that chance. There is magic…there is power in you. I've seen what you can do. You have to figure it out, and the sooner the better."

"What do you know about aether?"

"Nothing, except that the merfolk used it as a power source for their underwater city."

"So if anyone understands it…" Ginny glanced toward Ashe and Zamir who stood a slight distance away, speaking in lowered tones. The stiffness between mother and son was slowly melting into the closeness of family. "It would be the mer-king, right?"

Varun nodded.

"What is he like?" Ginny asked.

"Zamir?" Varun glanced over at Ashe and Zamir. "Like Ashe, he loves deeply, and like Ashe, that love can be used to manipulate him."

"What did he look like, before he took over Jackson's body?"

"An old man with a fish tail."

Ginny's jaw dropped. "What?"

"Zamir was almost three hundred years old—which is the maximum lifespan of a Beltiamatu. He had long white hair, a white beard, but he was vigorous, still strong. And then in the underworld, he had a different form, a man in his prime, but with the oddly angular eyes so distinctive to the Illojim. It was probably the First Commander's body as it had been, and what I saw was the visible merging of Zamir's consciousness and the First Commander's soul."

"And now he's a black man," Ginny finished. She

chuckled suddenly. "And I think I'm confused. Imagine how he must feel. And Ashe, too."

"I don't think Ashe is confused," Varun said. "She's had much more time to deal with the vagaries of shifting forms. The body's just the body. It's what's inside that matters. She looks at Zamir—and I think that, whatever body he wears, she often sees the baby, the child she left behind, the son for whom she risked everything, gave up everything. That kind of bond isn't easily broken."

"And he's forgiven her?"

"He's working on it." Varun smiled faintly. "And he's a great deal closer to forgiveness than he thinks."

"What did she tell him?"

"She explained. I'm not sure she actually apologized. Ashe isn't great with apologies. Sometimes, even explanations are a stretch for her."

"And the fact that she's a mermaid—"

"She's not a mermaid," Varun corrected. "Not anymore. She's not human either—her body is just a shell she's wearing. She's not like the other elementals. She's astral energy held together by her will, her consciousness."

"And wasn't it weird to..." Ginny bit her lip. "To love her?"

"To fall in love with her?" Varun shrugged. "It was terrifying, but I'm mostly over it now even though she can probably still kick my ass without trying too hard."

Ginny laughed softly. "She's remarkable."

"She's driven. She rants and rails at Inanna and Ereshkigal, blames them—at least outwardly—for the entire damn mess, but she's still at it, trying to fix it."

"It's our world," Ginny mused. "Our only world." She

tilted her head and studied the bubbling mud and spitting flames in the crater. "How are we going to get in there?"

Varun huffed out his breath. "I'm working on it. Or Ashe is."

"Is there a plan?"

"No. Usually we just make it up as we go, but with Zamir around, we might have a hope of a plan."

"You like him," Ginny whispered.

"I didn't, until I realized that he was as emotionally lost as his mother, and that his hurt, his pain was behind the destruction of the ocean. Twice, I saw more pain on his face than I'd seen on anyone's—when Ashe won and seized the trident from him, and when she chose to save my life instead of his."

"She did?"

"I'm still not sure why."

Ginny chuckled softly. "Because she loves you, you silly goose." She looked back at Zamir. "What happened after that?"

"In the underworld, it was different. Zamir had lost everything. He didn't think that his mother, who, in his mind, had rejected him three times, would ever return. But Ashe came for him."

"He wasn't expecting that, was he?" Ginny asked.

"No." Varun smiled faintly. "It changed him—not immediately, not even quickly—but it was in the underworld, ironically, where Ashe and Zamir started working things out. It's not perfect, and I don't think it will ever be—there's still a great deal of anger in him—but I think they both realize that despite their past, there is still room, in their present, for family."

"She doesn't strike me as the maternal type. The ass-kicking type, sure, but not the maternal type. Just goes to show how wrong first impressions can be."

Varun followed Ginny's gaze to the edge of the crater. "The Ginny I thought I knew would have been charging ahead, eager to see, touch, and do everything, but here you are actually chitchatting."

She frowned. "I wouldn't exactly term it chitchat…"

"You're afraid, aren't you?"

Ginny bit down on her lower lip. "Terrified." She looked at Varun. "How on Earth did a marine biologist and an ancient history scholar end up here at the Gates of Hell, with two merfolk—who aren't even merfolk anymore—trying to save the world from alien invasion?"

Varun shrugged. "We got lucky. At least I did…" His glance fell on Zamir. "You almost did. I'm sorry. I know it's confusing—"

"It's not confusing at all. They're different people. The fact that they look the same to me, physically, isn't relevant. Jackson was…" She swallowed hard. "We were almost something more. And Zamir is…he's just not…" Ginny sighed "He was friendlier as a ghost."

"Like Casper, huh?"

"At first, I thought it was just stray light, like a flicker you sometimes catch out of the corner of your eye, but then I realized I could see him even when I turned my face to look at him full on. That's when he realized I could see him."

"Did he ever try to communicate?"

"He pointed at lots of things. When no one was looking, I told him what they were."

"An English lesson?"

Ginny giggled, and Varun realized it was the first time, since Jackson's death, that he'd heard her laugh. "On the ship, he followed Ashe a great deal, watching over her. Now I understand why. He was trying to protect his mother." Ginny sighed. "It makes me feel a little bit better about him. He feels like less of an unfriendly ass."

"If it makes you feel any better, Ashe is a lot of an unfriendly ass. I'm not surprised Zamir takes after her. I think it has to do with being a merfolk, surrounded by humans, and royalty, to boot. Revealing their thoughts is just not a thing that occurs to them, ever. Which is why all our plans are made up on the spur of the moment."

Ginny stiffened as both Zamir and Ashe turned around to rejoin them. Her gaze shuttled between Ashe and Zamir, always quickly darting away from Zamir's eyes.

Zamir began, "I have a plan—"

"Oh, thank God." Varun grinned.

Zamir glanced at Varun, then Ginny. His brow furrowed in confusion; it seemed as if he were looking to Ginny for answers.

Ashe shook her head. "Don't mind him. It's a weird human thing."

"It's not a weird human thing," Varun said. "It's a communication thing, but hey, don't let me stop you."

"The ship is buried under boiling mud and burning gas," Zamir continued. "The excavation activity in the area shifted it, which means that I no longer know exactly where it is. It's going to require some searching."

Varun glanced at Ashe. "Ashe and I can likely pass through the heat, largely unharmed, but what about you and Ginny?"

Zamir turned his head to meet Ginny's eyes. "She'll have to change the terrain—carve a path through the heat and burning gas."

"But how?" Ginny asked.

"Aether. Dark energy is in everything, and manipulating the amount and form of energy within things changes its composition—its shape, even its elements."

Ginny stared down at her hands. "Is…that what I was doing?" She wet her lips and made a few false starts before getting the words out. "Do you know what aether can do?"

"In theory. The Beltiamatu royal family can contain it within their bodies, but we can't manipulate it. Only humans can." His smile was rueful. "The old stories say that the Illojim were worried that the merfolk would rise in rebellion, so withheld from them the ability to manipulate aether."

"And they weren't afraid of the humans rising in rebellion, huh?" Ginny asked.

"I guess humanity had yet to fully demonstrate what it was capable of," Zamir said. "I can tell you everything I know about aether, but I can't show you. That power has to come from within you, just as my mother's power, Varun's power, comes from within them and not from rules imposed by the universe."

Ginny drew a deep breath. "All right. Tell me what I must do."

Zamir knelt and with his finger sketched patterns in the sand. "This is where the *Dalkhu Libbu* was. Based on how the crater collapsed, my best guess is that the starship settled… this way." He drew an arrow in the sand. "Since the crater hasn't collapsed any further, it's safe to assume that the starship is still there—about two hundred feet beneath the surface. The entrance is here…on the far side."

"Naturally," Ginny muttered.

The corner of Zamir's mouth twitched in a hint of laughter. "My mother can insulate us in air, but it'll only get us so far before the heat becomes too much for anyone who can't just flash back into astral energy, so we'll actually have to open a path to the ship." He looked at Ginny. "And aether can do that."

"How?"

"Change it. Change the boiling mud and burning gas to something else."

Ginny's eyes flashed wide. Her gaze swept over the breadth of the crater. "All of it?" Her voice was a squeak.

Zamir hesitated. "Not all, but a great deal of it. I'll show you." He extended his hand to her.

Ginny did not move for a moment, then she reached out and placed her hand in his. Zamir led her close to the edge of the caldera. He gestured with his other hand. Varun could not hear the words, but Ginny was leaning in toward Zamir, listening intently.

Varun ground his teeth. "If the *Dalkhu Libbu* is buried, if we can't get to it, there's a chance Nergal can't get to it either."

"Do you want to gamble on that chance?" Ashe asked.

"So, we get onto the *Dalkhu Libbu*, we find the controls for the *Dirga Tiamatu*…and then what?"

"I'll destroy it."

Varun's gaze snapped to Ashe's face. "You? Alone? But we're all there, with you."

"Not at the end." Ashe shook her head. "I need Zamir's

help to navigate past the traps on the ship and to get to the bridge, but then you, Zamir, and Ginny have to get out."

"And then what? You'll destroy the *Dalkhu Libbu*, with you still in it?"

"Zamir and Ginny are in human bodies. They won't survive if they're not out of the ship when it explodes." Ashe's expression tightened. "I cannot lose my son. Not again. Never again."

"But I'm not human. Not anymore—"

"You have to get them out. Ginny's powers are too uncertain. And your control over your astral form isn't precise yet." She drew a deep, trembling breath. "And I can't lose you either."

Varun glared at her. "You losing me, and me losing you, is the same damn thing. Our best chance of getting through this is together." He shook his head. "You didn't tell Zamir this part of your plan, did you?"

"No."

"Of course, you didn't. He would never agree to it. Damn it, Ashe. You make terrible plans."

She glowered at him. "That's better than not having a plan, right?"

"In your case, planning's not an improvement on making shit up." Their eyes met. "I'm not leaving you."

"So you're going to let Ginny die?" Ashe shook her head. "She's the innocent in this, and for that matter, so are you. Zamir and I made choices that got us all to this point. But Ginny…this isn't her fight. She shouldn't have to die for someone else's mistakes."

"This is war, Ashe." Varun told her. "It's war against Nergal. It's a war to save this planet. My planet. Ginny's planet. We are soldiers—all of us, Ginny too—and soldiers die in war."

Ashe rolled her eyes. "That's a ridiculously human view, and it only works when you have the luxury of breeding like rabbits. We are trying to destroy the controls for the *Dirga Tiamatu* so Nergal cannot use it to destroy the Tree of Life, which is an aether core." Ashe pointed to Ginny. "*That* is an aether core. She's a walking, living, breathing aether core. If she dies in a massive explosion, the overload of energy will turn all of Turkmenistan—and more—into a crater." She raised her chin. "Ginny cannot be anywhere near the *Dalkhu Libbu* when it explodes. She's also the reason why simple air insulation won't work. We know the heat can be intense. We can't take any risks with her. Zamir knows more than I do about aether, but not enough. We've never had to deal with aether being inside a person before."

"So all those things that Zamir said, about the power having to come from within her."

"It's all true, but we don't know where the truth ends. If there are rules, we don't know it. Let us just *not* let her get killed."

"Why does she need to go down at all?"

"The Illojim, Beltiamatu, and Atlantean cultures were built around aether. Zamir believes that there are things on that ship that only she can manipulate with aether."

"I wish his inherited memories were more certain."

"It was enough to get us here." Ashe reached for Varun's hand, her fingers entwining with his. "You'll get Ginny out." Their eyes met. Her voice shook slightly. "Please."

"Zamir will get her out," Varun said, but even as he spoke the words, he knew that Ginny and Zamir's best chances of escape was if he—or Ashe—accompanied them. He squeezed his eyes shut. The ache in his chest stunned him. "*You* are going to leave with Ginny and Zamir."

"Varun—"

"We're not done." A muscle twitched in his cheek. He stared at her, and his grip tightened on her hand. "We're not at the end. After we destroy the controls for the *Dirga Tiamatu*, someone still has to take out Nergal. You're stronger. You have a better chance of going up against Nergal and winning. I'll destroy the *Dalkhu Libbu*. You get out. Take Zamir and Ginny with you. Then you stop Nergal."

"No, I won't—"

Varun pulled out the *Isriq Genii* from his utility belt, and offered it, hilt first, to her. "You losing me, me losing you, it's the same damn thing. I swear, either way, it's going to hurt like hell." He swallowed through the tightness in his throat. "This is war, Ashe. We send in the best person for the job. That final battle with Nergal…it has to be you. Inanna chose you to be the catalyst." He managed a faint smile. "That's why you have to end it. End the influence of the Illojim on what's left of the Beltiamatu, Atlanteans, and humans. This is *our* world, Ashe—yours, Zamir's, Ginny's, mine—not aliens who play at being gods. We're taking our damn planet back."

The fading light of dusk flickered, not with the final glow of sunlight but with streaks of purple lightning. Varun glanced toward Ginny. She stood at the edge of the chasm, her arms extended over the superheated mud. Her head was tilted back, and Zamir stood beside her, his arm around her waist, anchoring her.

Varun shook his head. "I thought I was afraid of what was in me, then I realized I am petrified of what's in her."

"It's just energy, Varun."

"You say that so calmly, *after* you tell me that she can't be anywhere near the blast zone because she might crater the entire country."

Ashe glanced over the bleak landscape. "I've seen fires raze thousands of acres, earthquakes level cities, hurricanes cover entire island archipelagoes, and floods sweep away every vestige of human civilization. The power to destroy is in you and in me. Just because you've seen it all before, just because it can be explained away as a natural disaster doesn't make it any less devastating. A life lost is a life lost, whether to fire, earthquake, hurricane, flood, or aether." Ashe waved her hand at Ginny.

"But neither of us can do that," Varun murmured as purple lightning arced over the crater. Wherever the lightning struck, the ground quivered. The air shimmered around it as boiling mud twisted into a spiral, winding deep down into the crater.

Zamir glanced over his shoulder. His nod beckoned them over.

Ashe started toward her son, but Varun held her back, his grip on her hand tightening. "One way or another, we'll get this over the finish line," he promised softly. He leaned forward and touched his forehead to hers. It was scarcely enough to hold each other, to share that moment of closeness—but it was all they had left.

They were out of time.

CHAPTER 21

Mud, bubbling and boiling, oozed down the walls of the tunnel that aether had carved through the burning gases. Tongues of fire danced overhead, coating the roof of the cavern in flame.

It was like nothing Ashe had ever seen. Unfortunately, she was not in the mood for enjoying the view, unlike Varun, whose head swiveled, wide-eyed with wonder. In spite of everything that had happened, he had never lost that innocence. Neither he nor Ginny, both of whom looked around, trying to absorb everything that was happening.

Humans. Ashe suppressed the exasperated chuckle.

And if there was any doubt that Jackson was dead and Zamir inhabited his body, it was swept away. Zamir, like Ashe, was focused on the possible threat, not on the obvious promise. He strode through the tunnel, leading the way with certainty that inspired confidence, although he was armed only with a platinum spear.

A king, Ashe thought. The Beltiamatu still needed a king, although there was no way Zamir could return to the ocean now. If Kai were still alive, he could take his grandfather's place and lead what was left of the merfolk into a new future.

Assuming, of course, that she, Varun, Zamir, and Ginny managed to save the Earth.

Fragments of Ginny's conversation with Varun drifted toward Ashe. "I'm not sure how I'm going to explain this at Thanksgiving dinner." Ginny managed a nervous chuckle as she stared down at the purple-streaked black cloud churning on her open palm. "It was bad enough dealing with all the questions about why I'm wasting my life buried in dusty manuscripts and ancient dig sites. What did you tell your parents?"

"Nothing yet," Varun said. "Although, I think my mother suspects something. Everything considered, she and my father handled the fact that Ashe was a mermaid pretty well. That I'm an earth and fire elemental, and that my body isn't really here, might prove more problematic though."

Ginny rolled her eyes. "Don't be ridiculous, Varun. Of course your body is really here. Just because you can scatter and reassemble your molecules at will doesn't make you any less here. You're transforming, just like aether transforms."

"Aether transforms," Varun mused. "Ashe thinks of it as astral energy, but perhaps astral energy is just another name for aether, for dark energy."

"Maybe, in the end, we're all connected?" Ginny grinned up at him. "That's a comforting thought. You know, maybe, once we're done with this, I should go find a physicist. Maybe he can tell me more about dark energy. It would be nice to not feel like I'm making up this shit every time my fingertips get tingly."

"You could get your second Ph.D. It seems like a university or a laboratory would be a good place to hide out until you get a handle on things."

Ginny's glance flicked to his face. "Are you sorry you left the university for field work?"

He shook his head. "No. There was an ocean to save, even if I'll be saving it in ways I didn't expect."

The air vibrated. Varun paused and looked over his shoulder just as Ashe turned around. She saw nothing, but the trembling air quivered with urgency, bordering on panic.

"Keep moving," she said sharply. "Ginny, stay close to Zamir."

Ginny gave Ashe an alarmed look before hurrying forward to stand by Zamir.

"What is it?" Varun asked, his voice lowered, as he strode up to join Ashe.

"I don't know."

"More fire imps?"

"I don't think so."

"People?"

"Almost certainly not. Judging from the amount of air displaced, it's too big to be a person. Definitely too big to be an imp."

"Let's get moving, then." Varun reached for her hand.

She tugged it out of his grip. "I don't think we want to lead it—whatever it is—to the ship."

"But I don't think you want to fight a battle in the middle of a corridor of boiling mud and burning gases that exist only because Ginny carved it out of her imagination using magic she doesn't fully control. The walls and tunnels shift when her concentration wavers. It could come crashing down if she panics."

"I heard that!" was Ginny's tart reply. "And I resent it. Even if it's almost entirely true," she added in a small voice.

"Come, Ashe," Varun insisted, taking her hand and tugging her down the corridor.

She raced alongside Varun, but the darting breeze became even more panicked. It brushed against her cheeks, tugged at her hair, pleading, begging—

Ashe spun around and hurled out a blast of air.

A humanoid form, at least three times the size of a person, staggered back.

Varun jerked to a stop. "What is that?"

"A golem." Ashe's eyes narrowed. "And that's not steel, judging by its gleam."

Varun shook his head. "It's the same color of the metal we saw at Atlantis. Orichalcum."

The golem's arms wheeled, steadying it, and it straightened, standing stock still for a moment, as if taking in its surroundings. Its slitted eyes passed over Ashe and Varun to fix on Ginny. It leaped to attack, but Ashe slammed it back with another blast of air. "Go," she told Varun. "Keep Ginny safe."

The golem leaned forward, almost hunchbacked. Its lower profile made it harder to knock backward—

Ashe smiled wickedly. She spread her arms, beckoning, and the wind rushed toward her instead, the momentum knocking the golem off its feet. It landed on its back, but did not have a chance to regain its balance when the wind picked it up. Its limbs flailed like a struggling human. The air swirled around Ashe, whipping her hair away from her face as she inexorably pushed the golem against the wall of cascading, boiling mud.

Mud oozed over the gleaming metal shoulders and down the golem's chest. Within moments, the metal seemed to glow, then bubble as if something beneath its surface was mottling. The golem's limbs wriggled. Its head twisted. The golden sheen of orichalcum gave way to a red, angry glow that superheated into blinding blue light a moment before the golem exploded, large fragments flying outward.

The wind wrapped around Ashe, cocooning her and deflecting the pieces that might have struck her.

The golem's arms and legs twitched on the ground for a few seconds before unfolding like a child's toy. The metal contracted into sections and four segmented legs emerged, followed by a long tail that twisted around like living serpents. Finally, a small, stylized head popped out.

The four creatures stood as stiff as statues, their backs to each other, in a circle. Their shape and stance reminded Ashe of the stylized lions she had seen in Ginny's drawings of Inanna's gate. Only the tails writhed. Their tips touched, and purple lightning streaked down the tails and into the animal golems.

The stiffness melted into pure fluidity and sleek motion. As graceful as living lions, the four animal golems leaped. Sharp talons popped out of their smooth paws. Their metallic jaws parted to reveal gleaming fangs.

Instead of fleeing, Ashe slid down toward the lion golems. Their momentum carried them over her head, but by the time they landed and twisted around, snarling, Ashe was already on her feet. The wind lifted her up. The flames dancing overhead were so close that she could feel their heat against her skin as the golems paced beneath her.

Occasionally, one would leap, but the wind battered it away, sending it tumbling onto its back or side. The creature would snarl as it righted itself and rejoined the others. As a pride, they blocked her progress forward, but no matter. She could just—

A gust of wind brushed against her, its quick touch alarmed, even panicked.

Something else was coming up behind her.

She glanced over her shoulder as the darkness melted back from around eight more lion golems, their tails swishing like angry snakes with purple-streaked tongues. In the poor light, the technological marvels gleamed like golden statues.

They, too, had come out to play.

And to kill…

~

The tunnel carved out of mud and flames narrowed as it twisted down into a cavern. Varun emerged from the tunnel and stared up at the Illojim starship, wedged against the roof of the cavern. The cavern was warm, but not hot. The starship had fallen through and then blocked a hole in the cavern roof. On the other side, burning gases scalded the uppermost portions of the ship, lighting it in an orange glow. The ship looked like a malformed heart, and with its upper sections bathed in pulsing light, it seemed to Varun that it continued to beat like a living heart—albeit one taller than a fifty-story building.

"The *Dalkhu Libbu,*" Zamir murmured.

"Were there other starships?" Varun asked.

For a moment, Zamir hesitated, as if wrestling off a half-formed memory, then he nodded. "Yes, but none that has survived to this day. The *Dalkhu Libbu* was the flagship of the An dynasty. The other starships were melted down to supply the needs of the Beltiamatu and Atlantean empires."

"Where's the entrance to the ship?" Varun asked.

"One of them is down here." Zamir pointed toward the base of the heart.

Ginny glanced over her shoulder at the way they had come. "Shouldn't we wait for Ashe?"

Varun drew a deep breath. "We don't have much time. I have to destroy the controls for the *Dirga Tiamatu* before Nergal can use it against the Tree of Life. Where in the ship are the controls?"

Zamir pointed to the top, the part blocking the hole.

"Go figure," Varun muttered. "Better get started, then. Can you open the door?"

"I will try." Zamir strode toward the ship and walked around its base, often stopping to examine one feature or another on the surface.

"What are you looking for?" Varun asked.

"The right door," Zamir said. He straightened his shoulders as if from a silent sigh. "You realize this is going to be highly problematic."

"What do you mean?"

"The First Commander's memories seem like intuition, except that I can't tell the difference between facts and guesses. We'll be counting on luck to get us through this day, and I've never had much luck with luck." He laid his hand against a panel.

Varun held his breath but nothing happened.

"There's another problem," Zamir said. "The ship's controls are coded for the First Commander's passage... except this isn't his body."

"Are you saying it won't open for you?"

"Not this way." Zamir looked at Ginny. "Are you open to experimentation?"

She slanted him a glance. "What do you mean exactly?"

"Aether magic transforms. Can you transform my physical appearance?"

"Into what?"

Zamir's voice changed; the words accented differently. "Into my memory of who I was."

"How exactly do I do that?" Ginny asked.

"Here, take my hand." Zamir extended his hand.

Varun stepped between them. "Wait. How do you know so much about aether energy?"

"Aether energy was the mainstay of the Illojim empire. Our civilization was built on it."

Varun frowned at the unfamiliar accents and the possessive tenses. "You're not Zamir right now, are you?"

"I am, and I am not. The more he draws on my soul and my memories, the more I become." The First Commander glanced at Ginny. "Are you ready?"

She took his hand in hers. "What do you want me to do?"

"Just pour out your energy into me. It knows what to do. And do not let go until it is done."

She nodded.

His grip on her hand tightened. "Ginny."

Their eyes met.

"Do not let go, whatever happens to me."

"Okay."

"Change is painful, even excruciating. Do not let go."

Ginny paled slightly. "I got it."

The First Commander smiled, but the curve of his lips was scarcely visible. "All right. You may begin."

Ginny closed her eyes, and the expression on her face transformed from anxiety into surprising serenity.

Varun, however, kept his eyes open. He saw the exact moment when Jackson's face began melting. Jackson's skin and flesh dribbled off the top of his forehead like wax. His eyes blended into his tears and ran off his face. His nose melted into the cavity of a skull. The scream on the tip of his tongue was silenced as his mouth vanished.

Varun clamped his hand over his mouth to silence his horrified gasp.

The melting transformation continued down Jackson's neck, his shoulders, his arms, and even his fingers.

Ginny's eyelids fluttered open. She stared at the molten featureless face in front of her.

Her scream was absolute denial. Absolute anguish.

"No!" Varun clasped his hand over hers, locking hers over Jackson's, not allowing her to let go.

"Please, I can't!" Ginny screamed. Her eyes squeezed shut and she flailed wildly, trying to push Varun away, trying to flee from Jackson. Her hand trembled, her muscles clenched against Varun. "It's melting. His hand's melting away! All of him. Oh my God, what have I done?"

Varun swallowed hard and tasted bile in his throat, but he tightened his grip on Ginny's and Jackson's hands—keeping them joined. "Just hold on, Ginny. We can't go back. We can only finish this. Don't give up now. Don't let go."

Ginny thrashed at Varun, but the motion melted into tears. She sagged against his chest, her shoulders shaking with each wrenching sob.

Varun stared at Zamir as the transformation ran its course, but said nothing until he was certain it was done. Only then did he stroke Ginny's back. "It's finished. You did great. You held on."

"I killed him," Ginny choked out. She did not look up.

Varun stepped back. "Ginny, open your eyes."

Her chest heaved, but then she straightened, lifted her chin and opened her eyes.

She stared, mouth agape, at the man who stood where Zamir had been, wearing Jackson's clothes, but not Jackson's body. The man appeared to be in his late twenties or early thirties. Smooth shaven, his hair was a deep blue-black, and his skin a bronzed hue. He might have appeared Middle Eastern, except for his oddly angular eyes. They were blue-green, flecked with gold.

Ginny stammered. "Zamir?"

"This, actually, is the First Commander's body," Zamir said. He looked at Varun. "You recognize it."

Varun nodded. "It's the body you had in the underworld."

Ginny looked at Varun, aghast. "How are you keeping up with this?"

"After a while, you learn to fake calm," he said.

"But you had all melted away. I could feel it…" She shuddered. "Your hand, your fingers, like soft mud in my hands."

"Aether transforms—and what I needed was a complete transformation, down to my fingerprints, to my genes. Everything changed."

"But you're still Zamir. And still the First Commander."

He nodded. "His soul is bound to my consciousness. We are one now." Zamir glanced at the ship. "And now, let us hope that transformation was worth it." He walked up to the ship and placed his hand against a panel. For several seconds, nothing happened, then a blue light emitted from the ship, passing over Zamir from head to toe.

The light vanished, then reappeared, moving over Zamir again.

Then for a third time.

Varun stiffened. "Is it supposed to take this long?"

"No," Zamir said. "I suspect the mixed signature in this body is confusing it. Step back. Just in case."

"Just in case what—"

The hatch swung up, but in that same instant, something shot out.

Zamir deflected it with his spear. He had been, Varun realized, ready for it.

Varun glanced at the circular projectile quivering in the cavern wall, still vibrating from the force with which it had struck the wall.

Zamir wedged his spear into hatch before it could close. "Get in!" he shouted.

Ginny and Varun dashed under the hatch.

Zamir glanced over his shoulder. "Damn it, Mother. Where are you?"

"There!" Varun pointed toward the tunnel entrance as Ashe dashed out, riding the wind.

Behind her raced twelve gleaming metallic animals, as sleek as lions, but with tails that waved like serpents.

"Come on!" Varun waved her over.

Ashe sprinted beneath the hatch. Zamir yanked his spear out as he leaped inward. The door slammed down in front of the animal golems' drawn-back lips and exposed fangs.

For a moment, the only sound was that of heaving breaths. Varun finally broke the silence. "What were those things?"

"Remnants of the humanoid golems," Ashe said.

"The defenders of *Dalkhu Libbu,*" Zamir added. "Inanna, for all her apparent recklessness, was actually an excellent strategist. She always believed in contingency plans for her contingency plans. That included layers of traps and defenses."

"Will the door hold them?" Ginny asked, her voice thin, and edging on fear, as the door thudded beneath the impact of the animal golems slamming their weight against it. Multiple small dents appeared.

Ashe drew in a sharp breath.

More thudding sounds; the dents deepened.

"No, the door won't hold them," Ashe said firmly. "Let's go." She looked at her son. "What was wrong with the body you had?"

Zamir shrugged. "I preferred the genetic prints on this one." He hesitated. "It doesn't change anything."

"Of course not." Ashe wrapped her arms around him in a quick hug. "Which way to the *Dirga Tiamatu* controls?"

"We're not going to use the elevators. They'll be death traps," Zamir said. "There is a central stairway in the middle of the *Dalkhu Libbu* that spirals all the way to the control room."

Varun held out the palm of his hand, and a bright flame coalesced. He held it up to light their surroundings.

Instead of polished metal, the interior walls of the *Dalkhu Libbu* was textured with indented ovals that formed arcing patterns, like the curve of a wave or the dash of falling raindrops.

Ginny ran her fingers over the surface. "It doesn't even feel like metal of any sort. It's almost like a soft resin."

"Only the outside is metal, and even then, it's only a layer of adamantine. The ship itself is organic."

Ginny looked sharply at Zamir. "Wait…what?"

"The *Dalkhu Libbu.* The demon's heart. You didn't just think it was merely figurative, did you?"

"I…did, actually. But this heart is taller than office buildings. How large was the demon whose heart it was?"

"I expect he was fairly proportionate," Zamir said, which offered no one any consolidation.

"Who…who carved out his heart?" Ginny asked.

Zamir frowned, and the swirl of his blue-green eyes brightened to pure gold. "Inanna did. The demon offered her his heart, and she took it—literally."

Ashe rolled her eyes. "Somehow, I don't have trouble believing it of the war-mongering goddess."

The door behind them shook. Ashe glanced back. Some of the deep dents were cracking under the pressure. "Let's go. We have a job to finish."

The flickering flame in Varun's hand was the only light in the empty darkness of the demon's heart.

CHAPTER 22

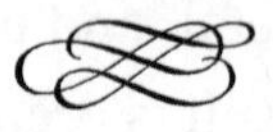

The *Dalkhu Libbu*'s walls curved and its corridors dipped and rose seemingly without reason, like something naturally made, not artificially designed. Ashe trailed her fingertips over the walls. It did not feel like flesh, yet the soft warmth in the resin-like material pulsed with life. The corridors split off into small alcoves and rooms that reminded Ashe of the towers in the royal palace of Shulim.

She caught Zamir's eyes as he glanced back at her.

It seemed as if the resemblance was not lost on him either.

"How many Illojim came to Earth?" Ginny asked of Zamir.

"Only the dynasty of An, twenty-five Illojim in all. But they brought many of their servants, most of whom chose to live in the ocean. They became the Beltiamatu—the mer-people—who eventually spawned the Atlanteans."

"And you?" Varun asked.

Zamir's voice shifted, taking on the accents of the First

Commander. "I chose to remain with the dynasty of An. With Ereshkigal."

"She said you chose not to return to Aldebaran when you died and your soul was set free from your body."

Zamir nodded. "It is the only way back to Aldebaran. Without souls, the Beltiamatu are trapped here on Earth. That's why Ereshkigal's punishment was so devastating. It barred their way back to the stars." He looked at Ashe. "You always sensed this even though the stories of Ereshkigal had faded into legend by the time you became a mother. Somehow, you knew that there should have been something more."

"I didn't expect this though." Ashe swept out her hand to encompass the ship. She glanced sharply over her shoulder.

Varun frowned, also tilting his head.

She heard nothing, but the air shifted, screaming a warning. "I think the lion golems broke in. When we're done here, I think I might have a word with Inanna about her excessive contingency planning."

"You're planning on arguing with the goddess of heaven and earth?" Varun asked, his tone lightly sardonic.

She, however, chose to ignore the tone. "Why not? Bad decision-making seems to be the trademark of Beltiamatu royalty; so why stop now? How far to the control room?"

"We've barely started," Zamir said.

"Is there only one way up?" Ashe asked.

"No, and this is not even the fastest way up, but it bypasses other more dangerous sections of the ship."

"But it's all connected. The paths intersect, don't they?"

Zamir nodded. "You're not suggesting we split up?"

"I am. Twelve lions are too much to take on all at once, but if I can thin their numbers, we'll have a better chance if we ever have to make a stand. You three go ahead. I'll handle this."

"We both will," Varun insisted. He looked at Ginny, then at Zamir. "We'll regroup at the control room. Take care of Ginny."

Zamir nodded.

Ginny glanced at Varun and Ashe, then nodded tightly before continuing with Zamir up the stairs.

"I think they'll be all right," Varun murmured. "His knowledge of the ship, and her control of aether might be enough if they don't have fight off snarling lions too. Do you have a plan, Ashe, or shall we just make it up as we go?"

"We could close off all the paths to the control room, except that I have no idea where they all are."

"So instead we split up and take out the lions, one by one?"

She nodded. "They're powered by aether."

Varun stiffened. "What does that mean?"

"That whether or not we destroy them, there will be pools of aether left in this ship when we blow it up. I don't think we can avoid a large explosion now."

"How large?" Varun asked.

"The crater will probably expand to three or four times its size."

"But that would swallow up the village of Derweze."

"I realize that."

Varun snarled. "You have a hell of a track record, but I don't want to just always leave destruction in my wake."

Ashe's chin lifted. "We're elementals. Sometimes, to save, we have to destroy."

~

The hell it was.

Varun was an elemental, but he would be damned before destruction became his default choice.

The elementals had spent too long defending and protecting the Earth. It was not going to go to hell just because they were up against the likes of Nergal. The god of fire and pestilence was determined to win the game by destroying the Earth.

One did not beat Nergal by destroying the Earth *first*.

Varun crept along a side corridor that branched off the main one. It wound up, then down, like a path through the hills. Alien-like beauty flaunted itself in the delicate arches that held up the corridors, and the double doors that swung open as he pushed through them.

Only after he had passed through several sets of swinging double doors did he realize they were the valves in veins. He was walking through a blood vessel. His thoughts shrank from the enormity of it all. What would the world's scientists do if they realized that a vast and technologically superior alien culture had hidden itself in myths and fairy tales?

The flame dancing on his hand suddenly quivered. It was just enough warning to spin him around.

The light cast the animal golem into flickering shadows. The creature snarled, baring gleaming fangs, as it circled him, moving lightly on soundless paws.

Varun stepped around, keeping an eye on the golem as another metallic beast joined it. He did not have an abundance of earth around, but fire was useful in a pinch. He conjured flame with a snap of his fingers and crouched low, watching and waiting for the creatures to make the first move.

A golem leaped for his throat. Varun hurled a flare, and the golem twisted aside to land gracelessly on its side. It did not snarl or hiss in pain, but the flames scorched the gleaming metal. Varun managed a grim smile. Real fire would not have hurt the beast. Perhaps Nergal's fire magic, however twisted, had some value after all.

The creature tried to rise but its limbs flailed, and it sagged to the floor, unmoving.

The second golem, warier, paced around Varun. Its eyes, mere slits, gleamed.

A sound clicked to Varun's left. For a split second, his glance flicked across the hallway.

An instant later, his head hit the ground. The weight of the golem pinned him down and adamantine jaws snapped at his face. He grabbed the lion's mouth a fraction of an inch from his face, wrestling it back as it hurled itself forward. His hands glowed blue.

The gleaming adamantine blackened, and instead of an attacking creature, Varun found himself holding on to a writhing beast, trying to escape. The glow of its eyes brightened, intensifying with the animal's thrashings, then suddenly blinked out.

Several dozen pounds of once-living metal crumpled down on Varun.

He grunted, but the remains of the golem hardly moved.

A familiar voice breathed huskily. "Trapped by victory?"

He raised his head as Ondine strolled into the room as casually as she might have while twirling a parasol along the

Seine. Four golems prowled at her feet, weaving around her like attack dogs waiting for an order to pounce.

Varun stared at the woman he had once loved. That tangle of feelings in his chest defied explanation. He did not know if it was joy, or relief, or fear, or panic. It was probably all of them, smashed together into a knot he could not unravel.

"Your parents are looking for you," he said softly.

She stiffened and blinked hard, several times, then waved her hand in a graceful and dismissive motion. "Things are not what they were. We are not the same people who boarded the *Veritas* all those weeks ago."

"This isn't you, Ondine."

She threw her head back, laughing. "Nothing has been me in the longest time, Varun. Ondine—the real Ondine—would have died as a child, drowned in the seas near Krakatoa. I lived only because I was possessed first by Neti, and now by Nergal."

"It's not the same thing. Neti did possess you, but Nergal's not in you. I've seen him—"

She chuckled softly. "Do you think that power can only be one place at one time? You—who possess so much of Nergal's power—do you really believe that he cannot give more of himself to others?" She waved her hand over her metallic lions. "His power, now *my* power, brought these golems back to life, pulsing liquid adamantine through their veins. I am the heir of Atlantis."

"Ashe might have something to say about that."

Ondine's chin lifted. "My pets will hunt her down and tear her apart. Unlike you, she cannot stop them. Although, you can't really stop them now, can you?" She waved her lions forward.

The four beasts lunged.

Now or never.

Varun deliberately let go of the tightness he always felt somewhere in the vicinity of his chest. The astral energy holding his body together burst out of him, and his physical body vanished. The golems jerked to a stop and circled where he had lay.

Ondine, her hands clenched into fists, screamed. "Find him!"

The cats paced silently, moving back and forth.

Varun looked down on the creatures—how odd to know that he was here, yet did not have a body. He wasn't just invisible; he had no physical form.

The real test was yet to come.

He felt the tingling—not at his fingertips, but at where he thought his stomach was. Blue flame appeared seemingly out of nothing. The golems stopped and stared up at it.

As did Ondine. She recoiled in upon herself. "Varun?"

For an instant, she sounded young, frightened, and just like the woman he had known and once loved.

But that was before a blast of blue fire surged toward him.

The flames, dancing at his command, spread out into a defensive wall. Fire blazed against blue fire, the heat so intense that the golems retreated, their gleaming adamantine coats singed.

Neither of us can win this, Ondine. Varun threw out his thought. *Nergal gave us both our powers.*

"Perhaps you are right. Perhaps you can hold out forever, but so can I. You will not pass, and without you, where will your friends be? They will need you at the end, but you will not be there."

CHAPTER 23

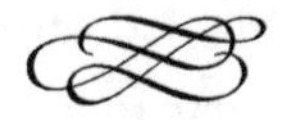

The red steps, decorated with blue filigreed patterns, wound steadily upward. Ginny had never paid much attention in her science classes, but the spreading blue against the red looked too much like the spread of veins in exposed flesh, so she tried not to think too hard about what she was stepping on.

It was a starship.

It was also a demon's heart.

But surely the Illojim would have cleaned up and renovated the place, right? Perhaps it was just the outside that looked like a heart.

Yet even she doubted it when their path took her past open spaces large enough to accommodate other ships. She stood on the steps, looking at both spaces, separated by a thick wall. Didn't the heart have large cavities where blood was stored before being pumped into the rest of the body?

She peered over the rail and visually traced the shape of the vast room—wide at the top, narrow at the bottom—

Yup, she was definitely standing *in* someone's heart.

"Are you all right?" Zamir asked.

"I..." She pressed her fist against her stomach. "Yes, I just got a bit queasy for a moment." She looked up, met his eyes, and once again, felt that painful punch in her chest. He was no one she recognized. Every last bit of Jackson—his quick, easy smile, his kind brown eyes—all gone. Even Jackson's deep bass had given way to a melodic tenor. "When we get out of here, will you ever...change back?"

Zamir's eyebrows drew together in the hint of a frown. "Do you want me to?"

Ginny mulled over his words. "I don't know. I didn't expect you to ask that."

Zamir looked away. "I did not steal his body. I did not even ask to be in it."

Her chest ached at the cool defensiveness in his voice. Had she put it in there? "I know," she murmured. "I saw. It's just...I wasn't ready to lose him."

"No one is ready for loss."

Ginny tilted her head as she followed him up the steps. Something in his voice told her he had lived through loss after loss. "You've lost people you've loved."

For several moments, he did not reply, and she was giving up hope that he ever would when he finally said. "First, my mother—who probably loved me more than she should have, and who definitely risked more than she should. Then my son..."

"What happened to him?"

"In Beltiamatu culture, the royal family does not marry.

We do not allow external influences to hold sway over the family. The partner…the mate…of the prince or princess is killed when their child is born."

Ginny inhaled sharply. "So, your father…"

"Was ritually sacrificed when I was born."

"And your wife?"

His shoulders stiffened, squaring as if against an ancient memory. "The mermaid who bore my son was killed after she gave birth to him."

"Okay." Ginny's eyes narrowed. "That's barbaric, you know that? At that rate, you're going to start running out of citizens. Besides, everyone knows people—men and women—are good for more than just one baby."

"It is our way," Zamir said, unapologetically. "But my son tried to deny it. He fought our culture and the laws that protected the throne."

"What did he do?"

"He fled with his pregnant mate. And I sent my soldiers after him to bring him back."

"He loved her?" Ginny asked, her voice soft.

Zamir did not reply, but his hand on the bannister, shook. "She had given birth far from the palace by the time the soldiers found them. My son refused to return, and he refused to let them take her. In the battle—" Zamir drew a deep breath. He stared at the stairs that continued to rise above them, but Ginny did not think he actually saw anything. "The soldiers returned only with the infant. My son and the mermaid he chose, over his kingdom and over his life, were killed in the battle."

Ginny laid her hand over his. "I'm sorry."

He shrugged his shoulders, a rough and surprisingly

awkward motion, considering how flawlessly graceful he was in all other things. "I chose it. I chose his fate when I placed the needs of my kingdom over the choices of my son."

"And your grandson?"

"Kai. I raised him. He was the captain of my personal guard and my heir. I thought I had I lost my mother to the love of a human man, and then my son chose to die for love, too. Love had taken my family from me, and I was determined never to let love take my grandson."

"Where is he now?"

"I do not know. He disappeared in that last battle, when my mother reclaimed the Beltiamatu throne after the *Dirga Tiamatu* destroyed Shulim, the capital mer-city."

"So, now…Ashe rules the merfolk?"

"She cannot possibly do a worse job than I have." A wry smile twisted Zamir's lips. "I made pacts that killed the ocean, infected my own people with disease, and led to the destruction of my city. I tried to rule without being swayed by emotion, and found that ruling without love is as wretched, if not more so, than ruling with it." He paused and looked down on the massive emptiness in the middle of the demon's heart. "I was dead, Ginny."

She jerked, startled to hear her name from his lips. Was it the first time he had spoken her name? "You were a ghost."

"That's no different from being dead," he said. "I don't know what magic made it possible for you to see me, but I never thought I would come back. Never imagined I would be here now."

"Never believed you would have a second chance?"

He looked up and met her eyes. "Is this a second chance?"

"Isn't it?"

Zamir shook his head and said nothing.

But Ginny thought she glimpsed something in his eyes—something more than denial.

Zamir continued up the stairs, and she followed him, groping for a peripheral topic. "You are going to find your grandson, aren't you?"

He hesitated longer than she expected. "If he is alive."

"What does he look like?"

"Beltiamatu breed true—fathers to sons, mothers to daughters. Like his father, and like me, he has black scales—a rarity among the Beltiamatu. Royalty breeds true too. His eyes are like mine, like Ashe's."

Blue-green eyes that mirrored the sea, and flecked with the gold of a breaking dawn.

Sculptured features, so precise, so beautiful that angels would have wept with envy.

The panicked flick of a long fish tail covered with iridescent blue-black scales that flared out into fan-tail softness. A lean, muscled body tensing with pain, then curling into itself to escape merciless spears.

Crimson on translucent blue.

Blood in the water.

Ginny shuddered and buried her face in her hands. Her stomach wrenched at the horrific vision that tossed somewhere between a nightmare and a memory. She staggered; her foot would have slipped on the steps if Zamir had not caught her.

"Are you all right?"

Ginny covered her eyes—but the image, seared in her mind, refused to go away.

Hands pressed up against each other—separated by a steel grate over a tank of water.

A dark cloud, slashed with purple lightning, passing from his hand to hers.

Aether.

She thought she had—or at last Varun thought she had—picked up aether magic while walking through the field of mushrooms in the Garden of Eden.

But what if she hadn't?

What if she had received it earlier—from the merman?

But when? And where?

"Ginny?" Zamir's voice was touched with concern. His glance snapped over her shoulder. "Down!"

He shoved her to her knees and swung his platinum spear like a pole over her head. One end of his spear struck a gleaming lion golem as it leaped through the air. The impact flung the golem over the bannister and down the central stairway. Zamir shoved his spear forward, and the sharp tip sank into the adamantine chest plate of a second beast. The creature pawed the air, its sharp talons coming within inches of Ginny's face.

Zamir grunted under his breath, then with a mighty heave, lifted the mechanical creature into the air and flung it down the shaft. Ginny peeked out. The golem clawed at the air, but fell without a sound, without any seeming anguish at its impending destruction.

"It appears that a couple of the creatures made it past Ashe and Varun." Zamir tugged Ginny to her feet. "Come. Quickly."

"But what if Ashe and Varun are hurt? We have to help them."

"We have to disable the controls for the *Dirga Tiamatu,* or the explosion will create a crater that will swallow whole continents."

"So we don't have to destroy the starship? I heard Ashe and Varun. They said they would have to destroy the ship."

"My mother can turn into air on a whim and eke out an escape from most tight spots. She tends to think in absolutes. Most of us can't escape as easily, so we have to be a bit more creative. If we can disable the controls, we don't have to take out the entire ship, but if we have to…" Zamir stared at her. "*You* are an aether core, Ginny. If I have to blow up the starship, you're getting out first."

I don't think there's time. But Ginny nodded. "All right. Let's—" Her gaze darted at something behind him. "Zamir!"

Zamir twisted into a battle crouch, his spear braced in front of him.

The leaping lion sank onto the tip of the spear, its flailing weakening by the moment.

Ginny pressed a hand against her heaving chest. "How did it get ahead of us?"

"I don't know." He straightened, his gaze swiveling as he stepped around her, guiding her away from the bannister. Four lions closed in on them, two from above and two from below "But we're trapped."

~

The chamber filled with incandescent blue light where fire met fire, neither Varun nor Ondine yielding. The remaining lion golems slunk away to crouch in darkness. The walls melted, the outer surfaces turning into a viscous goo that dribbled into slick puddles on the floor.

Varun grimaced. A stalemate would keep him alive, but it wouldn't help Ashe, Zamir, or Ginny. He stared at Ondine. Pale green light surrounded her; did he see it only because he was not looking at her through human eyes?

Was she even still human or was she merely a human-looking golem, animated by the powers of extra-terrestrial beings masquerading as ancient gods?

He did not know. Not anymore.

He knew only what he had to do. If fire could not defeat Ondine, then earth had to.

That surge of elemental power came from deep within him—like fire, emerging from his stomach, not from his chest. The earth, shifting in response to Varun's will, clenched around the Illojim starship.

The demon's heart pulsed.

A single, slow beat.

A terrifying beat.

Air whooshed through the chamber in lieu of blood.

Varun's consciousness stiffened. If he had a physical body, if he had eyes, he was certain they would have been as wide, as stricken as Ondine's.

"Varun?" she called out, her voice even more hesitant. She blinked hard, and confusion suddenly replaced terror. "Where…What is this place? Where am…?"

The lion golems bared fangs in silent snarls as they prowled from the shadows, circling Ondine, as if she were prey instead of master.

She drew a sharp breath, her face shockingly pale in the starship's dim running lights, and retreated until her back pressed against the gooey wall. Ondine glanced over her shoulder, her expression twisting in revulsion as she pulled away from the wall. Parts of it clung to her like tendrils of a broken spider's web. The stench of burnt flesh filled the chamber. "Varun?" Her voice shook. "Varun, are you here? Where are you? Please..." She cringed back as the golems advanced. "Please don't leave me—"

Turmoil churned though Varun. His astral energy jerked inward, and his physical body reformed. The lion golems swiveled toward him, but he blasted one of them back with a surge of fire.

"It never fails." Ondine's voice resonated with unnatural power, no longer a lost, terrified woman but a powerful avatar of a wannabe god.

Fool me once...fool me twice... Varun ground down so hard on his teeth that his jaw hurt. He circled slowly, his gaze alternating between Ondine and the lions. Ondine shifted too, perhaps unconsciously moving to keep him directly in front of her, until he stood between her and the lions.

He was surrounded. Trapped.

She sneered at him. "Your instinct to protect and to save will get you killed." At her gesture, the lions crouched, prepared to leap.

His earth elemental powers seeped out, sinking into the rock around the starship. "I hate to break it to you," Varun said grimly. "But it already got me killed."

The lions pounced, and he vanished. The golems smashed into Ondine, and all of them tumbled for an instant, thrown off-balance. Varun's earth powers slammed down hard, crushing the base of the starship. The demon's heart pulsed, the beat so powerful that air propelled through the blood vessels, hurling Ondine and the remaining golems upward, past the chamber, only the gods knew where.

Perhaps even out of the starship. Into the scalding heat of the surrounding earth.

Her wail of terror confirmed that wherever she was, she would not be coming down any time soon.

If she could die, had he killed her *again*?

Varun's silent curse was incoherent, a railing against the Illojim who made pawns of human lives. Ashe was right. It was time to end the curse the children of An had visited upon Earth with their vengeful histrionics.

First, Nergal.

Then the others…

Varun's physical body reformed, and he raced out of the chamber. Where were Ashe, Zamir, and Ginny?

~

Where the hell was everyone?

Ashe darted through the ship, weaving along the sloping corridors. There were no straight lines or sharp angles in the starship, and the surfaces were delicately textured, weblike indentations running just below the soft, warm surface. It was as if the demon's heart was still pulsing life through its veins.

The ship suddenly contracted, as if it really *were* beating.

Ashe's eyes narrowed. Was Zamir's story—the First Commander's distant memory true? Had Medea—*Inanna*—really spurned a demon and carved out his heart?

Ashe wouldn't have put it past that incorrigible goddess of love and war, of heaven and earth.

If only Medea was as good as cleaning up her messes as she was at starting them.

The demon's heart beat again. *Too freaky.* Ashe glowered. Was it going to keep doing that?

She wound her way up the corridor. The air grew warmer. No doubt, she was near the top of the ship, the part wedged into the crack in the earth, the part exposed to the burning gases and boiling mud. She kept an eye on the gleaming lights in the corridor. If they were traps, they were probably triggered by something more substantial than air—

The lights shifted, the colors altering subtly.

—Right?

Panels in the ceiling opened, and tiny streaks of too-familiar white lightning arced between the ceiling and the floor. If it was anything like the Beltiamatu energy weapons, it was going to make it impossible for her to shift into her astral form, at least for a while.

But if that is the only way through it—

Whatever form I wear, I am who I am. And I am enough.

More than enough.

Ashe plunged through the corridor, energy sizzling over her body, momentarily fusing her astral consciousness even more tightly with her physical body. The pain was still jolting through her when she stepped around the curve of the wall. The corridor widened into a large, multileveled room with clear windows that displayed a cascade of boiling mud, streaked with flames. An array of smooth panels and flat, seemingly empty tables covered the other half of the room—technology that had surpassed knobs, buttons, and even touchscreens.

Only one panel was lit. Text blurred over it almost too

quickly to read; Ashe recognized only a few words, but it was enough to make her catch her breath.

The *Dirga Tiamatu.*

A man stood with his back to her, staring out at the almost hypnotic flow of superheated mud.

"Nergal," Ashe said quietly.

"Asherah," the god acknowledged without turning around. "I'm not surprised you arrived without incident. My servant, Ondine, is far more obsessed with Varun than with you. I suspect they're renewing old ties now."

Ondine? Damn it! Varun had better be up to the damned task of taking Ondine down once and for all. Ashe stamped down the flare of panic and stood her ground. "Turn it off, Nergal. Stop the *Dirga Tiamatu.*"

He shook his head, and turned to face Ashe. "It's too late now. There is nothing worth saving on this damned planet."

"The humans beg to differ."

"The world is not theirs. The humans, like the Beltiamatu and the Atlanteans, are ours. We own them. We created them."

Ashe shook her head. "You lost control of them the moment they took their first breath. They are no different from children. My mistake was trying to frame Zamir's future within the constraints of my imagination. You're making the same mistake."

"Am I?" Nergal smirked. "I regret nothing. When the *Dirga Tiamatu* destroys the Tree of Life, it will—truly—all end. The Tree of Life is the largest aether core in the universe, and its reach extends to every continent on the planet. When it explodes, it will tear through the mantle and into the core. The oceans will evaporate, the continents will crumble. The cascade of devastation will extend all the way to Irkalla. It will kill Ereshkigal. It will kill Inanna, who is there now, rebuilding the gates to free her sister." His smile was whimsical. "The Earth began in fire, and it will end in fire."

Ashe held out her hands. Water pooled on one. Air swirled around the other. "Life began in the water. As long as there is water, there will be life."

She brought her hands together. The wind churned water into a torrent.

With a kiss, Ashe sent it on its way.

CHAPTER 24

Ginny heard only her breath. The circling lion golems made no sound; not even their metal paws clicked on the spongy floor. "Stay behind me," Zamir ordered.

She nodded, her cheek brushing against his back.

One of the lions leaped. Zamir caught it on the end of a spear.

In that same instant, another attacked.

Zamir twisted around with the lion still pinned on the end of his spear. The momentum swung the speared lion into the second, sending both slamming against the wall. With uncanny grace, they righted themselves even before they landed.

Their eyes were not any narrower. The golden gleam was not any brighter. But to Ginny, they looked irritated. The swish of their tails snapped the air, the crack as audible as a whiplash.

All four leaped. Zamir knocked two off their trajectory with wide swings of the spear, and hurled them over the edge of the stairs, but the third landed on his back. Teeth sank into Zamir's shoulder, and Ginny heard the snap of bone an instant before Zamir cried out in pain. He staggered. His knees hit the ground.

The fourth lion bared its teeth, poised to rip out Zamir's throat.

Ginny lunged forward, grabbing the beast's large head in her small hands.

The lion tossed its head, and started scrabbling backward, as if trying to escape. She held on even as it dragged her forward. She did not dare let go. If she did, it would attack, its jaws wide and teeth flashing.

"Zamir!" she shouted as the lion backed away, dragging her to the edge of the steps, toward a seemingly infinite fall.

Zamir raised his head, his eyes ablaze with agony. Blood ran down his shoulder, over his chest and back, and along the length of his arm. The lion was still holding on, its mouth locked on Zamir's right shoulder. Its right paw sank its talons in Zamir's right bicep, and its left claws pierced Zamir's left bicep.

Zamir reached for his spear, his motion slow and pained. He turned it so that its tip faced him, at a point just over his shoulder. Gripping the spear, he slammed his weight forward.

The spear pierced Zamir's shoulder and went clean through the lion's metallic skull before emerging from the back of its head.

Blood, spilling from the tip of a spear.

Blood in the water.

Ginny screamed in denial, shaking her head as if it would push the nightmare away. Her eyes closed. Her feet slipped.

Suddenly, the ship pulsed once, then twice, as if the demon heart were beating.

And then she was falling.

"Ginny!" Zamir's voice seemed to come from a long way away.

She jolted. Her eyes flashed open.

She was hanging upside down.

Ginny peered dazedly up at Zamir who was sprawled on the steps, his hands gripping her ankles.

"Let go!" he shouted.

Let go? But he was holding her. How was she supposed to let go?

"Let go of the lion!"

Only then did Ginny look down at her hands. She was still holding the lion's jaw. A black cloud, streaked with purple lightning, mottled around the golem's head.

"Let go!" Zamir shouted.

She let go.

The lion tumbled into the darkness, but not before Ginny caught a glimpse of its malformed face, as if it had melted where she had touched.

Zamir's breath sagged out of him. Slowly, he inched back, pulling Ginny up.

Ginny did not breathe easily until all of her was resting on the stairs.

For several moments, they slumped next to each other. Ginny stared at Zamir's injuries, at the deep gashes the lion's attack had left in his right shoulder and both biceps. And the self-inflicted spear wound—

She pressed her lips together. "Did you have to...?"

Zamir lowered his head. His breath escaped in a sigh. "I had only one chance, and my aim was too uncertain otherwise—but with its teeth on my shoulder, I knew exactly where its brain was."

"You're still human right?"

"Right now?" He stared at her. "Maybe?"

When had she become so blasé about receiving a reply of maybe to that question? Ginny shrugged the backpack off her shoulders and tugged out the first aid kit. "Here, hold it down." She pressed a bandage to the spear wound, which had gone through his flesh. "I'm going to tape around it."

"Do you know what you're doing?"

"Jackson probably would have, but you're going to have to settle for an ancient civilizations professor." Ginny's voice trembled only slightly. The ache in her chest, however, was ferocious and alive in a way she never imagined she would feel.

She squeezed her eyes shut and her hand shook at the unshakeable, unforgettable memory of Jackson's face melting like wax.

She had done that to him.

It wasn't Jackson, but Zamir. And he had asked for it, for perfectly obvious, logical reasons.

But still, she had done that.

There was no way to escape it, no way to purge that memory.

Ginny bit her lip. No doubt Zamir knew her hands were unsteady, but he said nothing of it. "How does it feel?" she asked after she bandaged the smaller wounds on his biceps.

He tried to roll his shoulders, but aborted the motion with

a wince. "Thank you for stopping that fourth golem before it got to me."

"I wish I could help more, but this aether…" She stared down at her hands. "I don't know what it's going to do when I touch things. It has its own mind. It changes things, and in horrific, terrible ways."

Zamir looked down at his hands. Was he thinking about how her touch had changed him, literally everything about him? When he spoke, his voice was quiet and reflective. "Once, I heard my mother tell Varun that there were no rules in elemental magic, because power—all power—is about relationships."

"Do you believe that?"

He was silent for a moment. "I failed when I allowed myself—my obsessions—to become more powerful than my relationship with my people. If I had put them first, Shulim would still be standing."

She heard the ache resonating in his voice. "It must have been beautiful," she murmured, reflecting what she knew were his thoughts.

"It was like no other city on Earth." He shook his head sharply. "I can't bring it back, but I can keep Earth's cities from facing the same disaster, the same fate." He rose easily to his feet. "Can you stand? Can you walk?"

Ginny stared at him. He was the one who was injured, with bandages swathed across the breadth of his right shoulder, and he was asking if *she* were all right?

Well, hell. She was not going to be a discredit to the human race, now, was she?

Ignoring his offered hand, Ginny leaned against the wall and scooted to her feet. "Let's go."

The stairs circled upward, then straightened into a corridor. The walls were patterned with overlapping waves, and red lights gleamed overhead. "Wait here," Zamir told her.

Ginny immediately jerked to a stop and watched as Zamir walked forward into the narrow, low corridor. The crimson light washed over him, undulating like waves. Yet there was deliberation in the motion. It was a scanner of some sort, Ginny concluded, and the red glow made it more ominous than it needed to be.

Zamir was about halfway across when the light stopped moving.

Zamir dropped flat to the ground as metal plates appeared out of the wall and sliced along the wavelike patterns on the walls, bending smoothly around the curves in the pattern. The precise pattern on both wall allowed the metal plates to undulate together and away from each other in a fluid, unpredictable patterns.

One of the plates dipped low. Its metal edge sliced the skin off Zamir's back.

Ginny clamped her hands over her mouth so she could not scream.

He might have arched in pain, if not for the constant waves of metal sweeping around and over him. Zamir grimaced. His grip tightened around his spear, and in a swift motion, he swung it vertically upright. The moving metal waves struck it from both directions and quivered against it, pushing at the spear from both directions.

The spear shook, but did not give.

Not yet.

Zamir leaped to his feet and weaved his way around the

metal plates. The end of the corridor seemed even farther because of the plates in his way.

Ginny's gaze darted between the spear which quivered, straining under the opposing pressures placed on it, and Zamir's rapid progress through the corridor.

Zamir was only three quarters of the way through when the spear snapped and the deadly metal plates began moving again.

"No!" Ginny screamed a warning. She darted forward, her arms outstretched. Purple lightning arced from her fingertips, striking both metal plates. A sizzling sound accompanied the dense smoke that filled the corridor.

No, not smoke, Ginny mused. She smelled roses—not real roses, but pungent perfume. She walked closer, her eyes narrowing when she realized that she had transformed thin, razor-sharp metal blades into a gauzy, translucent material. She bent her head down and drew a deep breath; the gossamer fabric was scented with a rose-like fragrance.

The mist cleared enough for her to see Zamir, standing partway down the corridor. She pushed her way past the material that wavered like white caps on the ocean.

"All in all, your solution might have been better than mine," he said.

"I used to play dress-up in layers of chiffon and pretend that I was a rich society lady going to a ball," Ginny murmured. "I used my mother's perfume. It smelled just like this." A lump blocked her throat, and she sensed his intent gaze on her. She had to get Zamir's attention off her. "What happened?"

"It's a security feature, intended to only give access to those permitted on the control bridge. I made it part of the way before it realized I wasn't really the First Commander. Maybe it sensed the other aspects of me."

"Like Zamir?" *And Jackson?* "Are there are other security features, like these?"

"Not quite like this, but there are others—" He stiffened. "Do you hear that?"

Ginny tilted her head. "Is that…thunder?"

"From the bridge. My mother must have made it past all the traps."

"And she sounds angry."

Zamir stiffened. "Nergal. He must have arrived before us." He grabbed Ginny's hand and sprinted down the twisting corridor.

Together, they burst onto the bridge. Ginny jerked to a stop at the entrance of the room that extended across several floors accessible from a large central platform. Technology gleamed, sleek and dark, except for one screen.

"He's turned it on," Zamir breathed. He leaped over the rail and dashed across the platform toward the one lit screen, oblivious to the titanic elemental battle raging over him. Ashe and Nergal circled each other in the air, neither paying any attention to the laws of gravity. Nergal blasted out black-green surges of energy at Ashe, but both air and water swirled around her, slapping aside Nergal's attacks.

Within an instant, Ginny was completely drenched. She darted down the steps and ran to Zamir. "What's going on?" she asked as he placed both hands on the screen.

"The *Dirga Tiamatu* is sixty-seven percent charged," Zamir said. The fear in his eyes belied the calm of his voice.

"You can stop it, right?"

"I'm trying." The screen changed, and he lifted his hands.

A faint smile of relief passed over his face. "It accepted my genetic signature."

"What now?"

"Shhh." Zamir stood still, his eyes staring ahead of him, wide and unblinking.

Ginny gaped at him. Was he communicating telepathically with the ship?

She stared at the number on the screen. Thank God she could read Sumerian. The number seemed to hold at sixty-seven percent, then it changed to sixty-eight.

Ginny yanked in a sharp breath. "It's going up."

"I'm trying," was Zamir's terse answer.

"We still have a long way to one-hundred."

"Nergal has locked in the target—the Tree of Life in the Blue Mountains. Only he can redirect it. I can still turn off the *Dirga Tiamatu,* but if it hits seventy-five, there's no undoing it. The built-up energy in the core must be released." Zamir closed his eyes and his fingers folded into fists.

Sixty-eight ticked over into sixty-nine.

Then seventy.

Ginny bit down on her lower lip. Behind her the titanic battle between Nergal and Ashe raged on, unnoticed by her. All her attention was focused on the screen.

Seventy became seventy-one.

Zamir groaned, a gut-deep sound of agony. It sounded as if he were wrestling with the ship, perhaps even nature itself.

The number flickered. Terror lodged in Ginny's heart as the number one trembled on the edge of indecision—

Then became zero.

Seventy. Ginny's breath sagged out of her.

Sixty-nine.

Zamir's face was contorted with anguish, but somehow, he was winning.

A flash of green light, tainted with black, blasted past Ginny and struck Zamir's side. He crumpled to the floor, his muscles contracting on the edge of a convulsion. Ginny spun around. Nergal hovered overhead, the anger on his face transforming to triumph.

And Ashe's face—Ginny would never forget the horror on Ashe's face. A mother's love. A mother's terror.

Darkness foamed on Nergal's open palm, and he drew his hand back again.

Ginny threw herself over Zamir to protect him, but Ashe physically tackled Nergal and slammed him onto the floor. His hand jerked, and the blast struck the ground an inch from Ginny, instead of going right through her and Zamir.

"Help me up," Zamir groaned, his voice scarcely audible.

Ginny wrapped her arms around his back and pulled him upright. His weight staggered her, but they managed to collapse against the side of the panel.

Her gaze flashed down. Her heartbeat skipped. *Seventy-three.*

Zamir's hands trembled as he set them on the panel. His breathing was labored, as if his body were struggling with itself. "Don't let me let go," he whispered.

Ginny's heart was pounding so loudly she could hardly hear anything else. She nodded, leaning her weight against Zamir to press him up against the panel. She laid her hands over his. Whatever happened, Zamir would not let go.

The sickly scent of rotting flesh emanated from Zamir's side wound. Whatever Nergal had done to Zamir, it was consuming him quickly from the inside out.

Seventy-three ticked over into seventy-four.

Zamir groaned again, his voice cracking from extreme, exquisite pain.

The number wavered, blurring, ready to change yet again.

Motion flicked in her peripheral vision. Flickering light heralded the presence of astral energy taking on a physical form. Ginny glanced up in surprise and met Varun's eyes as his body reshaped beside her. Her grip tightened protectively on Zamir. "He's hurt. He's losing the battle against the ship. Varun, you have to stop the *Dirga Tiamatu*. Tell the Earth to fight back, damn it."

~

"But I..." Varun's gaze fell on Zamir, then he glanced at Ashe who battled Nergal. Why did the job of saving the Earth fall to a marine biologist instead of the mer-king or the Lady of the Ocean?

It was supposed to be a simple project investigating the dead spots in the ocean...

A muscle twitched in his jaw. If this was the way it was supposed to end—

He'd already said his goodbyes to the person who mattered most.

Ashe.

Varun straightened and closed his eyes. His astral energy relaxed, and his body turned translucent, like the sparkling of stars in the universe, as his consciousness roamed free. It darted past the injured Zamir, and raced past Ashe, then he found himself outside of the ship, beyond the grip of living metal. His powers no longer constrained, he immersed himself in the embrace of fire and earth. Mud, seared with flame, slid past unchanging, unmovable, superheated granite.

His consciousness merged with that of the tortured Earth.

Far beneath, the core roiled with energy, tossing like churning waves.

The anger, the hate poured into it was a heartbeat away from breaking loose.

It's all right, Varun murmured. *Just hold on. Give it a moment. Let me help you. Let Zamir help you.*

The Earth snapped at him like a wounded animal, claws extended, fangs bared.

You know me, he whispered. *I am earth, I am fire, and at your core—you are earth and fire. Listen, do you hear it? The wind? The waves? Air and water are fighting to save you.*

He could almost hear the Earth hold its agonized breath.

Just hold on. Don't give up. Don't step over the edge. Just hold on. Let me…let us pull you back.

Anger and hate boiled, bubbling rapidly, spilling over, breaking over his feet. In that instant, Varun knew the truth.

It would take more than words.

Saving the planet he loved—and saving Ashe—demanded his life—

Without hesitation, Varun stepped over the edge, and then he was diving, straight into the core.

CHAPTER 25

Ginny held her breath. The blurring numbers froze.

Seventy-five.

An instant later, it moved again.

Seventy-six.

Her heart stuttered. Her grip slacked, but Zamir pushed forward, resting his weight against the panel instead of collapsing with her.

"It's too late," she gasped. "We have to get out of here."

He shook his head. "There's no place to run where we can be safe." He squared his shoulders and raised his chin. "This is *my* ship, not Nergal's. It obeys me." Standing upright in spite of what had to be excruciating pain, he closed his eyes and laid both his hands on the panel.

Were his thoughts linking up with that of the ship? Judging from the oddly serene, transcendent expression on his face, Zamir's consciousness was somewhere else.

Ginny looked down at the panel. It blurred into seventy-seven, but almost instantly quivered again, and the number changed.

Seventy-six.

Her jaw dropped. The *Dirga Tiamatu,* fired up beyond the point of no return, was somehow decharging.

Varun, wherever he was, had done something.

And Zamir was doing something.

Seventy-five...

"No!" Nergal screamed. He turned toward Zamir, pestilence and death pooling in his hands.

Ginny's head snapped up. *No doubt. No fear.* She stepped in front of Zamir, finally willing to die for him.

~

Ashe reached down to her waist. Her fingers wrapped around the *Isriq Genii.* A breath of wind swept past her, carrying Varun's final, fading astral energy. He was gone. She knew it with absolute certainty.

For us, Varun. And for the ocean. She snatched the blade up. The plain hilt felt sturdy and perfectly balanced in Ashe's hand as she slammed it into Nergal's back.

Cool metal sank into warm flesh, into Nergal's heart.

Nergal jerked upright, the fractional movement enough to send his blast astray. It scorched the network of panels.

The ship rumbled. The floor convulsed like a wounded creature.

Zamir shuddered as if he had been hit. "No," he gasped. His shoulders hunched over the console, fingers tensing until his knuckles were white. He poured his strength and will into the wounded ship.

Color leeched out of his face, and he would have reeled if Ginny had not propped him up. "Don't let go," she pleaded. Her hands layered over his, pressing his fingers down to the panel.

Nergal chuckled, the sound soft and amused. "The *Dalkhu Libbu* will kill him. The ship will suck the life out of him."

Ashe retreated as Nergal reached around to his back and pulled out the dagger. He stared at the *Isriq Genii,* then let it fall as if it mattered not at all. "You need to stop believing Inanna, or do you call her Medea?" His smile was as bitter and as tight as the knot in Ashe's chest. "She is a witch, in every sense of the word. A manipulator, a liar. She cares for nothing and no one. Unlike you, Ashe."

Nergal extended his arms. "You, Little Mermaid, care too much—but for the wrong people. For Zamir. For Varun. For people who have disappointed you, yet you spend yourself protecting them from the world, and worse, from themselves. From their own mistakes, from their reckless curiosity." His eyes burned into hers. "Are you done with children? Are you finally ready for someone worthy of you?"

Ashe circled, her gaze flicking from Nergal to the fallen dagger that lay between them. "You?" She tilted her head. A smirk twisted her lips. "You may think you're worthy of me, but I have higher standards." Ashe dived into a roll and snatched the dagger as she came up into a battle crouch. The blade gleaming in the pale light, she leaped at Nergal.

His hands caught her wrist as the blade descended. The wind screamed around her, trying—but failing—to tear off Nergal's grip.

"Why do you still fight me?" Nergal demanded. The harsh tone almost perfectly concealed the plaintive confusion beneath his question. "Your son is dying. Your lover is gone. Everyone you love, you have lost."

"Everyone I love I have lost fighting *you*. I couldn't protect them, but it was never for me to protect them from themselves, or even from you. It was enough to fight beside them, to stand beside warriors, to trust them to do everything in their power to stop you."

Nergal's eyes narrowed. His grip shifted in an instant, from her wrist, to close around her clenched fist. He spun her around in a swift motion, and pulled her toward him. Her back pressed against his chest.

Ashe pushed away, but *Isriq Genii* directed by Nergal's greater strength, quivered dangerously close to her heart.

"Not in the heart. Strike him in the stomach!" Ginny shouted suddenly. "In Sumerian mythology, the soul is in the stomach."

The soul. Ashe's heart clenched. She had spent 297 years slaving away for a soul…and all for nothing.

No, not for nothing. She had spent it, and was going to spend it, saving the Earth, saving its people.

Instead of pushing, Ashe pulled with Nergal, angling the cursed dagger so it plunged into her stomach. As the blade sank into Ashe, it ruptured the flow of her astral energy. Her body evaporated. Her consciousness scattered.

But the deadly momentum could not be checked.

The dagger slid, unchallenged, into the soft, unprotected flesh of Nergal's stomach.

~

Ginny watched, mouth agape, as Nergal stiffened. His limbs

splayed out as if an electric current had seized him. Starting from his fingertips, his body dissolved piece by piece to reveal incandescent golden light. It was as if he were being erased out of existence. The last part of him was his face. His eyes were wide, transfixed with horror and unimaginable pain. His mouth opened in a silent scream as the visible portions of his face shrank into nothing.

And all that was left was golden light in a dazzling humanoid form.

For an instant, its glory dominated the vast command room, then it exploded.

Fiery golden strands sprayed every direction, then slowly faded into nothing.

Behind Ginny, Zamir inhaled sharply.

She spun around and wrapped her arms around him to steady his violent trembling. "Are you…?" She glanced down at the console.

Seventy-four.

Seventy-three.

She did not breathe easily until the countdown plunged under sixty, then under fifty.

The death in the planet's core unwound and settled back into a low simmer.

Only when the countdown hit zero did Zamir lift his hands from panel. He staggered back, but Ginny supported him before he would have crashed to the floor. "My mother…" He looked around, but there was no sign of Ashe or of Varun. "I…" He closed his eyes, and his hands curled into fists.

Ginny wrapped her arms around him, and leaned against

his chest. Tears leaked from the corners of her eyes. The sobs that hitched her breath poured out of her.

It was not until the sobs passed that she realized that he was holding her, his hands steady against her back. "Are you..." *Dying?* How could she even ask the question?

"I'm all right," Zamir said quietly.

Ginny glanced down at the wound Nergal had inflicted in Zamir's side. The scorch wound no longer stank of rotting flesh, and it had closed cleanly, leaving only a faint scar. The miracle, however, did not extend beyond that injury. Ginny touched Zamir's shoulder, packed in bandages, and that light motion caused him to wince in pain. His back was still scraped raw, blood already drying on it.

Nergal's death must have undone the devastation he personally unleashed, but Zamir was still injured, and badly. "You are a long way from being all right," Ginny said. "We should get you to a doctor."

She supported Zamir as he clambered to his feet, and helped him from the command room. He glanced back only once as they passed through the door. His blue-green gaze swept across the empty room, resting briefly on the *Isriq Genii,* lying on the floor in the center of the room.

The cursed dagger, forged in a demon's heart from the core of a fallen star, had been restored to the demon's heart.

CHAPTER 26

A light breeze danced across the barren, gray landscape, stirring up the unmoving dirt.

Inanna scarcely glanced up from the aether draped like golden threads across her fingertips. The threads dangled, trembling like hope in the air, as she coaxed them into a complicated tapestry.

The wind whistled more insistently. Its snap almost sounded like the stomp of a little foot.

Was it her imagination or did the breeze seem to have something dangerously resembling a personality—

A perpetually irritated personality?

Inanna deliberately ignored it as she placed the final knot and stepped back to study her masterpiece

The gleaming threads formed the image of a gate several hundred feet tall and several hundred feet across. With a smile, Inanna called up more dark energy. Aether shimmered on her open palm like a black cloud seared with purple lightning. She extended her hand. The cloud floated off her palm and drifted toward the golden gate. It hovered next to the keyhole, then melted into it.

The glow around the keyhole faded as golden threads and raw aether combined and transformed into magic-infused granite. The glow rippled away like dying waves, until the only thing left in its place was a vast gate.

She had rebuilt the gate to Irkalla.

It swung open as she approached. On the other side, her older sister, Ereshkigal waited, flanked by Neti and Ninshubur.

Ninshubur hurried forward, a dazzling smile on her lips. She flung her arms around Inanna. "I knew you would come." Then, she remembered herself and dropped to her knees to kiss Inanna's feet.

Inanna treasured the first burst of Ninshubur's greeting far more. It came from her heart instead of from ritual. With her beloved handmaiden back by her side—oh, how she had missed Ninshubur when her handmaiden accompanied Ashe in the guise of a foul-mouthed gray parrot—Inanna turned to face her sister.

The queen of heaven and the queen of the underworld closed the distance between them.

Ereshkigal spared a glance up at the gates that once more, reopened the way between Irkalla—the Sumerian underworld—and the Earth. "They're grander than the ones Nergal broke on his way out."

"I thought it was time for a new look," Inanna replied.

"Nergal is dead," Ereshkigal said simply, stating what Inanna knew for a fact.

The Earth had shuddered with relief at Nergal's death,

and all the children of An had felt it. If anyone mourned him, no one spoke of it.

Her expression guarded, Ereshkigal extended her hands to her sister.

Inanna drew a deep breath. She had to have imagined that sudden twin bursts of pain and of joy in her chest. She was the goddess of heaven and earth, of love, and war. She didn't do pain or joy.

But she could do reconciliation and forgiveness.

Inanna reached out. The sisters' hands joined, and the Earth seemed to hold its breath.

Nothing broke. Nothing shattered. Nothing exploded.

Instead, a long moment passed in silence. The conflict and hurt of millennia took its first hesitant step toward healing. "Thank you for sending the Little Mermaid," Ereshkigal said.

The wind brushed against Inanna's cheek, drawing through the strands of her long, dark hair. "She had love, passion, and—in the final count—power enough to save the both of us."

"What will happen to her?"

"The *Isriq Genii* disrupted her astral energy, just as the power of the Earth's core disrupted Varun's when he poured himself into it to calm its anger. Their consciousness dispersed."

"Forever?"

"Nothing is forever. As long as the universe breathes, there will always be a second chance, although months, years, centuries may pass before their consciousness coalesces once more."

Ereshkigal looked thoughtful. "Will they find each other?"

The irritable, impatient breeze swept past Inanna, skimming low and stirring up the clear water as it darted toward the Isle of the Blessed and the Fountain of Life. Ashe's resurrection in the Fountain of Life had bound her—unknowingly and forever—to its sacred waters. As long as a sliver of her awareness had will and wit enough to find her way back to its waters, the second chance would occur sooner rather than later.

"Will they find each other?" Inanna echoed her sister's question. She scarcely concealed her smile. "Considering the Little Mermaid's ingenuity and her inability to take no for an answer, the answer is yes."

~

Ginny stood on the deck of the *Veritas,* staring out over the ocean. Behind her, the laughter of children provided a counterpoint to the rhythmic splash of the waves against the ship's hull, and the whistle of the breeze in her hair.

Her small hands curled into fists, her nails biting into the palm of her hand. Her breath hitched, and she blinked back the sting of familiar tears in her eyes. She could not listen to the wind or the waves without crumpling from that terrible ache in her chest.

Stopping Nergal's deadly assault on the Earth had cost Jackson, Varun, and Ashe their lives. Nergal's pestilence had also claimed the lives of millions of others. No one was untouched by what he had done.

There was no price too large to pay to stop Nergal—except that for Ginny, it was *almost* too large.

She did not turn around at the sound of footsteps. These days, Zamir was the only person who approached her. Her cloak of grief kept all others at bay.

"The navigator says we'll be at the port in about thirty hours."

Ginny nodded, the only sign that she had heard Zamir's oddly accented words. With a fierce swipe, she dashed the tears from her eyes. The *Veritas* had lost both its captain and first mate, as well as its reason for its initial expedition. Varun hadn't just been her closest friend through four years of graduate school. He had also been her key into and guide through a new and fascinating world. Now, he and Ashe were both gone, and she was left alone and in possession of magic she did not understand and could not control.

Jackson was gone too, and she was left wondering what might have been between them.

Zamir leaned his back on the rail and held out an apple.

She did not realize she was hungry until she took it from his hand and bit into it. Its sweet, tart flavor flooded her mouth. Ginny looked up at him, a murmur of thanks on her lips, but their eyes locked.

Blue-green, gold-flecked eyes.

The world blurred around her.

A breathtakingly handsome face.

Hands almost touching; a black cloud, slashed by purple lightning, passing between them.

The graceful flick of a long, black-scaled fish tail, with gossamer-like fins.

The sharp glint of spears piercing the water.

Crimson spreading against blue.

Blood— blood in the water.

Ginny drew her breath in sharply. The partly eaten apple hit the deck and rolled under the lifeboats. The tight, almost painful grip on her arms, recalled her into the present. Blinking hard, Ginny refocused her gaze on Zamir's eyes. "Are you all right?" he asked. "It's not the first time you've done this."

"Done what?"

"Mentally wandered away after looking at my mother, or at me."

"It's your eyes." Ginny pressed the heels of her hands against her temples. "They remind me…I keep seeing the same thing, and I think they're memories, not drug-induced visions. A merman, with a black tail, trapped in a narrow vertical tank." She stared down at the writhing black cloud that floated on her open palm. "I think he gave this aether to me. He had eyes…like Ashe's. Like yours."

"Kai?" Zamir's voice tightened. "You saw my grandson? Where?"

"In a tank…" She frowned. "In a cold, empty space, like a basement, but much larger. Everything else is hazy. I must have been drugged, which means that I must have seen him at the hidden base that belongs to the Temple of Ishtar."

"What temple?"

"The cult that Varun and—" Her voice caught. "Jackson rescued me from."

"Do you know where the cult is?"

She nodded. "Yes. It's in Colorado. Varun told me after we'd gotten away, and while I was recovering on the ship." Ginny drew a deep breath. "Zamir, they were…hurting him."

A muscle ticked in Zamir's smooth cheek. "The cult members are the descendants of Atlantis. They've always hated us. And now they have the mer-prince." His jaw tensed. "They won't kill him, but they will make sure he prays for death with every breath. I have to find him."

He turned to Ginny, but she laid her hand over his and spoke before he did. "I'll help you. We'll save him together."

EPILOGUE

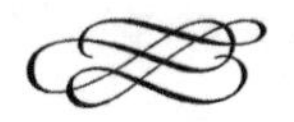

A solitary mermaid swam through the clear waters of the Levantine Sea, darting through the ruins of Shulim, the capital mer-city reduced to slag by the power of the *Dirga Tiamatu*. The seabed, ripped apart by fire and molten rock, was healing slowly, but a crack, no larger than the palm of her hand, still glowed red from the heat at the Earth's core.

Where *he* was.

Ashe leaned over the crack, and the gleaming tear at the corner of her eye—the priceless single drop she had carried from the Fountain of Life in Irkalla—dropped into the crack, plunging into the core.

It did not evaporate from the heat. She had known that it wouldn't, but could only hope that it did more than that.

She swam toward the surface, her body and long silver tail undulating through the water. The sun embraced her when she broke the surface. The wind swept around her like a long-lost friend, combing through the long strands of her blue and green hair.

Then, she climbed onto the islet formed by the explosion of Shulim, sprawled across the still-warm rocks, and she waited.

~

Varun was not certain at what point his consciousness had reformed enough to manage coherent thought, or at what point he realized it was probably a good idea to head toward darkness, away from the blazing heat and light at the planet's core.

With the return of consciousness came awareness—an innate understanding of the ways of the astral energy. Energy—such as he now was—could never be destroyed, but it could be dispersed until provided an anchor around which to rebuild itself.

And yet, Ginny had been right about the Fountain of Life. Its waters had changed Ashe, and it had changed him, linking their final sparks of consciousness to the fountain itself. A single drop of living water, released into the Earth's core, had given him an unshakeable foundation around which to anchor his astral energy.

Ashe. Somehow, she had brought the priceless drop of water to him.

He emerged in water, not cold but cool compared to where he had been. He glanced around. The gleaming metals scattered on the seabed, where they had melted and then solidified into puddle-shaped ores, triggered a single thought.

Shulim.

He was back where he had first fallen in love with Ashe, even if he had not fully realized it then.

If he was here, then perhaps she was still waiting for him.

The thought spiraled his consciousness toward the surface. Sunlight sparkled like gold on the water. As he broke the surface, he tugged astral energy toward him, the motion so natural that it felt almost instinctive. His body reformed as he emerged, physically reborn, from the waves lapping against the islet—where she waited for him.

She lounged on her stomach, looking like a mermaid out of a fairy tale, her tail curved until the diaphanous fins draped over her back. She tilted her head and blew him a kiss.

The wind darted around him, welcoming him like an old friend.

He waded through the shallows before joining her on the islet. Water dripped off his body as he strode over the rocks to settle down beside her as casually as if they had seen each other an hour ago. Who knew how much time had passed, but in that moment, the details did not matter.

Together, they stared out over the breadth of the ocean they had saved. Their shoulders pressed up against each other, the contact warm and reassuring. She turned her head to smile at him. Her blue-green eyes were flecked with gold. He cupped her cheek, then traced the slender line of her neck, before running his thumb over the tender hollow of her throat where the pendant had once rested, where it had always been in spite of her changing forms. Her black-scale pendant—her eternal tie to Zamir—was gone. What it meant he wasn't certain, but from the serenity in her eyes, he suspected she appreciated it as a change for the better.

"So, what now?" he asked softly, after he was certain she was not a dream, and that somehow, they had found their way back to each other.

"Almost three hundred years ago, in this little stretch of the sea, an overloaded boat tipped over in high waves, and I saved a man from drowning." A faint smile touched her lips. "I'm starting to believe that good deeds pay off—although you might have to wait centuries for it. But today—" She shrugged. "I'm just here to enjoy the sunset with you." Ashe leaned against Varun's shoulder, and together, they listened to the waves lap against the islet as the sun poured its blazing, burnished hues over the sea they both loved.

THE END

Join Zamir and Ginny in their search for Kai, the mer-prince and heir to a shattered empire, in **CURSED PRINCE...**

Never accept gifts from strangers...
Especially if it glows...

Ginny's first mistake was becoming one of the world's leading experts on ancient civilizations...

Her second mistake was getting kidnapped by Atlantean cultists who believed she knew more than she did...

Her third?

Accepting an energy vortex from a captive mer-prince.

Its reality-altering power entangles her in the millennia-long conflict between Atlantis and the Lords of the Ocean—the mer-people.

To free the mer-prince, she will have to trust a man afflicted with a chimeric personality and tormented by conflicted memories. She'll have to figure out how to control the devastating power the mer-prince entrusted to her…

Because if she doesn't succeed, Atlantis will rise again, and all the human nations of the Earth will fall.

Read **CURSED PRINCE** now!

If you enjoyed CURSED HEART, please leave a review. Reviews are critical for a book's success, and your review will help other readers decide if they'd enjoy the novel too. Thank you!

CURSED PRINCE

CHAPTER ONE SNEAK PEEK!

Never accept gifts from strangers...
Especially if it glows...

Ginny's first mistake was becoming one of the world's leading experts on ancient civilizations...

Her second mistake was getting kidnapped by Atlantean cultists who believed she knew more than she did...

Her third?

Accepting an energy vortex from a captive mer-prince.

Its reality-altering power entangles her in the millennia-long conflict between Atlantis and the Lords of the Ocean—the mer-people.

To free the mer-prince, she will have to trust a man afflicted with a chimeric personality and tormented by conflicted memories. She'll have to figure out how to control the devastating power the mer-prince entrusted to her...

Because if she doesn't succeed, Atlantis will rise again, and all the human nations of the Earth will fall.

~

CHAPTER ONE

How wretched did water have to be before a merman was forced to break the surface for air?

The water in the vertical tank, infused with blood and waste, was too polluted for even the sophisticated pump and filtration system. The machinery's low hum, amplified by the density of water into loud thumps, made rest impossible. The rapidly deteriorating quality of the water made breathing near impossible.

Kai twisted within the narrow confines of his prison, less than an arm's breadth across, and swam to the top of the tank. He tilted his head and allowed only his nose and lips to emerge from the water as he drew in a deep breath of the cold, musty air.

His heartbeat raced. He braced for a shouted curse and for the piercing stab of a spear.

Silence pulsed around him, alive, suffocating.

Nothing.

Yet.

Luckily, he had timed it well. His guards were on a break.

Did he dare push his luck?

He wrapped his fingers around the steel bars crisscrossing the top of the tank. His long, black-scaled tail beat against the water, pushing him upward as he shoved at the bars with all his strength.

One hinge popped, and the grate wobbled like a slightly loose tooth.

Just a little more.

Kai dove to the bottom of the tank. Looking up through the murky water, he could not even see the bars of his prison. He could only hope that the height of the twenty-foot tall tank provided him enough space to build momentum.

He launched up, and at the last possible moment, curled

his head into his chest so that his shoulders rose out of the water and slammed against the overhead grate. Pain rippled across his shoulders and down his back.

The second hinge jolted, but did not break.

Kai pressed his fingers against his aching shoulders, then glanced around the large room. The tank was the only thing in the cavern-like space, apart from the wooden platform that had been built at the top of the tank. On the far side of the room, a spiral staircase wound up.

How was he, tail and all, supposed to get up those steps?

He did not know—but he would never know, not unless he broke out of his tank.

One more try.

He twisted around sharply, grimacing against the pain in his back as he folded his body over the length of his tail and returned to the bottom of the tank. The constant pressure of the pump kicked up the filth that had settled there, but did little to clear it. The water, murky at the top, was foul at the bottom.

All the more reason to get out of here.

His fins beat against the water. The undulations of his muscular tail propelled him up, out of the water. His right shoulder took the brunt of the impact, but the hinge snapped. The steel grate hurled off the top of the tank. It rolled across the narrow wooden platform and dropped twenty feet to the ground.

Clanging echoes rolled around the room.

Kai gritted his teeth. Whatever hope he had in stealth was gone.

He gripped the side of the tank and pulled himself out of

the water. The air chilled against his skin as he dragged himself across the wooden platform and looked over the edge. His choices came down to the crudely made ladder leaning against the platform or a twenty-foot drop.

With a tail, that would give him zero chance of landing correctly.

Muted sounds drifted down to him. Doors slamming. Feet running.

He was out of time.

Kai gripped the wooden platform and lowered his tail over the edge. The weight pulled down on his aching shoulders and strained his back, but he was now only twelve feet from the ground, not twenty.

He let go.

His tail smashed into concrete. As he fell, he crumpled to absorb the impact. Pain screamed through every part of his body. His chest heaved as he tried to inhale the air punched out of his lungs. If he had broken any bones, he could not tell.

Not yet.

A door slammed at the top of the spiral staircase. Boots pounded against steel steps. Six men appeared on the far side of the room. A lean man, wearing glasses, shouted, "You bloody fools! I told you he was never to be left unguarded!"

Another man snatched up one of the long spears leaning against the wall and charged at Kai.

Kai twisted aside, grabbed the shaft of the spear, and swung back, flinging the man down. He flipped the spear in his hand and drove the spearhead into the man's chest. The man's hands clawed around his injury, then his head fell back and awareness blinked out of his eyes.

Motion flicked in Kai's peripheral vision. He leaned his weight forward and swung his tail. The power of his blow, which could force an adult orca into a hasty retreat, flung his second attacker across the room. The man crumpled to the ground, leaving a crimson streak against the wall.

Kai closed his fist around the spear shaft. The weapon was too long to be balanced and too ungainly to be hurled—an instrument of torture, not a weapon of war. Its long reach, however, allowed Kai to swing it like a pole at the two men charging toward him. One man managed to leap over it, but the second could not break his stride in time. He went down screaming, his hands clutching his knees.

An explosive sound tore through the room. Kai's breath caught from the shock of it an instant before the pain hit him. The spear fell out of his suddenly weakened grip. His gaze dropped to the bullet hole punched through his right shoulder. Blood leaked out slowly, as if his body scarcely comprehended what was happening to it.

The bespectacled man strode across the room to kick the spear away from Kai and smashed his fist, still wrapped around the grip of his weapon, across Kai's face. The impact dropped Kai to the cold concrete. His chest heaved as he struggled to breathe through the shock and pain. "Cuff him," the man ordered. "And get the weights."

Another man hurried to the staircase, but his steps hesitated at the top. "How much?" he asked. When he did not get an answer, he raised his voice. "Jacob, how much should I bring?"

Kai raised his head to find Jacob's narrow-eyed glare fixed on him. Jacob's lips tugged into a sneer. "Two hundred pounds, at least."

One of Jacob's men yanked Kai's arms behind his back. The motion wrenched a scream out of him. He was reeling, nauseated from pain, when cold metal locked his wrists together, but he scarcely felt them as Jacob wrenched his face up. "Where are they? Where are the others? Tell me where the merfolk hide."

Kai stared back at Jacob; self-loathing tightened into a sour knot in the pit of his stomach. The underwater city of Shulim, concealed in the depths of the Levantine Sea, had been the heart, soul, and crown jewel of the Beltiamatu empire. Except for a few scattered rural communities, the Beltiamatu—or merfolk, as Jacob called them—lived at Shulim.

Almost all of them, their blood tainted by ocean-destroying pestilence, had died there.

And by my hand.

His grandfather, the mer-king, had already activated the *Dirga Tiamatu,* the Beltiamatu weapon which unleashed molten rock and liquid metal from the planet's core. Its target was the Greek island of Kalymnos.

Varun Zale, the marine biologist who had swum to Shulim to disable the weapon, was a shadowy figure in Kai's peripheral vision—the only witness to the impending genocide as Kai reprogrammed the *Dirga Tiamatu.* Kai had redirected its growing fury away from Kalymnos, and into the center of Shulim.

"Where are your people? Where are the merfolk?" Jacob's hand closed around Kai's throat. The terror of suffocating yanked Kai back into the immediate crisis. "For too long, you have been a plague on humanity. You are monsters that think nothing of destroying human lives and lands to advance your sick, twisted ends. For thousands of years, we've tried to stop you, and this time, we will succeed. We can finally take the war to you." Jacob's grin was bright and vicious. His grip squeezed harder.

Kai's chest heaved uselessly, unable to draw breath. His vision blurred into sickly yellow.

Another voice resonated through the ringing in his ears. "Stop! If you kill him, we're back to square one. We'd be no closer to finding and destroying the merfolk."

Jacob's grip around his neck loosened, dropping Kai to the concrete. Kai dragged an unsteady breath into his burning lungs as his psychedelic vision faded into normal hues.

A third voice called out, "I've got the weights."

"Good," Jacob said. "Get him back up to the tank."

Two men hitched their arms under Kai's and dragged him up the ladder. Each wooden rung jostled against his tail, but the pain was nothing compared to the agony radiating from his injured shoulder and across his back and chest. They laid him on the platform beside the tank. His head throbbed; his vision swam. There was more motion beside him, but he could not focus on it.

Not until cold metal bands wrapped around the base of his tail.

Not until hands fumbled with the cuffs that bound his wrists behind his back.

Not until the sudden weight tore his shoulders out of their joints.

He screamed as the men dropped the iron weights into the tank. The weights yanked him off the platform, plunging him into the water. The water slowed his descent, but not enough. A hundred pounds of iron weights, lashed around his handcuffs, crashed into the base of the tank. Another hundred pounds, wrapped around the base of his tail, made movement impossible.

Jacob's voice, distorted by water, said, "Give me the spear."

Nowhere to flee. Nowhere to hide.

Bound and weighted down to the bottom of tank, trapped amid filth and waste, Kai closed his eyes as the men wrestled the grate over the top of the tank and welded it in place. Jacob's familiar footsteps rang against the steel bars. "When you're ready to tell us where to find the merfolk, raise your head, nod your submission, and we will release you."

Tightness clenched Kai's chest. If this was punishment for what he had done to his people, diseased though they were, he deserved it.

And if his silence saved the few untainted mer-colonies that remained, he would pay any price for their safety.

He drew into himself, curling tighter, not in defeat but in defiance.

Spears plunged into the water, the long shafts allowing the spearheads to pierce him. Blood spilled from the many cuts on his skin. Dazed with pain, he stared at the wispy crimson strands trailing through the dirty water. His thoughts wandered, as if through a haze, then shaped into the delicate features of the woman who had stumbled into the room days—or was it weeks—ago? She had pressed her hands against the tank and gaped as he uncoiled from his restless slumber to return her astonished gaze. Her eyes were dilated and unfocused, and her gait unsteady as she climbed the ladder to the top of the platform.

Had she been drugged? Was she a prisoner, like him?

He had swum to the top of the tank to find her fumbling with the grate, trying to yank it away. He heard the racing footsteps before she did, but she too glanced over her shoulder. Panic flashed across her face, and she pulled even harder.

She was trying to save him. He was certain of it.

He did not think she could free him, but perhaps she could keep the aether vortex, his people's power, from falling into his enemies' hands if he were killed.

Kai pressed his right hand against his chest, and as he drew it away, the living cloud of dark energy emerged, as magnificent as a lightning-seared night. It danced on the palm of his hand as he raised it to her waiting hands on the other side of the grate.

Aether passed through the steel bars between them. For several moments, she cupped it between her hands, then mimicking his actions, she brought it to her chest. The black and purple vortex swirled, its living tentacles writhing as if in protest, before sinking into the woman.

She looked up and met his eyes, her gaze uncomprehending. She was still staring at him when his captors clambered up to the platform and pulled her away, before driving him down to the bottom of the tank with their long spears. She screamed as they dragged her out of the room. Her voice, garbled through the water, begged them to stop hurting him.

Kai did not see her again.

The aether vortex was lost to him, to his people.

He had damned the Beltiamatu—not once, but twice.

His eyes flicked open. Water, tainted by his waste and his blood, surrounded him. Agony screamed through him. His heartbeat stuttered, exhausted by pain, drained by despair.

He was dying.

Read **CURSED PRINCE** now!

LORD OF THE OCEAN

CURSED PRINCE

Never accept gifts from strangers...
Especially if it glows...

Ginny's first mistake was becoming one of the world's leading experts on ancient civilizations...

Her second mistake was getting kidnapped by Atlantean cultists who believed she knew more than she did...

Her third?

Accepting an energy vortex from a captive mer-prince.

Its reality-altering power entangles her in the millennia-long conflict between Atlantis and the Lords of the Ocean—the mer-people.

To free the mer-prince, she will have to trust a man afflicted with a chimeric personality and tormented by conflicted memories. She'll have to figure out how to control the devastating power the mer-prince entrusted to her...

Because if she doesn't succeed, Atlantis will rise again, and all the human nations of the Earth will fall.

CURSED THRONE

He shattered his empire to save the world.
Rebuilding it could kill him...

To save the ocean and earth from a devastating pandemic,

the mer-prince Kai destroyed his capital city and its diseased merfolk.

Now, he wonders if he made the right decision.

Reduced to scattered colonies, the mer-people can no longer defend humans from the empire-building ambitions of their Atlantean offspring.

To rebuild his kingdom, Kai needs the aether core buried in the sunken ruins of ancient Atlantis, but the way is guarded by Ancients—gargantuan titans, monsters of myth and legend.

Yet the greatest peril lies not in the journey, but in the destination. A creature of immeasurable power is entombed alive within Atlantis.

And the only thing it craves, far more the priceless aether core, is absolute vengeance upon the royal bloodline...

CURSED LEGACY

Family is all he has left...
What—or who—will he pay to save the Earth?

Transformed by dark energy, the mer-king Zamir is a chimera—a seamless tapestry of skills...a mangled mess of memories.

Yet through all the catastrophes he has witnessed—many of his own making—he has learned one thing.

Family matters; especially the last of his bloodline, his grandson, Kai.

A straightforward quest to rebuild his shattered empire and set his grandson upon the throne is thwarted by the soul shards in his chimeric personality.

Zamir has enemies, far more than he imagined.

And their hate is brutally raw.

One of them, Marduk, possesses the power of a god, and in his attempt to right a perceived wrong, he will incinerate the Earth.

To stop Marduk, Zamir must draw upon all facets of his fragmented personalities, even the one he despises and cannot trust.

But nothing prepares Zamir for the devastating realization that sacrificing Kai may be the only way to stop Marduk's apocalyptic plans...

DAUGHTER OF AIR

"You will be swept away by this genre-blending masterpiece of urban fantasy, science fiction, fairy tales, and mythology."

CURSED TIDES

She no longer wants to be a part of his world. But he must convince her to save it...

Ashe is one mission away from earning her soul. Nearly three centuries after her disastrous on-land escapade, the former mermaid has a final assignment: protect a marine biologist on his quest to save the oceans. Perhaps it's pure coincidence that Varun Zale is the descendant of the prince she once chose not to kill.

Varun can't explain how storms obey Ashe or why her eye color changes to match the tossing waves, but he suspects she is more than the mute ship captain she pretends to be. His growing fascination leads him from the shallows of a fairy tale to the depths of a mystery older than recorded time. In the midnight reaches of the ocean, monstrous titans stir. An unstoppable disease becomes a weapon in the hands of the mer-king.

Nothing Varun has ever imagined or believed about mermaids is true. And being wrong could cost him everything...

CURSED BLADE

A cursed dagger. A desperate king. His quest will damn his kingdom, and the entire Earth.

The mer-king has bargained with demons, trading the death of the oceans for his soul. As the seas churn with disease, the marine biologist Varun Zale and the mermaid Ashe battle the mer-king's army across the black tides to the ancient stronghold of Atlantis.

They cannot hold back the mer-king forever, but there might be another way to end his rampage before the demonic bargain is fulfilled. When Ashe's cursed dagger claims a life, it can gift the soul to the king, and the way Ashe looks at Varun makes him wonder if she has identified him as the perfect target.

When the dagger finally strikes, it will rip the shroud of deception. For the mer-king, three centuries is a long time to live with hate, but it's even longer to believe a lie...

CURSED FLAME

When gods battle, worlds shatter. Now it's the Earth turn...

The queen of the underworld has stolen the mermaid Ashe's most treasured possession. To reclaim it, Ashe must unravel ancient mysteries to find the doorway to hell.

She doesn't need or want the marine biologist Varun tagging along. There is no safety for a mortal in a war between elementals and vengeful gods, but curiosity is one of his greatest vices, second only to his love for Ashe.

Love does not guarantee access to all her secrets. Without the facts, Varun cannot possibly understand the risks, especially when the queen of the underworld is convinced that Ashe is far more than she pretends to be…

…a goddess in hiding—the queen of heaven and earth.

CURSED HEART

Before aliens became gods and reality became religion, the war began. It's time for it to end—one way or another.

Pandemic sweeps the earth while humanity's ancient protectors watch helplessly. Societies and governments crumble before the advance of Nergal, the god of pestilence.

The mermaid Ashe possesses the power, the passion, and the audacity to challenge Nergal, but she is trapped in the underworld. Engineering her escape forces Varun, the marine biologist, to seek out unlikely allies, but freeing Ashe is only the first step.

The only weapon that can slay Nergal is a cursed dagger forged in a demon's heart from the core of a fallen star. And that dagger is buried in the depths of a living volcano…

URBAN FANTASY AND SCIENCE FICTION ENTWINE IN THE WORLD OF THE DOUBLE HELIX

"The Double Helix is the kind of series you'd expect to see with a movie deal. I loved, loved, LOVED it. I fell in love with the characters and will be reading all four books again in the future...a treat I reserve for my favorites."—Full Time Reader

"I wish I could award more than 5 stars. This phenomenal series continues to astonish and delight."—Hillel Kaminsky

THE DOUBLE HELIX COLLECTION

Finally available as a single collection, the books in the *Double Helix* series have gathered over 100 reviews with an average of 4.5 stars.

"Higher octane than Heroes. More heart than X-Men."

His genetic code sourced from the best that humanity offers, Galahad embodies the pinnacle of perfection. When Zara Itani, a mercenary, frees him from his laboratory prison, she offers him a chance to claim everything that had ever been denied him, starting with his humanity.

Perfection cannot be unleashed without repercussions; Galahad's freedom shatters Danyael Sabre's life.

An alpha empath, Danyael is rare and coveted, even among the alpha mutants who dominate the Genetic Revolution. He wields the power to heal or kill with a touch, but craves only privacy—an impossible dream for the man who was used as Galahad's physical template.

Galahad and Danyael, two men, one face. One man seeks to embrace destiny, and the other to escape it. But destiny has a name. Zara. Assassin.

The multiple award-winning *Double Helix* series, consisting of *Perfection Unleashed, Perfect Betrayal, Perfect Weapon,* and *Perfection Challenged,* will defy your notions of perfection and humanity and plunge you into a world transformed by the Genetic Revolution.

MIRIYA

Her destiny collides with a man who can kill with a touch...

Thirty years into the First Genetic Revolution, society's tolerance for human derivatives is wearing thin. Clones and in vitros are regarded with suspicion, and mutants with resentment. Yet in spite of the hostile environment, some alpha telepaths—like Miriya Templeton—have thrived.

Not for much longer...

Destiny has set her life on a collision course with Danyael Sabre, the alpha empath who can kill with a touch. Whether he becomes friend or foe, whether he and she live or die, will depend on the choices she makes. On her decisions hang the outcomes of the Second Genetic Revolution.

Miriya does not believe in destiny, nor want any part of the revolution, but she will risk everything to save a beloved friend, even if it means returning home to New Orleans. The decadent elegance of the Mardi Gras krewes conceal treachery and brewing death.

It's too much for a novice like Miriya.

Natural talent and courage won't save her.

Conviction might, but first, she has to decide what to believe in…and who to fight for…

PERFECTION UNLEASHED (Double Helix #1)

Winner of six literary awards, including Gold Medal, Science Fiction, Readers Favorites 2013

He shares a face with the perfect specimen. Together, they'll reshape a divided nation… or shatter it completely.

Years as an assassin taught Zara to steel her heart against weakness. But she believes no creature deserves to be caged and prodded… much less the man who embodies human perfection. Against her better judgment, she ditches a recon mission to spring him free. She wasn't counting on an irritating empath joining the chase.

Doctor Danyael Sabre hides his healing powers in plain sight. With tensions between unmodified humans and mutants intensifying, the empath vows to stay clear of the coming storm. But when his doppelgänger—a top-secret genetic experiment—escapes the lab, he is yanked into the fray. His only choice is to team up with his lookalike and the cold-hearted assassin who can't stand him.

As they fend off enemy forces and puzzle out the mystery of their past, Danyael faces an impossible dilemma. Should he use his healing powers to inflict pain or will he risk a lifetime in a cage?

PERFECT BETRAYAL (Double Helix #2)

1st Place, Royal Palm Literary Award 2013

One man's choice will shatter the impasse. He can defeat his enemies, but can he defeat his friends?

Danyael Sabre, an object of desire, would much rather not be. An alpha empath by birth, a doctor by training, and an empathic healer by calling, he is stalked by the military that covets his ability to kill, not heal. Bereft of two days of memories, he goes on the run under the protection of an assassin, Zara Itani.

The more he uncovers of his lost hours, the more he doubts everything that once anchored him. He knows only that he endangers those around him and that he is falling in love with Zara, who hates him for reasons he no longer remembers.

As forces—both powerful and ruthless—threaten those he cares for, Danyael has only two options. He can betray his values and abandon the path of the healer, or he can wait to be betrayed, not by enemies, but by his friends.

ZARA

1st Place, Royal Palm Literary Award 2016

She's an assassin-for-hire.
Everything has a price—
Except love...

When the U.S. ambassador's daughter is kidnapped in Beirut, a SEAL team is sent to retrieve her. Their "advisor" is the master assassin, Zara Itani. She has as many ties with the

Lebanese government as she does with the country's militant factions; friends and family on both sides.

She is pregnant—but that is nobody's business.

She is also torn by her inexplicable feelings for Danyael, the alpha empath she betrayed into a life-sentence in a maximum-security prison, but that is *definitely* nobody's business. After all, everyone knows that you can't trust anything you feel when you're around an empath.

The kidnapping is the prelude to far deeper treachery, and the mission goes terribly, desperately wrong. As international political conspiracy edges toward renewed military conflict, Zara's loyalties will be tested; her beliefs challenged. She could start a war, or she could stop it.

Or she could trust the difference Danyael has made in her life—

Tell me who you love and I will tell you who you are....

Zara will finally discover who she is, but what will her discovery cost the world, her allies, enemies, and ultimately, Danyael...?

PERFECT WEAPON (Double Helix #3)

Don't fear the army of genetically engineered perfect killers.
Fear the cripple who leads them.

An alpha empath, Danyael Sabre is powerful, rare, and coveted, even among the alpha mutants who dominate the Genetic Revolution. Betrayed by his friends and abandoned to a life sentence in a maximum-security prison, Danyael receives freedom and sanctuary from an unlikely quarter—

the Mutant Assault Group, an elite mutant task force within the US military. Physically crippled and emotionally vulnerable, Danyael succumbs to the warmth of friendships and the promise of love he finds within their ranks.

Friendship and love, however, demand his loyalty, and Danyael rises to the challenge of training and leading the assault group's genetically modified super soldier army. The super soldiers are faster and stronger than the military's human soldiers; their animal instincts spur ferocity and fearlessness in battle. Who is the perfect weapon, though, the super soldiers or Danyael, the alpha empath, who can, with a touch, heal or kill?

Adversaries swarm like vultures around carrion; the pawn is once again in play. The threads of betrayal that sent Danyael to prison spin into a web, ensnaring him. When a terrorist group strikes Washington, D.C., how far will Danyael go to defend a government that sent him to prison to die?

SILENCE ENDS

2nd Place, Royal Palm Literary Award 2013

When you choose your friends, you also choose your enemies...

Seventeen-year-old Dee wants nothing more than to help her twin brother, Dum, break free from the trauma in their childhood and speak again, but the only person who can help Dum is the alpha empath, Danyael Sabre, whom the U.S. government considers a terrorist and traitor.

The search for Danyael will lead Dee and Dum from the

sheltered protection of the Mutant Affairs Council and into the violent, gang-controlled heart of Anacostia. Ensnared by Danyael's complicated network of friends and enemies, Dee makes her stand in a political and social war that she is ill equipped to fight. What can one human, armed only with her wits and pepper spray, do against the super-powered mutants who dominate the Genetic Revolution?

As it turns out...*everything*.

In her quest to help her brother become normal, Dee will finally learn what it means to be extraordinary.

If she survives it...

CARNIVAL TRICKS

1st Place, Royal Palm Literary Award 2015

A genetic time-bomb.
A woman in the wrong place at the wrong time.
It's up to her to save the world.

In a world transformed by the Genetic Revolution, Kyle Norwood is an honest-to-God human and proud of it. His deadly skills come from hard work and not genetic sleight of hand. An easy mission to protect two Proficere Labs scientists turns into a shoot-out that leaves a scientist and a federal agent dead. Worse, the research data the scientists were carrying disappears.

In a world where human derivatives are hated and feared, Sofia Rios is almost human. When a fight during her waitressing shift turns fatal, a dying scientist launches her into the shady world of scientific espionage. The unwilling trustee of research that people would kill to obtain, Sofia turns to the man who steps out of the shadows to protect her, even though he appears as dangerous and disreputable as the people who hunt her.

Together, Sofia and Kyle must unravel the truth behind the illicit information she carries before one or both of them are killed. Their mutual attraction sparkles, but the spark could just as easily become an explosion if Kyle ever finds out that Sofia is a despised telekinetic.

SICARIUS SOUL

Some grudges live forever, and the worst enemies are the ones you didn't know you had...

Alpha empaths are dying, executed by an assassin who leaves no psychic trace. Zara Itani derides the mystery as sloppy investigation until Danyael is injured by the assassin's bullet. If he died, his empathic death throes would have driven everyone within ten miles to suicide.

The only solution is to imprison Danyael beyond the reach of assassins, damning him to physical solitude and emotional isolation. Zara, however, bets on her ability to use Danyael as bait to draw out the murderer. Kill the assassin, end the threat, right?

But nothing is ever easy in a world transformed by the Genetic Revolution. Sins of the past transcend decades and centuries to coalesce into a threat no one can contain. A vigilante driven by hate demands absolute vengeance—the suicide of millions of innocent people—and it will begin with Danyael's death...

PERFECTION CHALLENGED (Double Helix #4)

The 'perfect human' Galahad finally challenges his imperfect genetic donor Danyael—and only one will survive...

An alpha empath, Danyael Sabre has survived abominations and super soldiers, terrorists and assassins, but he cannot survive his failing body. He wants only to live out his final days in peace, but life and the woman he loves, the assassin Zara Itani, have other plans for him.

Galahad, the perfect human being created by Pioneer Labs, is branded an international threat, and Danyael is appointed his jury, judge, and executioner. Danyael alone believes that Galahad can be the salvation that the world needs, but is the empath blinded by the fact that Galahad shares his genes, and the hope that there is something of him in Galahad?

In a desperate race against time and his own dying body, Danyael struggles to find fragments of good in the perfect human being, and comes to the wrenching realization that his greatest battle will be a battle for the heart of the man who hates him.

XIN

3rd Place, Royal Palm Literary Award 2016

In pursuit of life and happiness, scientific experiments go terribly wrong.

And the innocent are paying the price...

When the trail of Danyael Sabre's stolen blood exposes illegal scientific research at a Chinese laboratory, it unleashes a designer drug with terrifying side effects and imperils the decades-long peace between China and America.

NSA analyst Mu Xin, the clone of a Shang-dynasty queen, steps into the fray to stem the chaos, but in a land where ancestral worship and beliefs in incarnation exist alongside cutting-edge genetic engineering, will Xin find herself trapped or liberated by her past?

She will risk her life; Danyael his sanity and his life.

And even then, their sacrifice may not be enough to hold back the tide of chaos and death that will consume China, and then the world...

AETERNAE NOCTIS

"...A stunningly original take on post-apocalyptic science fiction and fantasy!"

ETERNAL NIGHT

1st place, Fantasy, Royal Palm Literary Award 2014

Demonic overlords command vampire armies, but they are not the ones to fear...

For a thousand years, humans cowered beneath the rule of the Night Terrors, but Jaden's five-year-old sister is prophesied to stop them...if they don't get to her first.

To protect her, Jaden leads a rebellion against the Night Terrors, but when he is captured in battle and dragged before the demonic queen Ashra, he realizes that he has seen her face before...every night in his dreams.

Ashra is fighting her own battle for survival against enemies without and treachery within. But when Jaden stumbles upon Ashra's darkest secret and uncovers the truth about the city of eternal night, he realizes that nothing may be what it seems...including himself.

ETERNAL DAWN

Immortals and mortals struggle to co-exist.
An enemy is changing the rules...

All parents in Aeternae Noctis have lost children to the culling, among them, the herbalist Rafael Varens. Humanity's remnants rise in rebellion against the ruthless rule of the three immortal icrathari and their vampire army; yet again, they are crushed.

When the icrathari Siri seeks a salve for her chronic pain, she and Rafael strike a bargain. He will cure the poison in her blood if she expands the settlement and frees the children, including his son. Their tentative alliance ushers in unexpected friendship, until it is shattered by the cruelest betrayal.

From the darkness below the earth, an ancient and implacable enemy rises, twisting their pain and turning Rafael and Siri against each other—his first step in the destruction of Aeternae Noctis…

ETERNAL DAY

The only chance at survival demands an impossible reconciliation…

Erich Dale was once a poet, an artist, and in love with the night. Now, he's an elder vampire cursed into insanity by the icrathari warlord, Tera. Trapped in the fragments of his shattered mind is the key to healing a scorched and devastated Earth.

Only Tera can unlock his secrets, but she is a destroyer, not a nurturer. Erich, consumed by hatred and a desire for vengeance, will not be soothed. Together, they can end the thousand-year reign of eternal night, but unless there is forgiveness, there can be no reconciliation. Without reconciliation, hope perishes.

She created her worst enemy, and now, his hate will damn all humanity, forever…

OTHER SCIENCE FICTION AND FANTASY NOVELS BY JADE KERRION

CONFESSIONS OF THE UNDERWORLD BOATER

Losing my job wasn't the problem...
Being recalled was.

No one believes in the Greek gods anymore, which leaves me with nothing to do at the banks of the river Styx.

Boredom isn't an excuse for bad judgment, but I should have known better than to hang out in Fort Lauderdale.

The nightclub owned by my elder brother Thanatos —*Death*—is the hottest destination on the beach, until mortals inexplicably sicken and die—

—and show up at the Styx.

The displaced mortals are the first pawns in the long-overdue war between the gods of Olympus and the offspring of the Titans—the children of Nyx, my siblings and me.

My name is Charon, and my only power as the ferryman is to travel any path between Point A and Point B.

Unfortunately, that power isn't going to be enough to escape—or avert—the apocalypse headed my way...

ILLUSIONS

Sometimes, the truth begins with a lie...

Desperate to break the suffocating grip of eternal winter,

the fae prince Varian summons the most powerful witches and fae to shatter the icy shroud around La Condamine, but no one wants to die for the prince's cause. When he conscripts by force, they flock to Nithya, begging her to wrap her flawless illusions around their magic bracelets.

Nithya undermines Varian's tyranny until she realizes there is more to him than the façade of a merciless dictator. Even so, she's not the biggest traitor in the realm. The conspiracy that murdered Varian's father now turns its malice and hatred against him. Nithya finds herself entangled in treachery, betrayal, and illusions far more entrapping than anything she can conjure.

The prize is the soul of a nation, and the price is everything she cherishes—including Varian's love.

EARTH-SIM

1st Place, Young Adult, Royal Palm Literary Award 2013

*"**Earth-Sim** starts off awesome and just keeps getting even better…"* Cara Drake

A planetary management simulation program…
Two students who failed Communications 101…
What could possibly go wrong…?

Jem Moran has a reputation to prove and a secret to protect. The prestigious world simulation program seems the answer to both her problems, but only if she can succeed in spite of her slacker of a partner, Kir Davos, and the uncooperative human beings who populate her planet.

From the Great Extinction to the Renaissance, from world wars to intergalactic treaties, Jem's conflict with Kir will shape Earth's history, and their opposing management styles will either save or doom our planet.

This tongue-in-cheek, award-winning novel blends geography, history, mythology, and popular cultural into a breathtaking panorama of Earth. Read Earth-Sim, and you'll never see our planet the same way again... Either way, you finally have someone to blame for the shape our world is in.

MAGE'S LEGACY

He's desperate.
She's a fraud.
Together...they're a disaster.

To save his siren clan from the ravaging sea serpents, Gabriel must seek the help of a mage to recover the Legacy Stone and heal the oceans. That's how he finds himself at Kerina's doorstep, begging for her aid, and grateful when she reluctantly agrees.

Now Gabriel and Kerina must survive the perils of the cursed seas and challenge the demonic Tua and his seven monstrous children for control of the Legacy Stone—a difficult enough task for a lone siren warrior and a powerful mage...

Except, Kerina's not really a mage. The real mage died weeks before and hadn't even been cold in her grave when Gabriel arrived desperate for her help. Kerina hadn't exactly been eager to correct his mistake then, and now her lie of omission could leave the world in danger of complete extinction.

Kerina's not sure how long she can keep up the ruse, and she's running out of time to confess.

Fans of Kiera Cass, Neil Gaiman, and Faith Hunter will find this dystopian-fantasy siren adventure intensely addicting.

ABOUT THE AUTHOR

To join my newsletter and access exclusive content, visit me at http://www.jadekerrion.com

What readers are saying about Jade's books:

"...I wish I could award more than 5 stars!"–*Hillel Kaminsky*

"...This is the kind of series you'd expect to see with a movie deal."–*Full Time Reader*

At 3 a.m., when her husband and three sons are asleep, USA Today best-selling author JADE KERRION weaves unforgettable characters into unexpected stories.

Her debut science fiction novel, PERFECTION UNLEASHED, won six literary awards and launched the DOUBLE HELIX series which blends cutting-edge genetic engineering and high-octane action with an unforgettable romance between an alpha empath and an assassin. Readers continue their adventures in this dystopian Earth with the spin-off futuristic thriller series DOUBLE HELIX CASE FILES, starting with MIRIYA.

The DAUGHTER OF AIR and LORD OF THE OCEAN series, beginning with CURSED TIDES, blends fairy tales and mythology into urban fantasy. It's the story you always wanted to read: The Little Mermaid finally kicks ass!

Jade's award-winning fantasy novel, ETERNAL NIGHT, draws you in the post-apocalyptic world of AETERNAE NOCTIS where humans–victims of a war between immortals–are about to tip the balance.

LIFE SHOCKS ROMANCES, starting with AROUSED, features Jade's sweet and sexy contemporary romance series, which proves that, at the very least, she knows how to alphabetize books.

Jade's devious plan for world domination begins with making all her readers as sleep-deprived as she is.

OTHER BOOKS BY JADE KERRION

The Double Helix Collection

Perfection Unleashed

Perfect Betrayal

Perfect Weapon

Perfection Challenged

Miriya

Zara

Silence Ends

Carnival Tricks

Sicarius Soul

Xin

Daughter of Air

Cursed Tides

Cursed Blade

Cursed Flame

Cursed Heart

Lords of the Ocean

Cursed Prince

Cursed Throne

Cursed Legacy

Aeternae Noctis

Eternal Night

Eternal Dawn

Eternal Day

Other Science Fiction and Fantasy

Confessions of the Underworld Boater

Illusions

Earth-Sim

Mage's Legacy

East of the Sun

Shere Khan

The Seventeenth Slave

Life Shocks Romances

Aroused ~*~ Betrayed ~*~ Crushed ~*~Desired

Ensnared ~*~ Flawed ~*~ Graced ~*~ Haunted

Inflamed ~*~ Jilted ~*~ Kindled ~*~ Lured

Maligned ~*~ Nurtured ~*~ Owned ~*~ Prized

CPSIA information can be obtained
at www.ICGtesting.com
Printed in the USA
LVHW051508050619
620257LV00002B/459/P

9 781091 306738